I
Know
Your
Secret

D0932951

BOOKS BY RUTH HEALD

The Mother's Mistake
The Woman Upstairs

I Know Your Secret

RUTH HEALD

Published by Bookouture in 2020

An imprint of Storyfire Ltd.
Carmelite House
50 Victoria Embankment
London EC4Y 0DZ

www.bookouture.com

ISBN: 978-1-83888-224-2
eBook ISBN: 978-1-83888-223-5

PROLOGUE

The fire started on the duvet. A candle on a neatly made bed, scorching a black hole in the white cotton cover, burning through the synthetic fibres beneath. The hole grew as the flames spread, fanning out towarerds the rest of the room. She watched the fire reach out for the red dress that hung on the cupboard door, consuming it in one angry burst, before attacking the wood behind it. The flames licked the walls, scraps of wallpaper crinkling, blackening and then disappearing entirely.

She couldn't believe how easy it was to destroy, how quickly the flames devoured everything they touched. Elation overcame her, an intense rush. This was it. What she needed. The release was blissful.

She didn't know how long she'd been standing there. She could feel her skin heating up, her blood running hot through her veins, her eyes stinging. She must leave. The smoke was everywhere, in her hair, in her lungs. But a part of her wanted to stay, to let the flames consume her too.

She smiled as she turned to go, to walk out of the door, before the door frame itself was caught up in the inferno. Out of the bedroom and into the living room then quickly out into the corridor before the flames followed.

She could hear the sound of the smoke alarm above the roar of the flames. It started to dawn on her what she had done. She needed to leave now, before others appeared, asked her what she was doing here. Realised that she started the fire.

Running towards the stairs, she thought she heard something else. Screaming.

The sound was desperate. Hardly human.

Suddenly she felt sick, her feeling of power gone in an instant.

It must be something else, something caught in the flames, emitting the sound as it burned. It couldn't be a person.

As she entered the stairwell, she thought she saw the shadow of someone coming out of the lift. Had they seen her? She panicked then, finally thinking of the consequences of what she'd done. Then she ran down the stairs, careering down two at a time and then out of the building, into the street.

The cold air burnt her lungs and she stopped and looked up, her breathing ragged. In the orange glow from the window on the second floor a shadow stumbled.

There was someone inside the flat.

CHAPTER 1

BETH

'I can't do this anymore, Beth.'

I lift my soapy hands out of the washing-up bowl and stare at Richard in disbelief, a cup in one hand. 'What?'

Richard shifts his weight from one foot to the other. 'I'm sorry. I just can't keep going like this.'

I feel my jaw clench as my grip tightens on the cup. I know our relationship is in trouble, but I hadn't thought it would come to this. 'But we said we'd work to fix things between us. We said we wouldn't just throw it all away over nothing.' Since his affair with a woman he met in a bar, we've been trying to rebuild our relationship, trying to return to the way we used to be. I've been working so hard to keep everything together. How can he so callously tear it apart?

'Beth—'

'Keep your voice down,' I hiss, aware of Charlie watching cartoons in the living room. He's the reason we're still together. He's the reason I've been holding onto hope, clinging to the fading embers of our love. If it wasn't for our son, Richard would have been out the door as soon as I found out he'd cheated.

'I'm leaving tonight,' he says. He indicates the dining table and I see a suitcase parked behind one of the chairs. He must have brought it down while I was clearing up in the kitchen. It's our best one, the one we bought for our honeymoon. The biggest one.

'You've packed? Without telling me?' Blood pounds in my head, and I lose my grip on the cup. It falls out of my hand to the floor and shatters.

We both stare at its broken remains, but neither of us moves to clear it up.

'Look, I don't want an argument,' Richard says.

'You don't want an argument?' My voice quivers.

'We can talk another time. When you've calmed down. We're not going to resolve this now and like you say, we shouldn't argue when Charlie might overhear.'

I think of Charlie in the other room, oblivious to how his life's about to be turned upside down. Heat rises in my body and I dig my fingernails into my palm. 'How could you do this to him?'

Richard won't meet my eyes. 'Our relationship's over. We both need to face that.' His voice shakes, and for a moment I think he might have some compassion. I long for him to take me in his arms and say that everything will be OK.

Instead he turns away from me, grabs the handle of the suitcase and strides out of the kitchen. But I'm not ready for this conversation to be over. 'Are you going to *her*?' I call after him, the words muffled by emotion. 'Is that why you're leaving? To be with her?'

He doesn't answer. My pulse quickens as I follow him to the front door. I hear the closing bars of the theme tune from Charlie's favourite show coming from the other room and put my hand on the wall to steady myself.

'Are you going to her?' I repeat. My jaw clenches and my eyes burn from holding back my tears.

'Of course not,' he says impatiently.

'I don't believe you.'

'I'm not going to her. I'm not seeing her anymore. I've told you so many times.'

I'm not sure what to think. If I hadn't seen the photos of them together, then I'd never have found out about his affair. How can I believe him now?

'Where are you going then?'

'I've rented a flat not far from here. Don't worry, it will be easy for Charlie to visit.'

'You've planned it all out.' I think of him flat-hunting on his own, speaking to estate agents as a single man looking for a small flat, a bachelor pad. While I was frantically thinking of ways to save our relationship.

I grip the banister of the staircase for support. No matter what Richard says, it was his affair that was the beginning of the end of us. 'I can't believe it's come to this. She's managed to split us up.'

'No, Beth, it's not her. It's you. I can't live with you, can't live with your insecurity. We would have had a future if you'd just listened, just believed me when I said the affair was over.'

I feel like I've been punched. A wave of exhaustion washes over me. He's managed to turn everything around and blame it on me.

'Aren't you going to at least stay for Charlie's dinner?' I ask, desperate to keep him here a bit longer. Richard, Charlie and I always have dinner together, no matter what. It's been mostly a silent meal since I found out about his affair, the air thick with things we can't say in front of our son. I thought if we just pretended things were normal, repeated our daily routine, then eventually we'd get back to where we were.

'I think it's best if we have a clean break.'

I feel the burn of shame that, even after I've accepted the affair, I'm still not enough for him.

'I'll go now,' he says.

I glance over at the clock on the wall. I have clients coming tonight. New clients. And now I'll need to do everything alone:

feed Charlie, bath him, put him to bed. All before they arrive, expecting to find a calm and collected therapist.

Richard reaches down to pick up the suitcase. 'I want to get this all unpacked tonight.' Then he opens our front door and steps into the suburban street, and out of my life.

I put Charlie's fish fingers and chips in front of him and his eyes light up.

'My favourite,' he says happily, as he starts cutting his food up. My heart tugs. At four years old, he's so easily pleased.

I sit down beside him and tuck into mine. The fish is flavourless and I smother it in ketchup and then watch my son do the same. He's the spit of Richard with his dark curly hair and long eyelashes. He's only four, but he looks older, his long legs dangling under the table.

'Dad says I shouldn't have lots of ketchup,' he says as he squeezes the bottle.

'Well, Dad's not here.'

Charlie looks up at me, and for a moment I think he's going to ask where his father is. My stomach swirls in anticipation, but instead he squeezes the bottle once more and the fish fingers nearly disappear under a sea of sauce.

The house is silent, and I can hear the sound of the streets outside through our double glazing. The traffic rumbles down the main road a few streets away and high-pitched laughter rises and then falls as a group of schoolchildren pass by the house, most likely on their way to the park. I've always felt secure here, comforted by the constant noise of the London suburb, knowing that there is always someone around.

Charlie wolfs down his food as I push mine around the plate. How am I going to tell him his father's left us, that he lives somewhere else now? How can I say it in a way that will cause the least amount of damage? I remember when my own parents divorced, how convinced I'd been that it was my fault. I don't want him to feel the same way.

'How was school?' I ask, trying to keep things normal. I usually ask him on the way home, but I've been so distracted by the tension between me and Richard that I forgot today.

'It was OK.'

'Just OK?' His eyes are downcast. I reach across the table and touch his arm. He moves it away. A part of me wishes I hadn't said anything, that I could have just enjoyed his simple pleasure at being given fish fingers.

He's silent now, and I can see him swinging his legs back and forth under the table. I wonder if he's anxious because Richard isn't here, or if something happened at school. He had some trouble with a few of the other kids at the beginning of term, but I thought that had been sorted out.

I look at my watch. Forty-five minutes until my new clients arrive. I need to hurry up.

I rush through Charlie's bath, all the time wishing Richard was here to help. Even though there's not much time, I let Charlie play with his green boat and squirt me with his toy octopus. As I rub soap over my son's little body, I realise that this is the first day of the rest of my life. My evenings are going to be like this every day from now on. I won't have anyone to help. I won't get a break. And once Charlie's gone to bed, I'll face the evening alone, with just the television for company. I wrap my son in his towel and hold him tightly, breathing in his scent and the fragrant smell of his bath wash.

'I love you,' I say.

'I love you too, Mummy.' I wipe a tear on the back of his towel before he sees.

In his bedroom, I read him his favourite story about a dinosaur who's afraid of the dark and then kiss him goodnight. He wraps his little arms around my neck and kisses me on the cheek.

'Don't be sad, Mummy,' he says. 'Things will be better in the morning.'

He's repeating the words I said to him over and over again when he was crying because he wasn't fitting in at school. I thought I'd managed to keep my sadness hidden, but my kind little boy can sense it. I see the tiny frown on his brow, the perceptive eyes. And I can't stand the fact that my four-year-old feels the need to comfort me, when I'm the one who should be keeping him safe.

'I'm not sad,' I insist as I kiss him once more. Then I quickly turn off the light and escape to the landing, where I allow my tears to fall.

It's ten minutes before I manage to stop crying and go to the room at the front of the house where I conduct my counselling. I need to calm down before my clients arrive. Danielle and Peter. A couple visiting me for marriage counselling. If I didn't feel so full of despair, I'd laugh at the irony.

Instead I go through my usual routine to centre myself before they arrive. I light the candle on the coffee table and close my eyes. The calming scent of lavender fills the room, cleansing the air. I need to empty my head. I'm full of anger at Richard, that he could leave me like this, leave our son. How can I provide marriage counselling when my own relationship has just imploded? But it's too late to cancel.

I think of my little boy alone in his room. He didn't seem himself tonight, and I know he's worried about me. What if he wakes up and needs me? Richard would normally be at home to check on him. But if it's just me in the house, then who will go to him if he calls out? I'll have to leave the door ajar.

A wave of nerves threatens to overwhelm me, all my anxieties bubbling up inside me. I think of the couple coming to see me. I always feel nervous when I meet new clients. Before I open the door to them, I have no idea who they are. They could be anyone.

I open my notebook to the page where I'd jotted down some thoughts after my phone call with Danielle. Danielle Brown. Her husband's called Peter Brown. I pick up my phone and type their names into Google. I know I shouldn't, but I can't help myself. There's a huge list of Peter Browns on Facebook. The same for Danielle. I add *London* to the search term, but the list doesn't shorten much. It's pages long. I'm scrolling through the Peter Browns when the doorbell rings, making me jump.

After peeking into Charlie's room to check he's asleep, I rush down the stairs before the bell rings again.

'Hello,' I say, forcing a smile as I open the door. I wrap my arms around me against the cold blast of air that comes in from outside. 'You must be…' I hear my voice falter, as I stare at Danielle in surprise.

CHAPTER 2

DANIELLE

Beth does a double take as she opens the door, her mouth parting in surprise and her eyes widening. My pulse quickens and I step backwards, wondering if I should just turn round and leave, forget all about counselling, forget about trying to fix myself. But then I see her gaze resting on my cheek and I realise that she's just doing what everyone does now when they meet me for the first time. Noticing the angry scars that riddle my face and then pretending they haven't noticed at all.

I take a deep breath, hold out my hand and introduce myself. 'I'm Danielle,' I say with a practised confidence I don't feel. I've spent all day plucking up the courage to come here, to Beth's home, and start taking steps to address my past.

'Beth,' she says with a friendly smile, taking my hand and shaking it firmly. 'Come on in.' Her skirt swishes behind her as I follow her into her home. She can't be much over forty, but it feels as if she's older, with her sky-blue blouse and floral skirt. I've come straight from work, so I'm dressed more formally. Under my smart coat, I'm wearing a pencil skirt and a crisp white shirt, but I've left my suit jacket in the office, exchanging it for a grey cashmere cardigan before I left. Beth's brown curly hair has a natural bounce to it, unlike my straight bobbed hair, which sits flat against my head, no matter how long I spend styling it.

She pauses in the hallway, the cold air still blowing through the door. It looks like she's tried to tidy up but ran out of time. There's a pile of shoes pushed into the corner next to the shoe rack, and a messy collection of post, packages and small toys on a little table by the door.

'You're here for marriage counselling,' she says gently. Her voice has a soothing lilt, and I realise how easy it would be to fall under her spell, to immediately tell her everything.

'Yes.' I nod.

I notice the hairbrush strewn messily on top of the shoe rack, under the mirror, as if brushing her hair might be something she'd forget to do if it wasn't there.

'You mentioned your husband on the phone. Is he on his way?'

'No.' I look down at the floor, studying the dry mud on the mat in her hallway. It's days since it rained; the mud must have been here a while. 'He couldn't make it today. I hope he'll come next time.'

'No problem.' She puts her hand gently on my shoulder, a gesture that's almost motherly. My body tenses and I fight the urge to shake her hand off me. 'Let me take your coat and then we can go upstairs. How was your journey over? Did you have far to come?'

'Not far. I know the area.' I'd got here early and sat in my car for half an hour, staring up at the house, wondering if I would be brave enough for the therapy ahead.

I feel sick as I walk through her hallway to the staircase. There are children's wellington boots, next to a blue scooter. Crayon marks on the wall. The doors to the downstairs rooms are shut and I feel a desire to push them open, to peer in at the life behind them.

When we get upstairs, she leads me to a small, cosy room at the front of the house. Its pale green walls are punctuated by floating shelves full of self-help books. I study the spines, wondering if any of them have been read or if they're just for show. There's a sofa near the door and a chair and a desk opposite. A tissue box sits next to a candle on a coffee table in the centre of the room, its gentle flame flickering. I take a deep breath, absorbing the smell of lavender that scents the room. There's nowhere to hide. A part of me wants to run straight out.

'It's always hard the first time,' Beth says, reading my mind. 'Finding the courage to come.'

I nod. 'Thanks.'

'Take a seat.' Beth indicates the sofa. 'It's comfier than it looks.'

I lower myself onto the sofa and perch on the edge, back straight.

Beth sits down in the chair opposite, her long floaty skirt lifting and then settling.

We look at each other for a second and I smile nervously.

'So, Danielle, have you had counselling before?'

'Some…' I admit. 'A long time ago.'

'A long time ago?'

I don't want to talk about it now. I'm not ready. 'It wasn't particularly useful,' I say.

She waits for me to carry on, but I stare resolutely at the books behind her.

'OK, then. I find it helpful to run through a bit about therapy before we start, so we're both clear on what these sessions are for and what they are not for.'

I nod.

'As a therapist, I act as a sounding board for my clients, helping them hear their inner voice. I'm not here to provide guidance or tell you what to do. Rather, I'm here to help you work out what *you* want to do.'

Her voice washes over me, a voice so like my mother's. I close my eyes for a second, remembering. But I can't go back there. Not yet.

'OK.'

'All the sessions are confidential, but in some extreme circumstances, if I thought someone was in danger, I might have reason to break confidentiality.'

I frown. I'd thought that whatever I said would just be between me and her. I'm relying on it. 'What do you mean?' I ask. 'What kind of danger?'

'If I thought that you were at risk of harm from yourself or someone else, then I'd have to act.'

'OK,' I say. 'What do you mean by act?'

'It would depend on the situation, but if someone was in danger, I'd have to take it further.'

I stare at the floor, thinking about what I can say and what I can't say. How much I can share without consequences.

'What's on your mind?' Beth asks.

'I'm just thinking about what you said,' I say carefully. 'I'm a lawyer, I guess I like to know the details of how everything works.'

'Well, if there's anything else you'd like to know, then you can ask. Now, or at any time later.'

'Thank you.'

She smiles warmly. 'So, when you're ready, can you tell me what's brought you here today?'

'It's my marriage.' I put my hands to the scars on my face, feeling their jagged edges.

'Your marriage?'

'I'm sorry Peter's not here with me. I really hoped he'd come. He said he's caught up at work…' I pause, looking up at her. 'Would it be better to come back another day? When he's here too?'

She looks at me directly, her eyes meeting mine. 'Would you prefer that?'

I shake my head. 'No.' I want to get started.

'You look anxious.'

'I suppose I am.' It unnerves me being in this room with her, her gaze constantly on me. Watching me. Analysing me. I suddenly notice that the door is slightly ajar.

Beth's gaze follows mine. 'There's no one else out there,' she says. 'Except my son, but he's asleep.' She smiles. I imagine an innocent little boy, tucked up in bed. My heart aches.

'Can we shut it anyway?' I'm so on edge that I can't seem to get a grip on my own thoughts.

I see Beth hesitate, but then she goes to the door, peers into the corridor and then closes it gently. As she does, I notice a ketchup stain on the elbow of her blouse, dry and hard like an old splatter of blood. She sits back down.

'You were saying you were here about your marriage…'

'Yes… it feels like it's falling apart. We hardly see each other. We both work such long hours.'

'You're a lawyer, you said?'

'Yes, I work for a corporate law firm and do charity work on the side.' I feel myself start to relax. Law is easy to talk about.

'Charity work?'

'That's the bit I enjoy the most. I volunteer for a company which helps vulnerable people appeal wrongful convictions. I went into law because I wanted to help people, but in my corporate job I help companies, not people.'

'You take pleasure in helping people?'

'Yes, I actually thought about becoming a counsellor for a while. When I was really hating being a lawyer. But I realised that I didn't need to switch paths entirely. I could put more effort into the clients I volunteer with to give something back. At the moment I'm helping a care worker who's been convicted of Actual Bodily Harm for restraining a patient who was trying to attack him. We believe he should never have been convicted.'

She nods encouragingly.

'I want to help the people who need it most, the most vulnerable. Without help they'd really struggle.'

'I can see you enjoy it. Your face lights up when you talk about it.'

I nod. 'It's what sustains me, what makes me feel whole. Without it I… I don't really know that I'd be happy.' My voice breaks a little and I feel exposed, as if I'm sharing more than I intended.

'You wouldn't be happy without your job?'

'I don't know. Sometimes… sometimes I feel like I've planned out my life perfectly. And everything's worked out for me. On the outside I have the perfect job, the perfect life, but on the inside I feel empty. Like there's something missing inside me. Like my whole life is just an act.' I look up at her nervously, fiddling with my hair.

She nods. 'And how do you feel about Peter?'

I bite back the emotion that rises in me when I think of my husband. I remember the first flush of attraction when I met him, how much I wanted to be with him every second of every day. I remember our beautiful wedding day, tinged with the grief of getting married without either of my parents to see it, but the joy of joining with him forever, imagining building our own family together.

Things changed a few months ago when Peter had asked to take a break from our relationship. We'd been arguing a lot back then, but I'd still been devastated. Luckily we got back together again. But now it feels like we have separate lives, like two strangers existing in the same house.

CHAPTER 3

BETH

Danielle stares at the ocean of grey space beside her on the sofa, the place where Peter should be sitting. She takes a while to gather herself, pushing her straight blonde hair back behind her ears and smoothing her navy pencil skirt before she replies.

'I'm glad I married Peter, but... we hardly see each other. Because of work. He's a lawyer too. Sometimes we're so absorbed in our jobs that we don't see each other for days. I want to get the connection back that we had at the beginning. I want to fix our marriage. I thought he did too. But he's not here, is he?'

'Why couldn't he make it today?' I ask gently.

She's silent, staring at the wall behind me. I've been watching her as she speaks, taking in her movements, the moments when her breathing quickens and then slows, her nervous tapping on the sofa. I'm glad now that I didn't have time to cancel tonight's session. I can already see how much Danielle needs this space to talk, how much I can help.

'He's at work,' she says, twisting a strand of hair around her finger. 'Like I said, we hardly see each other these days. I think he's avoiding me.'

'He's avoiding you?'

'Yeah. It's because he doesn't want a baby anymore. He promised me we'd start trying soon after we were married, but I think he's changed his mind. Why would he do that?' She looks at me desperately, as if I might know the answer. Tears form at the corners of her eyes.

I hold out the tissues towards her and she sniffs, taking one.

'I can't answer that for you,' I say. 'I can only help you work out how to answer it yourself.'

'He says it's because I get angry easily, and jealous. But he's always either working or out late drinking with friends. It's no wonder I get jealous when I never see him. I work late often too, but I want us to try and make time for each other.'

She's silent for a moment and I'm careful not to interrupt her thoughts. I wonder if she thinks he's having an affair, or if I'm just so caught up with what's happened with Richard that I'm jumping to conclusions. I stiffen as I remember how unreasonable he was. I grip the side of my chair.

'Do you think he might be cheating on me?' she asks eventually.

I wouldn't know, I think. I didn't even know about Richard. 'That's not a question for me to answer.'

'But you've seen lots of married couples, haven't you? You must have an idea.' I wince, her words stinging. I had no idea about Richard until I saw the photos.

She puts her hand to her head and the sleeve of her stylish grey cardigan falls down slightly. I catch sight of a flash of darkness on her wrist. She sees me looking and quickly pulls it down. I wonder if she has scars on other parts of her body as well as her face, or if this is something else, another injury.

'What makes you think he might be cheating?'

'It's just a feeling. We split up for a bit a while ago. It was just supposed to be a break. He suggested it. And I wondered if it was because he'd met someone else. But then he came back to me. We'd both seen other people when we were apart, but it wasn't the same. We agreed that the break-up was a mistake, that we were meant for each other. When we first got back together we were all over each other. But it didn't last for long. Now we're both working such long hours we never see each other. And I wonder if he's really working at all, or if he's met someone else.' She wraps her arms around herself as if to comfort herself.

'Have you been cheated on before?' If she has, it might cloud her judgement, make her see signs that just aren't there.

'Yes,' she says quietly, staring at the floor. 'Years ago I was in a relationship with someone who was seeing other people all the way through. He used to shout at me too, accuse me of all sorts of things. I could never please him.' She glances up at me, meeting my eyes and searching for understanding. I nod, and shift my seat closer towards her, narrowing the gap between us. I want to reach out and comfort her. I've been that person too, when I was younger, dating men who didn't love or respect me.

'The thing I'm worried about is… well, I want a baby. Peter won't even discuss it. I wanted us to start trying a long time ago. And when we got back together I thought we would at least talk about it. But he won't entertain the idea. Recently, more and more of my friends have got pregnant, and each time I've wondered why it couldn't be me. Why Peter isn't interested.'

'That must be hard,' I say, looking at her intently. When I'd become pregnant with Charlie, it had been a surprise. Richard and I hadn't even considered having a family together, but once we'd had time to adjust, we'd both been delighted with the news.

'So hard—' Her voice breaks.

'He won't talk to you about it?'

'No. The only thing he's said is that I wouldn't have time for children as I work too many hours. Which is ridiculous, because he works just as hard. We'd both need to cut down.'

I nod.

'I've wanted a baby for so long,' Danielle says. 'When I married Peter, I thought children would follow.' She wipes a tear from the corner of her eye, trying not to smudge her make-up. Her body has hunched in on itself on the sofa and she looks so alone.

'I'd change if a baby came. If I had a child, they'd be the centre of my universe. It would be so different from my childhood.'

My ears prick up at this, wondering what kind of childhood she had, wondering how that's influencing her desperation for a baby. If she's subconsciously trying to put something right, trying to correct something.

'OK,' I say, hoping she'll continue.

Danielle looks at her feet. 'There's something else. Something he says to me. I know it's not true, but it makes me feel rubbish, it undermines my confidence.' She shifts her weight from one side to the other on the sofa.

'What does he say?' I speak softly, encouraging her to open up, to tell me whatever it is that is hurting her so much.

'He says I wouldn't be a good mother.'

I resist the urge to tell her that of course she'd be a good mother, like I would say if she was a friend, not a client. She needs to find that self-belief on her own.

'He says he knows me,' she continues, her speech quickening, as her tears turn into sobs. 'He says he knows me better than anyone, and that because of that, he can tell I won't be a good mother.'

I wait as she dabs at her eyes once more. 'I'm so sorry,' she mumbles. 'I didn't mean to break down. I've just been trying to keep everything together.' Her body shakes.

'It's OK to feel this way,' I reply, my words sounding inadequate in the face of her distress.

She stands suddenly. 'I think I need to go.'

Anxiety radiates from Danielle and I speak softly. 'This is a safe space. You can say what you need to say here. Feel however you need to feel. There's no judgement.'

She hesitates for a second, then shakes her head.

'Why don't you take a minute to calm down?' I indicate the sofa.

'Can I go to the toilet?' she asks. 'Have some time to regroup?'

'Why don't you do that here?'

'I need the toilet anyway.' She smiles through her tears, suddenly calmer. 'Two birds with one stone.'

I pause for a moment, reluctant. I forgot to clear up after Charlie's bath. I don't want her seeing his bath toys, a reminder that I have a child and she does not. But I can't think of a reasonable objection.

'Sure,' I say, pulling the door open. 'It's at the end of the corridor.'

I hear her feet padding down the corridor past Charlie's room, then the bathroom door shutting behind her.

I stand and walk over to the window. On the street outside, I see suited commuters hurrying back from the Underground station, heads down, and I imagine them rushing back to their families. I feel a stab of jealousy and I fold my arms, comforting myself. Tonight I'll be in this house on my own. No Richard. Just me and Charlie. Suddenly everything that's happened today comes rushing back to me.

I think of our son in his bedroom alone, without Richard here to keep an eye on him. I must check on him.

The door to Charlie's room creaks as it opens and I hold my breath, hoping it won't wake him. He's snuggled up, his little chest rising and falling under the duvet, his mop of dark curls resting against the pillow. His arms are wrapped round his cuddly penguin and his other soft toys line the bed behind him. He won't part with them no matter how many times I suggest that he might have too many. I straighten the duvet around him and then turn to leave. My heart aches for him, as I think of the baby he was and the man he'll become. I feel the weight of responsibility for him, my child. He looks so peaceful, unaware of what the future holds for him, unaware that tonight will be the first of many without his father.

I reach down and stroke his hair, then put my face in his curls. I didn't have time to wash his hair tonight and there are still remnants of the earthy scent of the playground mixed with the fragrance of his bath wash. I try to imagine his day; lessons and chatter and games. Or being ignored in the playground. I just don't know. Already he shares less than he once did with me. He's not desperate to tell me what happened at school anymore, no longer dying for me to hear all about his day, instead just wanting to curl up in front of the TV when he gets home. I feel like I lose a little more of him each day. And as much as I want to hold him close and keep him as a baby forever, I know he needs to grow up, to find his independence without me. I imagine the future, ten years from now. Charlie a teenager and Richard gone. I feel an intense sense of loss and I hug Charlie close. Who will I be then?

'I love you,' I whisper to his sleeping form.

I stand to go, but I can't take my eyes off my son. This moment seems so precious, and I want to cling to it, knowing it can't possibly last forever.

A cat screeches outside the window and I turn.

There's a shadow in the doorway, silently watching me.

CHAPTER 4

DANIELLE

I watch Beth with her son, see how difficult she finds it to leave him. I want all of that for me. I want to love a baby the way Beth clearly loves her child. I know I'm intruding on an intimate moment, but I can't seem to pull away from the scene in front of me. Her son looks so small and fragile beneath the duvet.

It took a while to control my tears in the bathroom, surrounded by the evidence of Beth's happy life with her son; a little green boat and a purple toy octopus by the side of the bath, the tiny red toothbrush sitting next to the adult one by the sink. It all seemed so unfair. That she should have what I so desperately want. And then, on the way back, I'd seen the door to this room ajar and I couldn't help peering in.

Beth turns suddenly, her eyes widening as she sees me. She draws her hands into her body defensively and jumps back. She hadn't realised I was here.

'He's beautiful,' I say quickly.

'They grow up too fast.' She reaches down to straighten a soft toy on his bed and then turns to me and smiles. 'How are you feeling? Ready to continue?'

Ten minutes later we're finishing up, and Beth gets up to let me out. She puts her hand on my arm and looks me in the eye. 'Thanks for coming today, and for sharing so much. The first session is always the hardest.'

I nod and draw away from her, exhausted by my whirring emotions. I never normally talk about how I feel and it's drained my energy. 'Thanks.'

'I hope to see you next week.'

'I'll get Peter to come along next time.'

'That would be helpful. But if he can't come, I think you'll find the sessions useful on your own.'

I smile. 'I think so.' A part of me is sad to leave, despite everything. There's so much left to say.

'Some of my clients find it useful to keep a diary when they start counselling. Tracking the highs and lows of their emotions can help to get to the bottom of what's bothering them.'

I nod. 'I can do that.'

We say goodbye at the door, and I step outside into the cold air, wrapping my scarf around me. When I get out my phone to order an Uber, I see a message from Peter.

I've got out of work earlier than I thought. I'll pick you up. I'll be outside in the car at 9pm.

Headlights flash across the street and I see him sitting behind the wheel of our car, his phone lighting up his face.

I climb in the passenger side and Peter leans over to kiss me. I turn my head away, my thoughts still spinning.

'How did it go?' he asks, as he starts the engine and pulls into the street.

'OK,' I say, suddenly feeling guilty about everything I've said about him.

'Do you think it will help?' he asks.

I pull at the long sleeves of my cashmere cardigan, extending them out under my coat, appreciating the comfort of the soft material on my fingers. I don't know the answer to that yet. 'I hope so. Beth – the therapist – she was a good listener.' I hadn't been expecting to tell her so much, so soon. Now I'm worried; about saying the wrong thing, confiding too much.

'That's good. I want you to get better.' He reaches across the gearstick, resting his hand on my leg for a moment.

'There's nothing wrong with me.'

He sighs. 'That's not what I meant… I love you, you know. I just want you to feel happier.'

'I want to feel happier too,' I say. I reach into my handbag, and my hand grips the bottle I've taken from Beth's cabinet. Antidepressants. I hadn't been planning to take them. I'd seen them in the cupboards when I'd been looking for more toilet roll. They'd been staring me in the face. Two full bottles of them. Both prescribed to Beth. I'd thought about how together Beth seemed, and I wondered if the drugs would help me too. I'd shoved them into my handbag on impulse.

Maybe they'll help. Maybe they'll improve my relationship with Peter. Maybe they'll help me forget the past.

I remember when Peter and I first met. We were desperate for each other's company, wanting to talk for hours, spending all day in bed. But now there's a distance between us that seems almost impossible to bridge. It's been this way for at least a year.

'Dani?'

'What?'

'I said I love you.'

'I love you too,' I say automatically, turning my head to stare out the window at the row of terraced houses rolling by. And then I wonder if it's true. I did love him at the beginning of our relationship. I spent every waking moment thinking about him, fantasising about him. And I loved him on our wedding day, I remember that so clearly. But do I love him now?

CHAPTER 5

BETH

After Danielle leaves, I lock the door of my therapy room and go downstairs to the living room, sit down and take deep breaths. I feel unsteady, just glad to have got through the session. As I try and relax, all the thoughts I've been keeping at bay come crowding in. Richard has left me. The man I love, the man who I thought I would grow old with, doesn't want to be part of my life anymore. Richard has always looked out for me, but now there's no one. I'm going to have to look after Charlie alone, without anyone there in the evenings to talk through the stresses and strains of bringing up a four-year-old. I feel the panic rising inside me, and I try to calm down by telling myself that I can keep going, I can hold it together.

I make myself a cup of tea and take it upstairs to check on Charlie. He's fine, still sleeping peacefully. Somewhere in the house I hear the clunk of a pipe and I jump, glancing behind me, remembering Danielle standing there earlier. I think of how much she longs for a child, and I feel sorry for her. But there's another feeling there, a kernel of fear. Maybe it was the way Danielle was looking at Charlie. I didn't like the way she came into his bedroom without asking.

I push the fear away, recognising its irrationality. A lot of people say you should trust your instincts, but mine can let me down. I was delusional once, spiralling out of control, convinced someone was out to hurt me. I ended up in hospital. These days, I'm better most of the time, but I have to remember to take my pills.

I think about how I can help Danielle, and a warm feeling spreads through me. The thought that I can make a difference to her life, help her through a tough time, goes some way to alleviating some of the emotional pain coursing through me. Even without Richard, there is still lots worth living for. I can focus on my job, on my clients. If anything's going to get me through this, it will be that.

I take my tea into the bedroom, pick up a novel from the bookcase and flick through the pages, unable to concentrate. Thoughts of a future without Richard swirl round my head. The drawer in my bedside table tempts me. It's where I lock away my grief, the things I try not to think about as I go about my day-to-day life. Happy memories, smiling photos and Charlie's drawings are scattered round the house. Only the painful memories make it into the drawer. Moments I want to hide from, never confront. As a therapist I should have dealt with all my own problems, but the truth is I've found some things insurmountable.

Most of the drawer is full of Nick; pictures and cards, theatre tickets and restaurant receipts. When I was in a relationship with Nick I was the happiest I've ever been. I laughed and joked as if I didn't have a care in the world. He helped me realise that not all men were like my violent ex, that the world could be a good place. He taught me how to live.

Much later, I moved into this house with Richard. It's in the suburb where I used to live, where I first met Nick, but I didn't tell Richard that. I was heavily pregnant by then, and we'd chosen the house thinking about the baby's quality of life. I brought my bedside table with me when we moved in, so the photos were never far away.

But now the pictures only make me sad. They remind me of what I once had. What I can never get back.

Soon the drawer became a repository for other painful things: the hospital identity band which they'd put round Charlie's little foot when he'd had to stay on the ward because he wouldn't feed and was losing weight. And the other photos. The photos I got in the post. The ones that showed me Richard was cheating.

I take a gulp of tea and then reach into the drawer, to the bottom, to the envelope containing the photos. My name's scrawled on the front in messy, rushed handwriting, and in the corner there's a first-class stamp, the postage mark smudged and illegible. It had rained that day and I had been struggling to manhandle Charlie into his raincoat to take him to preschool when it had dropped through the letter box. I was running late, and I'd put it to the side, but it had played on my mind as I dropped Charlie off. I wondered if it was someone from the past, a teacher from the school where I used to work who had tracked me down, or a friend from my counselling training. By the time I got back home, I'd been excited, eager to see the contents of the envelope. I'd practically torn it open before I'd even started brewing my morning cup of coffee.

The photos had fallen out the wrong way up and for a brief second I'd hoped they were photos of Nick, rediscovered on someone's memory stick. Pictures that would give me another piece of the puzzle, return another part of him to me.

I turned the photos over. But they weren't of Nick. There were of Richard. I felt a jolt of disappointment.

And then I looked at the first image more closely. Richard wasn't alone; he was walking side by side with a woman, her back to the camera. I didn't recognise her. In the next one the girl was still faceless, but Richard's image was clear, his arms encircling her.

My heart almost stopped. Was it a mistake? Not what it seemed?

I turned to the third photo. Once again the man was clearly Richard. And this time the woman had her head tilted back. They were locked in a kiss.

CHAPTER 6

DANIELLE

I rub moisturiser into my face, slowly working it into the damaged skin of my burn. The doctor told me to do it twice a day, but I often do it more. I want it to heal as quickly as possible, so I can return to the me I was before the fire a year ago. I grab a glass of water from the bathroom and knock back one of the antidepressants I took from Beth's house. I'll need it to get through today. I apply light make-up, avoiding the burnt skin. I try to smile at myself in the mirror, but I can't quite manage it. All I can see is the slightly distorted edge of my lip and my rough, injured cheek.

'Ready to go?' Peter says, coming up behind me.

I nod. A year ago I would have asked him how I looked. But I don't dare to now. I sometimes wonder if, when he suggested we have a break, it was because of my scars, because he couldn't bear to look at me anymore. We split up nine months after the accident. Time enough for people to think it wasn't because of my injuries, so he didn't look like the bad guy. But I still wonder if my scars were the real reason.

I push the thoughts away. All that matters is that we're back together now. We walk down the street together and I take his hand, feel the warmth of his fingers interlocking with mine. We should have worn gloves. But I never look like I'm dressed for the weather anymore. Despite the cold wind and the grey skies I wear a wide-brimmed hat and dark glasses to keep the sun off my fragile skin. I hate that it draws attention to me, makes people glance at me curiously. And then they see the scars and look away.

I walk to the Underground station like I do every day to commute to work. On the weekday commute everyone minds their own business, nobody stares. But at the weekend, the tube is different, full of tourists and curious children. When I get on the train with Peter, the kids point at me and ask questions of their parents who flush and tell them to be quiet.

I take my hat off, push my sunglasses up to my forehead and sit down, leaning into Peter's body on the seat beside me. He runs his hand through my hair and kisses the top of my head.

'Nervous?' he asks.

'Yes,' I admit. This is the first social event we've been to since the fire.

'I am too,' he says, and I wonder why. Is he ashamed of me? Of the way I look now?

I lean away from him and distract myself by reading the news on my phone until we reach our stop.

Jessica answers the door of the flat with a huge smile on her face, her pregnant belly already prominent and her face glowing. Her face drops slightly when she sees my scarred cheek, but she quickly recovers.

'Hello!' she says, and she reaches out to hug me, her belly getting in the way, an extra person between us. She doesn't kiss me like she would usually, not daring to go near the burns. I feel left out as I watch her kiss Peter on each cheek.

I used to be so confident, but now I feel self-conscious. A part of me wishes we weren't here, that I could spend all weekend working on my client's appeal instead.

'I'm so glad you made it,' she says.

'Wouldn't miss it for the world.' I smile and hand her my wrapped gift. A tiny pair of blue booties and a babygro with a colourful drawing of a playground, complete with a climbing frame, slide and swings. I feel a sense of longing, wishing I had bought it for my own baby. I dismiss the thought, guiltily. This isn't about me. It's about Jessica.

'Thank you,' she says. 'Come through.'

We go into the living room and we're offered champagne. I grab a glass and take a sip.

'I haven't seen you since—' Jessica begins.

'The fire,' I finish. 'No. I was in hospital for a while. And we haven't been out much.'

'It must have been so scary.'

I glance at Peter, who's staring at his shoes. 'It really was.'

She nods towards my face. 'And it's all healing OK?'

'As well as can be expected.'

'That's great.' There's an awkward pause and then she changes the subject. 'I love your hair,' she says. 'Never thought I'd see you with a blonde bob, but it really suits you.'

'Thanks.' I reach my hand to my hair, remembering when there was nothing there, when most of it had been burnt off. It's taken ages to grow back. More guests arrive and I move away, but I find I have to repeat the same stilted conversation about how awful the accident was with friends and acquaintances. Heat rises to my face, and I wonder why I can't seem to confide in them about what really happened. Some of them have been friends for years. Maybe if Peter wasn't here I'd be able to tell them the truth, but somehow I can't face it.

The conversation soon turns to babies and baby names. Jessica's mother tells me how much she and her husband are looking forward to having a grandchild. I nod politely and smile, but I can't help thinking how unfair the world is. If I was pregnant now, my parents wouldn't be around to admire my bump, eagerly awaiting the arrival of their grandchild. I blink back tears.

Yet I still want a baby. So much. It would be a new chapter of my life. Creating a new family, starting again. I wouldn't repeat the mistakes my parents made.

The girl next to me, who I've just met, starts to tell me about her struggles with IVF.

'We're not getting any younger,' she says, clutching her partner's hand. 'But we're hoping this time it will work.'

I nod. I'm thirty now. It's not too late for me, but I need to know that Peter wants children too. He's on the other side of the room, chatting with Julian, the father-to-be. I wonder if Julian's excitement makes Peter feel differently, if he could see himself being a father too.

'Do you want children?' the girl asks.

I nod. 'I do.' I glance over at Peter. I'll just have to persuade him that I'm up to it. I can reduce my hours at work if I have to. But I know there's more to it than just that. I used to ignore him when he said that he didn't think I'd be a good mother, that I need to learn to calm down, control my temper. But his words have been getting to me lately. Maybe he's right. Maybe I'm just not cut out to be a mother.

CHAPTER 7

BETH

'Charlie! Put your shoes on now!' I shout from the kitchen, as I desperately try to prepare his lunch box, shoving cheese between sliced bread and throwing in an apple and a packet of crisps. When his lunch is made I run up the stairs and swallow an antidepressant with a swig of water from the bathroom tap. I put the bottle back in the cupboard. It's the last one. I was sure I had more. I got a few months' supply when I last went to the doctor's. But when was that? Maybe it was longer ago than I thought. I'll have to book another appointment.

When I return to the hallway Charlie is still shoeless, playing with a dinosaur which should be out of the way in the living room. I run a brush through his hair, grab his shoe from where he threw it down yesterday, undo the Velcro and start to push his foot into it.

'No!' he screams, kicking at me.

'Charlie, just cooperate, please. We're going to be late.'

'I don't want to go to school.' I wonder if the other boys are giving him a hard time again. A good mother would sit him down and get to the bottom of *why* he didn't want to go. But I don't have time. I refuse to watch the school receptionist raise her eyebrows at me when I sign him in late for the second time this week.

'We're going to school,' I say forcefully, 'whether you like it or not.' I grab the shoe and put it on him as he cries, then put the other one on.

'I'm a big boy. I can do my shoes myself,' he mumbles through tears.

'I know you can.' I stroke his curly hair, wondering when my little baby got so old. It feels like only yesterday I was taking him home from the hospital.

I put his coat over his shoulders, encourage his arms through the sleeves, slide my feet into my slip-on shoes and open the front door, grab his hand and pull him outside. The drizzling rain blows into our faces as we hurry down the street, me two paces ahead, geeing him along. I arrive at the school red-faced and breathless, the only mother without a coat on herself, just in time for the bell. Charlie lets go of my hand and runs towards his friends at the entrance.

I breathe a sigh of relief, and watch as he chats happily to the other children. I don't know what the tantrum was about this morning, but he seems fine now he's at school. Maybe Richard leaving is affecting him more than I thought. I nod to the gaggle of mothers chatting by the gate and then hurry away again, embarrassed by my unbrushed hair.

Back in the warm house, I calm down and make myself a cup of tea. I need to sit down for a moment after the rush of the morning routine without Richard. Doing it all on my own isn't easy, and it hasn't helped that Charlie has been in a bad mood all week. It must be because he misses his dad.

But as soon as I sit down I realise my first client's due in ten minutes, so I get up and speed round the kitchen tidying up the breakfast things, managing the occasional sip of my tea.

Three hours later after back-to-back clients, I'm exhausted. I've had two sets of couples this morning. Extramarital affairs are a common issue in marriage counselling, and usually I can see both sides, understanding that each relationship has its own complications. But since Richard left I've found it much harder than normal to take a neutral stance. It's difficult to switch off my thoughts about my own life. I miss Richard, miss having someone in bed beside me at night, someone to talk to and share my day with. This week, other than my clients and Charlie, I've only seen the mums at the school gate. I'm emotionally exhausted and I have no one to talk to. A part of me is jealous of my clients this morning, because, despite their difficulties, there is hope for them. They are still turning up to counselling, trying to fix their relationships. Whereas Richard has made it quite clear there's no going back. I know I should hate him, but a huge part of me still loves him, still craves his company. I love the way he used to make me laugh, the way he takes his own work as a therapist so seriously and genuinely cares about his clients. I don't understand how he can be so heartless towards me when he treats his clients with such kindness.

The wife I've just seen had begun a forensic investigation into her husband's affair. She knew every detail of every time they'd had sex. It made me wonder why I had buried my head in the sand about Richard's affair, accepting his explanation that it was just a fling, not asking for any details. Not wanting to know.

Now I'm curious, suddenly feeling an overwhelming need to know who it was Richard slept with, who broke us apart. She was someone he'd met in a bar. That's all he'd told me. I go upstairs and retrieve the photos from the drawer. I look at the picture of Richard kissing her. How could he do that? But no matter how long I stare at the images, they don't offer me any more clues as to who the woman is. They are standing in front of the glass windows of a building. It looks like it's in central London, but the design of the building is so common that it really could be anywhere.

I'm getting nowhere with the photos, so I load up Richard's computer, determined to look for other evidence. There must be emails between them, or messages on social media. I try and hack into his email, guessing again and again at the password, until I finally give up. It's the same with his social media. I sigh with frustration. I go through folder after folder on his hard drive, not even sure what I'm looking for. While I'm searching, my phone beeps and I jump. There's a missed call and a voicemail. I stare at the number in disbelief. Genevieve Price. The head teacher at the school where I taught art a few years ago. I should have deleted her number. Why would she be contacting me? I feel a headache starting to form behind my eyes. The last time I spoke to Genevieve she'd been so angry, furious that I'd brought the school into disrepute.

I pick up the phone and listen to the message, holding my breath. But her voice is friendly. She's moved to London after the death of her husband and wants to meet up. I feel a stab of pity. They'd been married at least thirty years, with two grown-up children. But I'm still not sure why she wants to meet up with me. Not after everything that happened.

I return to the computer, the message still playing on my mind. I have a few more attempts at getting into Richard's emails. No luck.

I stare at the computer screen for ages, lost in thought, remembering my teaching days. It's only when my phone beeps again with a text from the bank to say I've gone into my overdraft, that I notice the time: 3.16 p.m. I'm going to be late to collect Charlie.

I grab my keys and run out of the house.

The evening is a battle. Charlie refuses to eat his dinner, have his bath or go to bed. I can tell he's angry with me for being late collecting him. I'd fought my way through the hordes of parents leaving with their children to find him waiting on his own with his teacher in the classroom. After a telling-off from her that made me feel like I was the one still at school, we'd trudged home together, Charlie refusing to speak to me.

I'm angry with myself too, for getting so caught up in trying to find out more about Richard's affair and thinking about the past that I forgot the time. I swallow my guilt and try and remain calm while I attempt to persuade Charlie to go upstairs before Danielle and Peter arrive. Eventually I get him into his bedroom and into his pyjamas. I read him his favourite book about dinosaurs. He never grows tired of it. No matter how many times I've read it to him he still laughs in the right places, and always wants a hug from me when the T-Rex appears. I love the way he sees me as his protector. He doesn't know yet how fragile I really am. That I'm afraid of things too. That I can break down and fall apart.

I read the book two more times but he won't go off to sleep.

'Again, Mummy,' he says insistently.

'No, sweetheart. It's time for sleep.' He's tired and I can see his eyes starting to shut, before he snaps them open.

'Again!'

I stroke his dark curly hair. Danielle and Peter will be here any minute. 'There's no time today.' I point to the dinosaur clock on his wall, which I'm using to teach him to tell the time. 'See the big hand is on the twelve and the little hand is nearly on the eight. That means it's way past your bedtime.' He's supposed to be in bed by seven thirty, but things have slipped since Richard left. I know the doorbell will ring any minute.

'I want another story.'

I shake my head, bend over to kiss his soft cheek. 'Sleep well.'

'Mummy – don't leave me.'

I feel a stab of guilt that I was late to collect him from school. Had he thought I'd left him? Then my heart fills with anger at Richard. The bottom's fallen out of my son's world, his security taken away. This is all Richard's fault. 'I'll never leave you. I promise.' I place his toy penguin in his arms. 'Pengie will keep you company at night. You can cuddle him if you feel lonely.'

Charlie squeezes the soft toy tight.

The doorbell rings and I give Charlie a kiss, not wanting to leave his side when he's feeling alone. I give him another kiss. 'Go to sleep,' I say gently.

Then I hurry downstairs and answer the door.

Once I'm in my counselling room, I explain that I need to leave the door ajar as Charlie's not yet asleep and Danielle nods her understanding. She seems on edge. Once again, Peter hasn't turned up.

'Is Charlie ill?' she asks politely, ignoring the sofa and walking over to the window.

'No,' I say. 'He's just upset because I was late to pick him up from school.'

Danielle doesn't reply, staring out the window.

'What's on your mind?' I ask, stepping over to stand beside her. Outside the window it's foggy and I can hardly see the street below, the amber street lights barely cutting through the mist.

Danielle looks smart in her perfectly tailored suit, but the way her manicured hands grip the windowsill gives her away. A Victorian jade brooch is pinned to her lapel. I recognise it because I have my own collection that Richard has bought me over the years for birthdays and Christmases. That specific type of brooch is hard to find and expensive. The people who buy them are usually collectors.

'Everything and nothing,' she says. Her features contort into a worried frown and I can see her scar tissue stretching and puckering.

'It was an accident,' she suddenly blurts out.

'What was?'

'I'm sorry, but I could see you looking, and I know people always wonder. About my scars.'

'I didn't mean to—'

'No one ever does.'

'Do you want to talk about it?' Perhaps she's bringing it up for a reason.

'It was a fire.' She falters. 'They're burns. Third-degree.'

I feel sick, images flashing through my mind. Flames climbing up curtains. Shattering windows.

Fear claws through me. I reach my hand out to the wall to steady myself, trying to get the images out of my mind. I focus on the tree just outside the window. It needs cutting back, its branches like tentacles, reaching out towards the glass.

'I'm sorry to hear that.' I only just get the words out; they're barely a whisper. I can feel the blood draining from my head, the humming in my ears. I'm sure I'm about to faint. I slide down into my seat.

Danielle turns from the window and moves to the sofa, giving me a chance to get my breath back.

She touches her cheek, running her finger over the jagged edge of the scar, avoiding the angry centre. 'It was weird,' she says. 'At first I couldn't feel anything. It was only later it hurt.'

We both stare at the burning candle on the desk. I'd lit it before Danielle arrived, to cleanse the air in the room. Silently, I get up and blow it out.

Although the desk lamp is on and the candle wasn't casting much extra light, the room suddenly seems much too dark. I desperately need to stop the images ricocheting round my head. Stumbling towards the light switch by the door, I catch my leg on the edge of the sofa and knock into Danielle's elbow.

'Sorry,' I mumble as I reach for the switch. Light floods the room and I'm aware it will have revealed my red, flustered face, signs of tears that I've been holding back.

Danielle blinks rapidly.

I take a deep breath. I can do this. I can focus on my client; I can put aside my own history and help her.

'You said it was an accident?'

A tsunami of emotion rumbles inside me. *At least she didn't die*, I think. And then I feel cruel; I can't imagine how awful it must have been for her.

'We were having a barbecue, Peter and I. It was just over a year ago.' She pauses, digging her nails into the palm of her hand, before forcing herself to continue. 'Lots of people were coming. Friends, family, colleagues. I'd spent weeks planning it and all morning getting ready. I think a part of me was showing off really. I wanted people to see my perfect home.' She laughs bitterly. 'That taught me.'

I swallow, imagining the scene. Imagining what happens next. The smell of burning fills my nostrils as if I am back outside that building twenty years ago. I blink it away.

She continues. 'And then, just before the guests were due to arrive, the barbecue wouldn't light properly. The wind kept catching it and putting it out. Peter and I argued. I'd planned everything so carefully, and I felt like he was messing up his part. And then… he had this idea. There was petrol in a container in the shed. For the lawnmower.'

Tears fill her eyes and she squeezes them shut, her hand reaching to her face once more, as if she's still struggling to believe what happened. I watch her in silence, sensing her urgent need to tell her story.

'He took the petrol and poured it onto the coals. He can't have been thinking straight. The whole thing went up in an instant.'

CHAPTER 8

DANIELLE

By the time I get home I'm exhausted, my mind spinning with memories of the fire. It's the first time I've talked about it properly, the first time I've allowed myself to remember.

I'm on autopilot as I put the dinner on and shove some washing in the machine. When Peter gets home I just about manage to greet him with a smile.

'Good day at work?' I ask.

'Busy,' he says. 'It's intense at the moment. We don't have enough staff. We're trying to recruit some more juniors. How was your day?'

'I was at therapy tonight.' He's probably forgotten it was even on.

He nods. 'Nice for you to have the time.' Peter lowers his face towards the pan to smell the curry. 'What did you talk about?'

'Not much.'

'You don't want to talk about it?'

'Not really.' Even though I brought up the subject, I'm not sure I'm ready to talk to him about what Beth and I discussed. Not yet.

He wraps his arms around me from behind and my shoulders tense.

'You have to be able to trust me, Danielle,' he says. 'I'm your husband.'

'I do trust you.' I can feel an argument brewing, the same way you can sense the moisture in the air when a storm's coming.

We're becoming like my parents used to be, always looking for an argument, for an excuse to release the anger that bubbles under the surface of our relationship. Luckily our house is detached, so there's no one on the other side of the wall to hear it.

'Tell me about the therapy then. Tell me what you told her. How can we fix our marriage if you won't even talk to me?'

'We talked about the fire.'

The silence that follows feels heavy. Once my bandages were taken off at the hospital, we never mentioned the fire again. It's an unwritten rule. The words we've needed to say to each other, that we should have said to each other at the time, have remained unspoken. It's like it never happened. Except for the scars on my face. The scars he has never acknowledged. The reminder of what we both want to forget.

I check on the dinner while Peter gets the cutlery and sets the table.

'I'm glad you talked about it,' he says finally. 'You needed to.'

'Perhaps we both need to talk about it. In therapy.'

'I think it's you who needs the therapy. Not me.'

I nod. He's probably right. 'I think the fire affected me more than I realised.' I put my hand to my face, feeling the hard edges of the scar tissue. 'It's changed everything for me. My appearance. My confidence.' A tear runs down my cheek and I wipe it away.

'I still can't believe it happened,' Peter replies. 'The petrol… I don't know why—' His voice has a sharp edge to it – one I've become more and more used to as our relationship has progressed.

'We can't change what happened,' I say. 'We have to accept it.'

'That's what I've been trying to do. But I still don't understand.' He steps closer to me.

I step back and shake my head, fighting back the fear as I remember the flames engulfing me. Back then it had felt unreal, as if it was happening to someone else, but now my feelings are so intense it could be happening right now.

'It's so hard to talk about, to even think about,' I say.

'It must be. It must be hard knowing that something so awful was preventable.' He stares at me, his eyes cold and unforgiving. 'You need to get yourself under control,' he says quietly, 'or I dread to think what will happen next time.'

CHAPTER 9

BETH

After Danielle leaves I feel uneasy, unable to keep my own memories at bay. I go round the house, checking all the doors and windows are locked. I've always felt safe here with Richard, but since he's left I've become aware of my vulnerability, knowing that if there was any kind of intruder I would be the one who had to fight them off. Before Richard, when I lived in my flat, there'd been days when I was too scared to leave because I was convinced someone was watching me. I'd see a shadow pass the window and think it was them, waiting outside. It's been years since I felt like that, but now the familiar fear is creeping back.

I go and check on Charlie, moving the duvet back gently to see the rise and fall of his chest. He shifts slightly under the covers and murmurs something in his sleep.

'It's OK,' I whisper, stroking his hair.

He rolls away from me. 'Daddy…' he mumbles.

I feel tears prick my eyes. 'He's not here right now.' I think about how Richard isn't here to put him to bed at night or wake him up in the morning anymore. I wonder if he'll have a room at Richard's flat too, a whole life with his father I'll know nothing about. My tears get heavier and I cover my mouth with my hand. I can't bear for Charlie to suffer. He's still my baby.

My eyes wander to the bedside table, trying to distract myself, to find something else to focus on. I remember reading Charlie his story before bed, his favourite one. I go to pick the book up from the bedside table. Its familiar words comfort me too, a lullaby when I'm feeling down. But it's not there.

Instead there's another book. An old Thomas the Tank Engine one. Richard used to read it to him when he was little, and I feel a surge of nostalgia and regret.

But why is the book here? I'm sure I didn't put it there. Perhaps Charlie got up in the night, pulling it off his shelf to read. He wouldn't be able to read the words, but he likes to look at the pictures. I imagine him here on his own looking at the book and I feel a shiver of guilt. I had the door open when I was speaking to Danielle, but I was still oblivious to what he was doing in here. Shouldn't I have heard him get up?

Then a thought flits across my mind. Danielle. She's been in Charlie's room before, during the first session I had with her. Today she'd gone to the toilet just before she left, and I'd locked the therapy room and gone downstairs to start clearing away the toys. What if she'd seen Charlie had woken up and she'd passed him the book to comfort him?

I push the thoughts aside. Charlie must have got up in the night. I need to calm down, tidy up some more and then go to bed. There's no way anyone's been in my son's room. It's just my anxiety talking. I've become paranoid since Richard left. With only my own thoughts for company, my mind wanders to my worst fears. I need to get out more, meet new people. I lost so many of my friends when I was dismissed from my teaching role and I never really regained them. Richard and Charlie kept me busy. Now I'll have to make an effort to connect with other people. It's what I often suggest to my clients when they get lonely.

I think of Genevieve's call earlier. We used to be close when we worked together. Perhaps I should phone her back, arrange a time to meet up. But surely we'd have to discuss the past? I can't face that. Not now. I don't want to even think about it.

I leave Charlie with a light kiss and hurry out of the room. I go downstairs to the kitchen and find my gratitude journal, reaching over to the cookery books that line the windowsill where it rests horizontally across the top of them. I want to spend ten minutes trying to focus on the good things in my life. I haven't picked up the journal since Richard left, but tonight I feel it's important to take stock. I always write down three things I'm grateful for and three things I've achieved. It helps keep me in a positive frame of mind before I go to bed.

I'm about to sit down at the dining table when I freeze. I'm sure I heard footsteps. Is there someone outside? I go to the window and look out at the dark street beyond the house. Aside from the glow of a feeble street lamp, it's pitch-black, the parked cars just vague outlines. I draw the curtains quickly, cocooning myself in the safety and warmth of my house.

Perhaps I should increase the security. Install an outdoor camera, add a burglar alarm, put up an outside light. I'd done all that at my flat when I'd thought someone had been watching me. But it turned out there was no one watching at all. It had all been in my head.

Even so, I can't stop myself checking that the windows in the living room are shut and locked and then checking the front door again.

Once I'm completely certain everything is locked, I start to relax, sitting on a dining chair made from reclaimed wood that I bought at an antique shop, my feet on the Persian rug which belonged to a great aunt of Richard's. I'm safe and I'm at home, surrounded by the objects that make up my life and give me comfort, with my son upstairs.

'*I'm grateful I live in a house that's safe and warm,*' I write in the journal.

I stare at the words, contemplating them. My feet sink into the soft fibres of the rug and I wonder if Richard will eventually come back and reclaim all his belongings, taking the rug with him.

And then I feel the hand pressing down on my shoulder. Fingers squeezing my skin.

'Hello, Beth,' someone says softly.

A terrified scream slips out of my mouth before I can stop it.

CHAPTER 10

DANIELLE

I stare at Peter in disbelief. I can't believe he'd say that, implying that the fire could happen again if I didn't keep myself under control. But what if he's right? What if something awful does happen to me?

I need to get out of the house, to escape from him. I can't cope cooped up with him anymore.

I grab my handbag, open the front door and run out into the cold air.

'Where are you going?' Peter shouts.

I don't reply and shut the door behind me.

Outside a winter frost is setting in. Above me the sky is clear and cloudless and the moon casts a dim light. I can't walk anywhere in this weather. I reach into my handbag for my car keys and unlock my two-seater Audi. I bought it for myself when I was promoted at work. I open it up, climb into the driver's seat, turn on the engine and put the heating up to its highest setting. At first cold air blasts out at me, but then it quickly warms and I hold my fingers over the plastic grates. I stare at my house, shivering. In my years in foster care, I always dreamed of living in a house like this. I wanted plenty of space. I wanted it to be neat and tidy and full of designer items. But most of all I wanted it to be full of love. I wanted to find a space in the world where I was loved and accepted. At first Peter made me feel like that. Our marriage was the security I craved. I thought we'd have children and a picture-perfect family life.

I realise then that there's somewhere I need to go. I pull on my seat belt and flick the indicator, pulling out of the space outside our house. I drive a couple of miles until I reach the house I grew up in, before I was moved to foster care. It's huge, bigger than the house I live in now. It doesn't look too different to how it did back then. The curtains in the bedroom have been switched to blinds, but little else has changed.

I shiver as I look up at it, remembering my father. I can hardly bear to think of him. He worked non-stop to buy this house, and then he died and left it all behind. He never got to retire and enjoy the lifestyle he'd worked so hard for. He didn't even get to see me grow up. Even now, some days I can't believe he's gone. The pain lives deep inside me. It never goes away.

I'd give anything to hug him one last time. I close my eyes and try to remember what he sounded like, his deep, comforting voice. But I can't hear it anymore, not even in my head. With my eyes squeezed shut, I can only remember my parents' arguments, their voices echoing around the draughty house. Whatever I do, if I have a child I will give it a better childhood than I had.

CHAPTER 11

BETH

My screams keep coming and my pulse races. My whole body tenses, preparing to be attacked. I don't have a weapon. I'm in the house on my own with Charlie. And someone has their hand on my shoulder.

I can't bear to turn round, can't bear to face the monster behind me.

'Beth,' a voice says. 'Beth.' It takes a moment for my brain to stop panicking and for me to recognise it. Richard. It's only Richard.

'Are you alright?'

'You scared me,' I reply, finally turning round to look at him. And then I feel a flicker of hope. Has he changed his mind about leaving me? Does he want to come back?

'I'm sorry,' he says with a frown. 'I thought you heard me come in. It was about half an hour ago. I called out to you. I've just been looking for some course notes in my filing cabinet.'

'I was with a client.'

'Oh, yes,' he says absently. 'I saw the light on in your room when I went upstairs to check on Charlie. He was awake. I read him a story.'

'It was you who left the Thomas the Tank Engine book by his bed?'

'He wanted me to read to him.'

At first I feel relieved, but then anger rises in me. 'You can't just come in and read him a story without telling me. You shouldn't have let yourself in. You should have told me you were coming.'

He must have known that he'd scare me. He knows my history, knows how anxious I get.

'I used to let myself in all the time,' he says with a frown. 'And I wanted to see my son.'

'But we've split up. I thought I was alone, and then suddenly you appeared. Imagine how terrified that made me feel.'

'OK, OK,' he says, irritated. 'I'm sorry. I just wanted to talk to you about a few things. We need to sort out custody arrangements, for a start.'

'Custody arrangements?' It all sounds so official. And it hits me then. Richard's never coming back. We're never going to be a family again. Our relationship really is over.

'We need to work out when I can see Charlie.' He's so matter-of-fact, as if two weeks ago we weren't still trying to make our relationship work.

'I'll let you see Charlie, of course.' I'd never deprive our son of his father. But then I hesitate, horrified by a new thought. 'You don't want him to live with you, do you?'

'No, no,' Richard says hastily. 'You can be the primary carer. And besides, the flat I'm renting is far too small. Just a one-bed. That's something else I need to talk to you about. You know this house belongs to me.'

'It's *our* house.' I'd thought we'd grow old here together.

'But I paid for it, didn't I?'

I stare at him, incredulous. 'Are you saying you wanted to leave me, but now you've come back to claim *your* house?'

He puts a hand on my arm and I shake it off.

'No. But I've been thinking about it. And it does seem silly for me to be living in a tiny flat when you're here in this huge house. Especially as I was the one who paid for it.'

My whole life is in this house. It's close to Charlie's school. It's where I see clients. It's been my refuge since Richard and I moved in. Until recently, I've always felt happy here.

'What are you trying to say? I'd keep the house, wouldn't I?' I say, doubt creeping into my voice. 'I'll be the one looking after Charlie most of the time. And he'll need a big enough place to run around in.'

Richard squirms. 'It's not that simple. The house isn't yours to keep, Beth.'

CHAPTER 12

DANIELLE

I check my face in the mirror in Beth's downstairs cloakroom. The skin around my scars is flushed, but otherwise I look as presentable as I ever manage to look these days. I wash my hands under the tap and hurry out and up the stairs. I don't want to keep Beth waiting. It's a week since I've seen her last, and I've been thinking about therapy a lot.

'Ready to start?' she asks, as I take a seat.

'Sure.' I nod. I see her looking at the empty space beside me on the sofa. 'Peter's not coming today,' I say. 'He sees therapy as more for me than for him.'

She raises her eyebrows ever so slightly. 'And what do you think?'

'I suppose I agree.' Peter never had any intention of coming to these sessions. And a part of me never wanted him there, never wanted him to tell his side of the story.

The silence lengthens.

'What's on your mind today?' Beth says eventually, smiling warmly. For a second I think she sees right through me, that she can hear my spinning thoughts.

'Everything and nothing. Lots of things.' I pull down the sleeves of my suit, aware of the injuries below, the scars I try so hard to hide.

'Anything you feel ready to share?'

She looks at me, waiting as the silence fills the room. It's a technique we use in the courtroom too. Very few people can endure a silence without trying to fill it, and in doing so, people trip up, make mistakes, reveal too much. But I resist the urge to speak.

'Last week we talked about the fire…' Beth says eventually.

'Yeah,' I say, staring down at the cream carpet. 'It was awful… to relive it.'

'You said Peter started it by mistake.' I hear the slight emphasis she puts on 'by mistake', and I know she is already starting to question the story, already starting to doubt Peter.

'We talked about it afterwards. He was glad I'd spoken about it here. He thought it would help me.' I don't say that he said something terrible could happen again if I'm not careful.

'But he didn't want to come tonight? Talk about it too?'

'No. Like I said, he thinks I'm the one who needs therapy. And he's right. I feel like I lost a part of myself in the fire, a part of my identity. My scars mean that people look at me differently. I used to draw confidence from my looks, but now I feel embarrassed by my appearance. And I don't know what's left behind. I don't know who I am anymore.' I blink back tears.

She looks at me kindly. 'That's a big thing to say, that you don't know who you are.'

'Yeah.' Sometimes I feel like no one knows the real me, no one understands the emptiness inside me, not even me. 'The fire… it changed everything. How I felt about myself. My relationship with Peter.'

'It must have been very difficult for you both.'

'Peter blamed himself. He couldn't understand how it had happened. How he had made such a big mistake. He came with me to the hospital, saw what the fire had done to me. He felt awful.'

'Do you blame him?'

'I don't know.' I pull at a thread in my suit jacket absent-mindedly. 'We'd argued just before the fire.'

Beth meets my eyes and I see the concern in her face.

'I was scared afterwards,' I say quietly.

'Scared that it would happen again?'

'No, scared of Peter.' I let the words hang in the air between us, unable to say more.

'Of Peter?'

The silence grows. 'I don't want to talk about it,' I say finally.

She waits for a beat, studying my expression. I feel exposed under her gaze.

Finally she speaks. 'We can revisit that another time. When you feel ready.'

I nod, but I doubt I'll ever get there.

'Perhaps instead it might be a good idea to go back to your childhood to talk about how you formed your ideas about relationships.'

I feel my entire body tense, and the room starts to feel smaller. 'My childhood?'

'Yes. It seems to me that it might be relevant to your experiences now. All of us form our ideas about relationships from our own childhoods. I'd be interested to hear about yours.' She leans towards me, her eyes meeting mine.

'My childhood was… fine.' I manage a half-smile.

'Fine?'

'I got through it.' I take a deep breath, try to calm my racing heart. 'I'm still here. Still fighting. I was in foster care for most of my teens. I lost my parents.'

Beth smiles gently. 'I'm sorry. How old were you when that happened?'

'Fifteen.'

Without speaking, she reaches out and touches my hand, but I pull it away. I can't bear the physical contact.

She's silent, waiting for me to tell her more.

'It was so long ago now…' I say.

She hands me a tissue. I hadn't realised I was crying. I think of my parents, their unhappy marriage. What would things be like if they were both still alive? Would I feel differently about myself? Would I be happier?

I try not to think about it too much. But sometimes when I'm alone, I imagine speaking to my father, imagine trying to put things right between us, apologising for my teenage mistakes. I miss him so much sometimes, it's like a physical pain.

'What happened?'

'It was an accident…' I say quickly. 'A car crash.' I look away so I don't have to meet her eyes. If she looks at me she might see right through me, see that everything was my fault. Suddenly the sofa feels uncomfortably hard and I shift in my seat.

'That must have been so difficult for you. Especially when you were so young.'

I feel my defences coming up, the defences that got me through a series of foster homes, that stopped me from talking about what had happened. 'Yeah.'

She swallows and I can see she feels sorry for me. Seeing my own grief reflected in her eyes cuts me to the bone. Tears flow freely down my face.

'What was it like afterwards?' Beth asks softly. 'After they died?'

'Pretty awful. But I tried not to think about it. I threw myself into my schoolwork instead. Even though they were gone, I still wanted to make them proud. Especially my mother.'

Beth nods.

'We were always at loggerheads before. She wanted me to study harder, but I was too focused on impressing my friends – you know what teenagers are like. It was only after she died that I started concentrating at school.'

'It sounds like you dealt with your grief by distracting yourself with schoolwork.'

'There was no choice. I had to get on with things when I was in foster care.'

'You went straight into care after your parents' deaths?' I can hear the surprise behind the question, the thought that no one else loved me enough to look after me, not aunts or uncles or grandparents or friends. No one wanted to take me in.

'Yeah,' I say. 'My relatives came to see me, but they didn't want me living with them. None of my aunts and uncles had children, and they didn't want a teenager messing up their lives.'

'That must have been hard.'

I shrug, a forced nonchalance that I've perfected over the years. 'I survived.' There were people who could have helped, people I had trusted. But they'd let me down.

'You seem angry.' Beth stares at my hands, which have clenched into fists of their own accord.

'I am,' I say simply.

She nods, waiting for me to continue.

'There was something else. I found out a lot after they died.' I look at her directly now. 'Secrets they'd rather have kept hidden.'

'Secrets?'

'I suppose everyone must have them. Things they'd prefer other people not to know. Maybe I was naive to think otherwise.'

'It's fair to say that a lot of people have things they hide,' Beth says softly. 'It's a normal part of being human to want to keep some things private.'

I stare at her, struck by what she's said. She has her own life, her own problems. I'm sure there are things she hides too. I realise I don't know enough about her. I've shared so much of my own life without her sharing anything in return.

'Do you have secrets?' I ask.

'This isn't about me.' She shifts in her seat. I know there's something underneath. I wonder if it keeps her awake at night, the way the past stops me from sleeping.

'What did you find out?' she asks.

I hesitate, wondering if I can truly trust her. She waits.

'My father had been having an affair,' I say finally. 'He was planning to leave my mother.'

'How did that make you feel?'

'Angry, I suppose. But there was so much going on. I was grieving at the same time. And I was trying to adapt to a new life in foster care. Different people, in a different place. Everything had changed in an instant. It was like I couldn't really feel much at all. I just had to get on with things.'

'You blocked it out?'

'Yeah. But it's coming back to me now and I feel angry all over again. And sad.' I look up at her. Her kindly eyes meet mine and I feel the emotions swirling around inside me, threatening to overflow.

'Perhaps you're only allowing yourself to process your emotions now.'

I change the subject. 'I've come a long way since then. With my job. I'm at the top of my field.'

'I'm sure your parents would be proud of you,' she says, and again I get the sense she feels protective towards me, almost motherly.

My tears fall harder. 'Sometimes I feel like I'll never repay them.'

'What do you mean? You feel you owe them?'

'A part of me blamed myself.'

'For what?'

'For the way I lost them. There were things I wish I'd said. I wish I'd told them I loved them instead of always arguing with them…' I trail off, overcome by emotion.

Beth looks at me over her glasses. 'Danielle,' she says, 'it's very common for children to blame themselves for the traumatic events they go through. They think that if they'd done something differently they could have prevented a death or a divorce, or some kind of tragedy. But that's not true. It's never their fault.'

I wipe away my tears with a tissue and she reaches out and touches my knee. I recoil.

'It wasn't your fault.'

I take a shaky breath. 'I know,' I say. And I do know. I've been telling myself it wasn't my fault for years.

'It was an accident,' she carries on. 'You said so yourself. And there's no one to blame in an accident.'

But that's where she's wrong. Because there is someone to blame for what happened to my parents. But it's not me.

CHAPTER 13

BETH

When we finish, I'm emotionally drained. It's been hard to listen to Danielle talk about her childhood, yet I feel like we made progress. I managed to help her begin to process what happened to her parents, to shift some of the blame from her. As she gets ready to leave, I want to wrap her in a hug, tell her that everything will be alright. But I stop myself.

'Don't be too hard on yourself,' I say, in the hallway. She nods, shrugging on her coat and pushing her hands into her pockets. 'Thank you.' She smiles warmly.

The sound of a phone ringing shatters the moment. My landline.

'I'd better get that.' I go to the study, but the phone handset isn't in the stand. I can hear it ringing close by, but can't seem to find it. The desk is littered with papers and boxes of junk which I've moved in here out of the way. Finally I see it on one of the shelves of the bookcase.

I answer it. 'Hello?'

But I'm too late. The other person has rung off.

I go back into the hallway and see Danielle, her coat wrapped around her securely, her heavy rucksack on her back. She's reaching for the latch.

'See you next week,' she calls back to me as she steps outside.

I can hear the sound of the television from the living room. Charlie point-blank refused to go to bed this evening, so I'd put him into his pyjamas and let him stay up and watch *Paw Patrol* on the understanding that he'd stay still and keep quiet during my session. He was almost falling asleep when I'd left him curled up under a blanket on the sofa. I dread the thought of waking him and the tantrum that will inevitably ensue.

I push the door open to the living room. 'Time for bed,' I say gently, going over to the sofa.

But he's not there.

'Charlie?' My eyes scan the room.

Perhaps he's hiding. He used to do that when he was little and he didn't want to go to bed. I look behind the sofa, behind the curtains.

'Charlie?'

He's not in the living room.

'Charlie!' I shout. Maybe he was so tired he took himself up to bed. I run up the stairs to his room, pull the covers from his bed. He's not there.

I race round the house, checking the kitchen, my bedroom, the utility room. I even look in my therapy room in case he wandered in there when I was downstairs. There's no one there.

I run back downstairs, rechecking the living room. No sign of Charlie.

The garden. He must be in the garden.

Panic rises inside me and my heart pounds. What if he isn't there? What if someone's taken him? I think of the long argument we had about bedtime before I eventually gave in and settled him on the sofa. What if he's run away? I think guiltily of how engrossed I was in Danielle's story, how I never thought to check on him.

Our garden is long. At the back there's a swing and a climbing frame that Richard assembled one Saturday afternoon, but I can't see them in the dark.

I don't bother with shoes, my socks absorbing the dewy grass, soaking through. Adrenaline pumps through my veins and I can hardly feel the bitter night air. Somewhere on a backstreet a siren wails and my stomach clenches in response.

'Charlie!' I call, more desperately now. 'I'm not cross with you. Just come out.'

At the back of the garden the swing and climbing frame are shadows against the night sky. My eyes dart around. He's not here either. There's no sound except the buzz of the traffic on the ring road a few streets away.

I run back into the house, heart hammering, and pick up my phone. I'm about to call Richard, and then I wonder if I should call the police first. I have lost my child. How could I have lost my child?

Guilt sweeps through me once more. I wasn't watching Charlie. I was working upstairs. What will Richard say? What will the police say?

My mind's a jumble, but I swallow my fear and press call anyway. Richard's phone rings and rings but he doesn't pick up.

The doorbell goes and I jump.

Is it Charlie? My heart leaps.

Holding the phone to my ear, I open the door.

I see Danielle first. She must have forgotten something. 'It's not a good time,' I say hurriedly. But then I see who's standing behind her. Charlie. Relief floods me.

I hang up the phone and wrap my arms around him. He's in his pyjamas and his small body shakes in my arms, his tears forming a wet patch on the shoulder of my jumper. I squeeze him tightly, trying to warm him up. I clutch his freezing hands, rubbing his cold fingers between mine. My poor boy. How could I have let this happen?

'Thank you so much,' I say to Danielle, my heart bursting with gratitude. What would have happened to him if she hadn't been there?

'He was out in the street. It was so scary, Beth. He was nearly hit by a car.'

'Oh my god,' I say. 'Charlie.' I squeeze him tight. 'Why did you go out?'

'I was looking for Daddy,' he says, unable to meet my eyes. He can't seem to stop shaking. It must be the shock.

I look up at Danielle. 'What happened?'

'When I came out of the house, I saw him step out from between two parked cars. He was crossing the road. He didn't see the car coming. I pulled him back. It was so close, Beth. I was terrified.' Danielle looks like she's close to tears herself.

I hug Charlie tighter and he buries his head in my chest. 'It's OK,' I say. 'I'm here now. Everything's going to be OK.'

'How did you get out of the house?' I say, more to myself than to Charlie. Every scenario is running through my mind. Had I left the door ajar when I let Danielle in? Had he managed to unlatch the door himself? He'd never done it before.

'Wasn't someone watching him?' Danielle asks gently, but I think I hear a ring of accusation in her voice.

'I was in the house… I thought he'd be alright downstairs.' I'm shaking now too, hardly able to believe what's happened. My arms are wrapped tightly around my son, unable to let him go. I feel a surge of shame. I shouldn't have left him downstairs alone.

'I'd better go,' Danielle says. 'Will you be alright?'

I nod mutely and she hesitates, unsure.

'I'll see you next week then,' I manage finally.

She smiles, then turns and walks wordlessly down the path.

CHAPTER 14

DANIELLE

I dress carefully, my heart thumping with nerves. My hands shake as I put on the earrings my mother gave me for my twelfth birthday, pairing them with a necklace I bought for myself when I first qualified as a lawyer. I look at myself in the mirror in the office toilets, staring at the angry scars across my face. Beneath them I look so much like my mother. When I look into my eyes, I see my mother's determination reflected back at me. We used to argue a lot when I was a teenager, and I'll always regret that. But I used to think that the two of us could get through anything together.

No one knows where I'm going today. Peter will think I'm at work, and I've told my colleagues I have a hospital appointment. I consult the map over and over. It will take two buses to get to the other side of town. I didn't want to show up in an expensive car, it would be too conspicuous. No one in my new life knows anything about my old life, and no one would understand the reason for this trip, why I have to do this.

The first bus is full of commuters, but on the second the passengers are different. Mums with pushchairs at first, manoeuvring in and out of the buggy space. Elderly people with sticks and shopping trolleys. Once we get out of the city centre, they get off one by one, until only a few of us remain. There's a man who sits right at the back, tapping his fingers to the beat coming from his headphones, and an elderly woman on the seat nearest the front. And me. I stare out the window watching the scenery go by. An estate of low-rise flats. A park. A children's playground. A row of small shops: a newsagent, a dry-cleaner, a cafe.

I feel sick, wondering if I should turn round. My life is exactly as I want it. I have everything set up. A job that I enjoy, charity work where I make a difference. A calm, tidy home. A husband. Why am I taking this journey back here? Shouldn't the past be left where it belongs?

But I can't do that, not anymore. If I don't visit, don't have this conversation, then I know she'll come and find me. And what will I do then? How will I explain my absence all this time? How will I explain that I wanted to forget it all, and to do so I had to forget her too? I thought I'd moved on and left everything behind. I thought marrying Peter and changing my name would have meant I was no longer that girl, Sophie Loughton. The girl whose name was instantly recognised. The girl journalists tried to track down all those years later.

I look anxiously at my phone, watching the dot of the GPS moving closer to my destination. I want to turn round, but I can't. Not easily. That's another reason why I didn't bring my car. So I couldn't change my mind and drive straight off again.

We're nearing the destination now. Outside the window, I see the tall brick walls, the barbed wire on top. The prison's been here since Victorian times, and countless inmates must have passed through.

I get off the bus, my heart hammering. It's forty-five minutes until visiting hours start and I kill half an hour walking around the outside of the prison, thinking of all the people shut inside, how endless it must seem, counting the days until you're released. I can't imagine it.

I don't know how she's coped, how she's got through day after day, locked up. She liked the finest things in life. She had everything. But now she has nothing. She has no one. Except me.

I go up to the main gate fifteen minutes early, knowing I'll need to be processed first, details taken and searched. I shiver as I approach the huge gates and then go through the innocuous wooden door on the right-hand side.

'Hi,' I say to the person on the reception desk. 'I'm here for visiting hours.' My voice shakes as my confidence trickles away.

'Take a seat,' he says.

Gradually the chairs around me fill up and then we're taken through, one by one, to be searched.

Entering the room, I scan the rows of prisoners sitting behind desks. Some of them anxiously look up, watching for their visitors, while others pick their nails or slouch nonchalantly in their chairs. They're dressed in everyday clothes: jeans, jumpers, blouses, sweatshirts. If they weren't behind bars, they'd look like ordinary women. There's nothing that stands out about them. I see movement in the middle row, a tentative wave. I meet her eyes and her face breaks into a smile.

The guard's shoes squeak on the polished floor as he walks me over. I can feel the tears welling up in my eyes as she reaches out to put her arms around me. The guard coughs and we pull apart and sit down.

I look at her, her eyes a mirror of my own.

'Hi, Mum,' I say.

CHAPTER 15

BETH

It's Richard's afternoon off, and I've invited him round so he can see Charlie, and we can talk. I know how much Charlie misses his dad and I need to talk to Richard about the house. There's no way I'll let him sell my home from under me.

Before he arrives, I look around the living room, trying to see it through his eyes. I haven't had time to tidy up. I've been so worried about Charlie nearly being hit by a car yesterday. I've tried to talk to him about it, but he won't tell me anything. He's sitting in the corner of the room playing with his toy trains, rolling them round the track one after another, completely immersed in his game.

While he's occupied, I start clearing up, gathering up Charlie's toys and putting them into the cupboard. Richard will be appalled by the mess, books and toys shoved to the side of the room in ever-expanding piles. But other than that, nothing really seems to have changed. A professional photo of the two of us staring blissfully into each other's eyes still sits in pride of place on the side table, amongst all the other family photos. That won't do. I go over to the side table and shove the picture into the drawer beneath. Amongst the other frames, there's a windswept family photo of us on the beach on the South Coast, squinting and happy, cheeks tinged with sunburn. I ruthlessly sweep it off the table and put it in the drawer too. I rearrange the remaining images, but the table seems empty.

I look at the pictures that are left: me and Charlie in front of a country house, Charlie in his school uniform, him on his first birthday. And then it occurs to me. The person who's missing. The most important person who's been in my life, the man I still miss every day. Nick.

I dash upstairs and pull his photo out of my bedside drawer, staring into his intense eyes for a second before taking it downstairs and placing it with the others. I don't need to hide him away anymore. I can acknowledge our love and remember all the good times we had together.

Charlie's still playing happily. I stare at the picture. I remember how that smile was reserved just for me, how much we meant to each other. I think about how we planned to get married, have a family. He always seemed so much older than me, so much wiser, but when I look at the photo now he looks young. He must have been about the age I am now when it was taken. I have lived and he hasn't. It seems so unfair.

When Richard lived here I used to wait until he was out before I secretly took out this photo. I'd talk to Nick about my relationship with Richard, tell him about Charlie, tell him what we were doing, what my life was like now. How I'd built it up again, that I was working as a counsellor. I know Nick would be proud of me. He always said he admired how much I wanted to help others.

The knock on the door startles me and Charlie runs to it, getting there first.

I open it and Charlie flies into Richard's arms. 'Daddy!' he screams, wrapping his arms around him.

'Richard,' I say, and then stand awkwardly, unsure how to greet him.

'Beth. Can I come in?'

I wince. It's like he's a stranger. 'Of course,' I say.

He follows me through to the living room, as Charlie talks to him excitedly about his day at school, telling him far more than I could get out of him. Richard asks all the right questions.

'Do you want a drink?'

'I'll get myself a water.' I watch as he goes to the kitchen and turns on the tap. It already feels odd seeing him here. I must have got used to him not being here, because now he seems out of place.

'Why don't you go to the other room and watch *Paw Patrol*?' I say to Charlie.

'I want to see Daddy!' I think about yesterday, how he'd gone out onto the street to look for Richard. He must be desperate to see him.

'You can see Daddy once he and I have had a little talk,' I say to Charlie.

'I want to play with Daddy… now!'

I sigh. 'Why don't I get you an apple juice? You can have it in the living room.' Charlie brightens, as I fetch the drink and poke the straw through.

Richard looks at me and then turns back to our son. 'Why don't I come and turn the TV on for you? Then I'll speak to your mum and I'll be back to play with you in no time.'

Charlie nods, and I'm sad to see how grateful he is for this tiny piece of attention.

When Richard returns he sits down at the dining table and I take a seat beside him.

'So…' I say. 'How have you been?'

'Good,' he nods. 'I've been good.'

'Clients OK?'

'Fine.' There's a pause, and I think he might ask me about my life or even Charlie, but he gets right to the point. 'We need to talk about money.'

I nod. 'We do. And there's no way you're selling this house.' I look him in the eye, and he flinches.

'I know it will be difficult for you, but it's what needs to be done. I can't pay the mortgage on this house *and* pay rent on my flat.'

'I've done some research. I have a beneficial interest in the house. Which means I'm entitled to live here.'

'Have you consulted a lawyer?' he asks.

'Not yet.' I've only looked everything up online, but I need Richard to realise I'm serious. There's no way I'm leaving this house. 'I'd prefer to come to an agreement between us, but I'm more than happy to take things up with a lawyer if I need to.'

He smiles wryly. 'I'm not going to stay in a tiny flat forever. Not when I'm still paying for this house.'

'Is it the mortgage that's the problem?' I ask. I've been studying our bank statements trying to work out if I can afford to contribute more to the mortgage, so Richard won't have to sell the house.

'Well, yes, that's part of it. If I wasn't paying the mortgage I'd be able to afford to rent somewhere bigger. But in the long term I want to release the equity from the house to buy somewhere else.'

'Right. Well, I've been running some calculations and I think I can afford the mortgage, if I just take on more clients. I can show you the spreadsheet if you like.' I hate the waver in my voice, how I've always felt inferior beside him. Richard had been my counselling tutor when we met, and our relationship has always felt unbalanced as a result. I used to look up to him so much.

'When do you think you could take on more clients?'

'Daytimes and evenings. I have a few slots open in the day, and if you looked after Charlie a couple of nights a week then I could have more clients then too. At the moment I have to wait until he's gone to bed.' But since Charlie escaped from the house the other night, I've been wondering if it's even safe to see clients after he's gone to bed. I need to make sure I always double-lock the door so he can't get out.

He frowns. 'I wanted to talk to you about that too. I'd like to see more of Charlie. I miss him. I'd like to spend the day with him on Saturday. I thought I could take him to the new soft-play that's just opened up the road.'

'Saturday?' I don't want to lose Charlie at the weekend. I'd been looking forward to a lazy morning, when I'm not rushing around getting Charlie ready for school, shouting at him for not putting his shoes on. I don't see why I should do all the hard work, dealing with him when he's tired and hungry and needs putting to bed and Richard just takes the fun 'quality time' at the weekend.

'It would be more helpful if you took him one evening. If you collected him from school.'

'You know I work then.'

'You could do it on your afternoon off. Or else, could you pick him up from here when you finish work and take him to stay at yours? Or come here and look after him while I work?' That would solve my problem of Charlie being alone in the house while I'm working. At least some of the time. 'You could do it every week if it works.' I smile at him.

'I'm not sure that's convenient for me.'

'Why? Do you have other plans?'

'No, but—'

'We have a son, Richard. He's our joint responsibility.'

'I suppose I could look into it.'

'And there's the safety aspect too. I feel uncomfortable leaving him alone. Charlie tried to get out of the house the other day, while I was seeing clients.' Guilt stops me from telling him he succeeded, that I didn't know how long he'd been out there, alone in his pyjamas, that he was almost run over. I don't want Richard to think I'm not coping on my own.

'Why did he try and get out?'

'He was looking for you. He misses you.' I feel so sad for my son and angry at Richard for leaving. 'So why don't you come over one evening next week when I'm working?'

'OK. I'll check my diary and get back to you. We can try it and see how it goes.'

'Thanks, Richard.'

'Right, I'll go and see Charlie now.'

I follow him to the living room, where Charlie's on the sofa, looking sheepish. He's covered in apple juice, his clothes and skin sticky.

'Charlie!' I say, berating him. 'What happened?'

'I spilled it.' I wonder if he's done it on purpose, for his dad's attention.

'You're so sticky.' I reach for the baby wipes, but I already know they won't be enough.

'I can give him a bath if you like. Clean him up,' Richard says.

'I think that's a good idea.'

Richard takes Charlie upstairs and soon laughter fills the house. I imagine Richard tickling him and swallow the lump in my throat, trying to remember the last time I heard Charlie laugh like that. I hate thinking about how much Charlie's missed out on in the last couple of weeks without his father.

Instead I busy myself, going back to the tidying I really should have finished before Richard arrived.

My phone rings as I'm putting everything back in its place and I answer it absent-mindedly.

'Hello?'

'Beth. I'm so glad I got hold of you. It's Genevieve.'

'Oh, hello.' I remember Genevieve, the head teacher at the school I used to work at, calling a couple of weeks ago. It feels like she's calling from another life.

'Hi… I left a message, a while ago. Did you get it?'

'I did. I'm sorry I didn't get back to you. I've been so busy.' I hadn't called her back because I hadn't wanted to think about the past, how she'd dismissed me from my teaching post. 'I'm so sorry about your husband,' I say quickly, remembering that he'd recently passed away.

'Thank you. I've moved out of our old home now, down to London… and, well, I don't know many people. I thought you might want to meet up. For a coffee or something.'

'I—' I have no idea what to say. I'd thought she never wanted to see me again.

'Or maybe you're too busy. Like you said. It seems everyone's always rushing about everywhere. Considering how many people there are in London, it's very hard to meet people.'

Is that why she wants to meet? Because she's lonely?

'I'm not too busy,' I say, feeling a stab of pity. 'It's just—' Doesn't she remember how nasty she was when we last spoke? I'd thought we'd been friends. I'd trusted her.

'I know we parted on bad terms,' she replies. 'But it couldn't be any other way. I had to dismiss you. I didn't have any choice. It's all water under the bridge now.'

I frown. I thought she couldn't stand me anymore, that she thought I was a bad teacher who'd abused my position. Is it possible that it wasn't that straightforward?

I remember how well we used to get on. How we had the same vision for the school, believing that pastoral care was just as important as the academics. I'd like to meet up with her. It's not as if I've made many new friends since I left teaching.

'OK,' I say. 'Let's do coffee.'

'Brilliant,' she replies, breathlessly. 'I'll message you with a few dates.'

'Great.'

'Enjoy the rest of your day.' She hangs up and I stare at the phone, surprised and pleased at how the conversation went. I'd never expected to hear from her again after what happened.

Upstairs, Richard is running the bath for Charlie. I get out the vacuum and run it over the living room. When I turn it off, I hear Richard calling out for me.

'Beth!'

I frown in irritation. Can't he give Charlie a bath without my help?

I go to the bottom of the stairs and shout up, 'What is it?'

'Have you seen this?'

I go up the stairs and into the bathroom, curious.

'Look at this,' Richard says. He points to Charlie's upper arm and I see a smattering of blue and purple bruises. Almost like fingerprints.

I shake my head and peer in closer. 'Charlie, how did this happen?'

'I don't know,' he says, staring into the bathwater.

Richard turns to me. 'You need to keep a proper eye on him. How can you not know about this? You're supposed to be his mother.'

CHAPTER 16

DANIELLE

My mother looks frail, her smile stretching over her sallow face. Ten years in prison haven't been kind to her. She's lost some of the softness at her edges, become thin and brittle. And old. She looks much older than her mid-fifties.

I fight back tears as I think of all the moments we've missed together. Me finishing school. My graduation from university. And then from law college. I've only ever been able to show her the photos.

'It's been a long time,' I say, and immediately feel guilty. It's been over a year. I should have come to see her. I really should have. But this place, I can't stand it. Can't stand to see her in it, to see her suffering. I remember when she was first arrested, how shocked I'd been. I'd known she hadn't done it. She couldn't have.

'Your face,' she says, reaching across the table to lift up my chin and look at my cheek. 'What happened?'

'It's nothing,' I say, pulling away, leaning back in my seat. 'An accident.'

'It looks like a burn.' She smiles grimly. 'To match mine.' She pulls up her sleeve and I see the scars that run up her left arm.

'I fell over. Scraped my face. I was so busy with work that I didn't treat it properly and it's healed badly.'

'I can see it's a burn, Sophie. But you're such a good liar I almost believed you.'

I still haven't told her I've changed my name. I don't know how she'd react.

There's a silence between us and I stare at the clock on the wall, watching the second hand count the time. Do we really have nothing to say to each other?

'I like your hair,' she says. 'Blonde suits you.'

'Thank you.' The silence lengthens. I should have thought of conversation topics before I came.

'I'll be out soon,' she says suddenly.

'That's good news.'

'Yes, I think so.' I can see the questions in her eyes. Where will she go? Our family home was sold long ago to pay her legal fees.

I reach out to touch her hand. 'I'm sorry you've been in here so long.'

'It doesn't matter. None of it matters. You've got nothing to be sorry for. I can't imagine what it's like to have to come and visit me here, when other people your age just pop in to see their mothers for Sunday lunch. It's not fair it's so different for you.'

I nod. It's not like I've visited often. 'We can do that once you're out. Go for Sunday lunch.' The words hang between us, as if neither of us quite believes them.

She manages a half-smile. 'It's so hard to imagine now. It's been so long. I hope I can become the mother you need. I'd love to cook for you again, feel like part of a family.' She looks at me hopefully.

Is she coming to live with me? I don't know if I want that. I know she loves me but I can't help remembering how volatile she could be. She used to be up one minute and down the next.

'I can't wait,' I say, trying to sound convincing.

Her voice falters as she says the next words. 'I know you don't need me, Sophie. I know you've had to cope without me for a long time, since you were young. You're successful, and I'm so proud of you. But I hope you can find a place for me in your life. I'm your mother and I've missed you. All I've been dreaming of all these years I've been locked away is being with you.'

I nod. I'd like to say the same, but the truth is I haven't been dreaming of being with her. I've just tried to forget that she's in here, get on with my life.

'You're wearing the earrings I bought you.'

'Yes,' I say, reaching up to touch my ears.

'They look good on you.'

'Thanks.'

I see tears in her eyes. 'You've grown up.' She reaches out and strokes my arm, and I have to stop myself recoiling. Her love seems stifling after I've been starved of it for so long.

'Not long to go now,' I say again, stuck for things to say.

'It will be different, won't it?' she asks. 'When I'm out. Without your father.'

Tears well up in my eyes. We'll be a family of two, me and Mum. I feel a sudden surge of guilt, the familiar feeling creeping over me.

'You mustn't blame yourself,' she carries on. 'You were just a child. None of it was your fault.'

CHAPTER 17

BETH

Despite the winter chill, bright sunlight streams from a cloudless sky as I walk to collect Charlie from school. There's hardly been a day without rain in the last few weeks, and I feel grateful for the warmth of the sun on my face. I think of Nick, how he will never get to feel the sun again. When he died I couldn't find any joy in anything. I hardly went out, hardly saw my friends. All I could think about was how unfair it was that he wasn't there to enjoy life with me. I left the area in the end, found a teaching job far away, at the school where Genevieve was the head, tried to start my life again.

I smile at Charlie when I see him across the playground. He comes straight to me. I notice he isn't with his friends today and wonder if that's connected to the bruises. I've spoken to his teacher and asked her if he's being bullied, and she said she'd keep an eye out.

'How was school today?' I ask.

'Fine.' He doesn't speak another word to me on the way home, despite lots of fruitless attempts to get something out of him about what he's done today. I'm sure something's wrong.

We haven't been home long when Richard arrives. Charlie runs straight into his arms as soon as the door opens. I feel my heart breaking. He misses his father so much. And despite myself, I miss him too. He's treated me so appallingly, but I can't seem to just switch off my love for him, as much as I want to.

'I'll leave you two to catch up,' I say, forcing myself to break away. Richard is here to help out with Charlie while I do some admin and see Danielle for her therapy session. I give Charlie a quick kiss on the cheek. 'There's some pasta in the cupboard and vegetables in the fridge for his tea,' I say to Richard.

Upstairs, I shut the door of my therapy room and light the candle. I stare at its gentle flame, trying to calm myself as the soothing lavender scent fills the room. I feel on edge. There was a time when I was afraid of candles, of their potential for destruction. But Richard helped me overcome my fear. I swallow back my emotions, trying not to think how much I miss him. I hate sleeping alone at night, the house silent without the comforting sound of his breathing. I miss the warmth of his body next to mine, the feel of his arms around me, the way he listened to me when I was feeling down, relieving my anxiety and calming my fears. Nick was the same. He knew exactly the right thing to say to make me feel better. I thought that perhaps I'd got over him when I met Richard, but the truth is I never really have.

My thoughts turn to Danielle. I remember her rushing off after the last session, after she found Charlie outside and he was nearly hit by the car. I've wanted to email her all week to explain that I don't know how Charlie got out of the house, to tell her it's never happened before. But I've stopped myself, knowing I was overreacting.

I use this time to catch up on admin, updating my website to show my increased availability in the evenings and submitting an advert for my services to the school newsletter. If I can just find enough new clients, I think I should be able to pay the mortgage and then Richard should let me stay in the house a bit longer. I rack my brains for other places to advertise. I could get Richard to put up an advert at the university. He teaches counselling there when he's not seeing his own clients. It was where we met. I google the university and browse through the website to see if there's a section for advertising online. I'm on a page dedicated to the administrative side of the university when I see the photo. It's of the outside of the main teaching block. The university building is glass-covered, generic-looking, hardly distinguishable from so many other buildings in London. The picture shows students talking outside happily, holding textbooks in their arms. But it's what's behind them that interests me. The water fountain. It's placement against the building. I recognise it.

I can hear Richard laughing with Charlie downstairs. I go to the bedroom and pull out the photos of Richard and his lover from the bedside table and take them back to the therapy room. I look at the first picture of Richard and the blonde girl in conversation, her back to the camera. There it is. The same water fountain. The photo was taken outside the university.

I swallow. Richard must have met up with her after he finished teaching. I feel sick at the thought of how blatant he was, meeting up with her at the university, where so many people he knows could have seen them. I wonder how many dinners out they had together while I was at home, looking after Charlie.

A thought occurs to me. What if the woman was a student, like I was? I feel a burst of anger. After we'd had Charlie, I'd learnt that I wasn't the first student Richard had slept with – there'd been many before me. But he'd told me he met the woman in a bar. Had he lied to me?

The doorbell rings and I hurriedly shove the pictures in my desk drawer and race downstairs to open the door to Danielle.

'Hi,' she says as she steps over the threshold. She seems preoccupied as we go silently up the stairs, not bothering with the usual small talk.

'Thanks so much for finding Charlie last week,' I blurt out as soon as we're sitting down. 'I'm so grateful.'

'Anything could have happened,' Danielle says quietly. 'If I hadn't been there…' She shivers. 'He would have been hit by that car, Beth.'

I swallow the bile that rises in my throat. I can't even contemplate the idea. 'I—' But I have no explanation, no excuses.

'I worked on a case once where a woman had neglected her children. It was heartbreaking. She hadn't fed them properly, or given them regular baths. And she'd let them play outside in all weathers.'

I don't know why she's mentioning that. Is she saying I was neglectful? 'I honestly don't know how Charlie got out.'

Her expression softens and she smiles sympathetically. 'How's he feeling after the whole ordeal? Is he alright?'

'He hasn't really spoken about it.' I wish he'd talk to me, but all he will tell me is that he left because he wanted to see his Daddy.

'Poor boy. I'm sure he'll get over it.'

I nod, keen to change the subject. 'Right, shall we begin?'

Danielle looks at the floor. 'Yeah. I wanted to talk to you about Peter. I'm starting to question my relationship with him. Whether it's right for us both.'

'Has anything in particular made you think about it?'

'I suppose the counselling has made me think about how I really feel about him. I feel trapped. We argue a lot. But all couples argue, don't they…?'

I sense she wants to say more, but she's struggling to find the words. I wait, hoping she'll speak first without me having to ask a direct question. I stare at the closed curtains, the silence building. In my head I count the beats of my ticking watch, audible in the quiet room. I listen for other sounds in the house, Richard moving around, Charlie stirring. There's nothing.

She looks at me, meets my eyes. 'Sometimes… I feel a bit afraid of him.' She tugs at the sleeves of her shirt and I remember the injuries I saw on her wrists the other week. I'd thought they'd been scars from the fire, but could they have been something else? Something to do with Peter?

'Afraid?' I lean in closer. I wish she'd trust me with whatever it is she's worried about.

'I don't know. It's just a feeling.'

I'm going to have to be more direct with her. I think I know what she's hinting at, but I need to be sure. 'When you say you argue, what do you mean? Just words, or physical arguments?'

'Words mainly.'

I remember what she said last week about how she'd argued with Peter before the fire. Had he thrown the petrol on the barbecue because of their fight? As some kind of punishment?

She's staring at the floor again, tears flowing.

'Danielle,' I say, leaning forward, 'if I think you're in any danger at all I have a duty of care to tell someone. Has he ever hurt you?'

She frowns as if she's contemplating what to say, how much to tell me. 'No,' she says quietly. 'He's never hurt me.'

I'm sure she's lying. 'But you're afraid of him?'

'Yes, but I don't think it's his fault. I think I'm afraid because of the past. I didn't have an easy time of it after I came out of care. I was looking for love, I suppose, someone who'd care about me. And I met the wrong man. He used to cheat on me, hit me. Since then I've been a bit, well, afraid of men in general.'

I nod, feeling sad for her. I'd had a partner who'd hit me too, before I met Nick. Nick had truly rescued me, made me feel like a real person, worthy of his love. But then I lost him, and I crumbled all over again.

'I think…' Danielle says, 'I think that questioning my relationship with Peter… it brings it all back. I'm scared his temper will explode into something more. I'm always tiptoeing round him, trying not to upset him.'

I sigh, feeling a huge well of sadness building up inside me. None of us escapes our past. Danielle is just like me, still affected by men who hurt her years before. Our early relationships mould us and we find ourselves subconsciously repeating the patterns, subjecting ourselves to the same abusive relationships over and over.

I wipe a tear from the corner of my eye. I can help her to break the pattern. This is why I became a therapist. To help people like her.

'I don't think Peter wants a baby,' Danielle says. 'Not really.'

'Have you spoken to him any more about it?'

'Not recently. I'm too scared to bring it up. Too scared of what he might say. If he doesn't want a baby then I'm not sure I want to be with him.'

I can hear the emotion she's holding back. Her voice is choked. 'A baby is so important to you,' I say, leaning in towards her and listening intently.

'I keep thinking back to other people I've met in the past, others I might have been with. I love Peter, but I'm beginning to wonder if I'd be better off with someone else. And I hate myself for thinking that, for thinking of ending it all, breaking my marriage vows.'

'Someone else?'

'There hasn't really been anyone serious other than Peter. There was a guy I had a fling with when Peter and I were on a break, but he wasn't right either.'

'OK...'

She smiles, the first genuine smile I think I've seen from her. 'He used to say I reminded him of Reese Witherspoon. Not because of the way I look. Obviously I don't look anything like her, with my scars and my short hair. He used to say that my energy reminded him of her. My lust for life.'

Richard used to say something similar to me. He used to say my smile reminded him of Kate Winslet. I don't look like her, but I liked the way he compared our smiles, the way he said that when we both smiled we lit up a room. I thought that was something unique to Richard, this way he had of complimenting me without it sounding superficial. But it must be more common than I thought.

She laughs. 'I fell for the compliment, but he probably just wanted to get me into bed.'

My face flushes. I'd thought Richard's words had been romantic.

'He wasn't right for me,' Danielle continues. 'He got on my nerves in the end. But I suppose the fact that I'm even thinking about exes means that maybe the relationship with Peter isn't working as well as I'd hoped.'

I think about Peter telling her she wouldn't be a good mother, how he threw petrol on the barbecue. There are a lot of things that sound wrong in the relationship.

She looks at me directly. 'What would you do if you were me? I feel so trapped. What would you do?'

I shake my head. 'I can't answer that,' I say, thinking how trapped I feel myself, in my own life, since Richard left. 'I'm just here to help you work through your feelings, work out what you want to do. I can't make the decisions for you.'

She looks dejected. 'I need someone to help me work it out.'

'I can continue to support you,' I say. 'You know you can talk about anything in here.'

'I know you understand. You're a single mum, aren't you, to Charlie?'

I nod, taken aback.

'That's why he's left on his own, isn't it? During our sessions.'

I feel my whole body tense.

'Oh, I'm sorry to be so nosy,' she says, seeing the look on my face. 'When I was in your bathroom, I saw there was just one adult toothbrush there. And I thought you must live on your own. I've wanted to ask you about it ever since, but it's never felt appropriate.'

'Oh,' I say. 'Well, yes, I am a single mum.'

She nods. 'I shouldn't have asked. It's none of my business. It just bothers me sometimes that you know so much about me and I know nothing about you.' Her eyes bore into me. 'It makes me curious about who you really are.'

CHAPTER 18

DANIELLE

I'm sitting in the living room on my laptop when Peter gets home from work. I still have loads of paperwork to do on the appeal for my client at the charity, but I thought I'd bring the work home so I could spend more time with Peter. I've hardly seen him this week, and since my last therapy session I've been plucking up the courage to have a heart-to-heart with him. We have a lot to talk about. I need to know where I stand in our relationship. What he really thinks about having kids with me. And I'm going to have to tell him the truth about my mother, now she's getting out of prison. He thinks we're estranged because she couldn't cope and put me into foster care. I told him she lived abroad, in Sweden, that I never intended her to be part of my life again. But now she's getting out of prison. And she wants to move in with us. I'll have to tell him the truth.

Although I've got lots of work to do, I've hardly been able to concentrate all evening. I keep imagining my mother living here with me and Peter. I just can't picture it. But she has nowhere else to go. And I want to rebuild my relationship with her. I have to take her in. She's spent all those years in prison. I'm her daughter. The least I owe her is compassion.

By the time Peter comes in at 10 p.m. I'm exhausted. I've been feeling a bit off colour lately and I think I'm run-down from the stress of my relationship with Peter and my mother's imminent release from prison. I feel like I could curl up and sleep for a week.

When Peter comes through the door, he throws himself down on the sofa beside me.

'Have you eaten?' I ask.

'Grabbed something at the office. You?'

'No. I thought you'd be home earlier, that we could get a takeaway together.' It's not his fault, but I still feel angry. It's symptomatic of the problems in our entire relationship. We both work so hard we've almost become strangers. And when we are together, we argue.

'I'm sorry. I got caught up. Looks like you were busy working anyway.' He moves the large Orla Kiely cushion from one sofa to another.

'Don't put that there. That cushion matches the other sofa.' I take it and move it to the green sofa that I bought it for.

Peter shakes his head. 'This is what I mean.'

'Sorry? What do you mean?'

'You can't relax. Everything always has to be just right. I really don't know how you'd cope with a baby.'

'What?' I feel the anger bubbling inside me. I know he's wrong.

'Look at you. You like everything just so. Perfect. A baby would mess it all up.'

'No it wouldn't. We'd have to adjust a bit, but I'd be fine.'

'We'd have to adjust a lot. You'd have to reduce your hours at work. I probably would too. And you'd need to take maternity leave to spend time with the baby.'

'I know that. And you could take paternity leave too.'

'It would be difficult with my job.'

'No more difficult than for me. We're both lawyers.'

'You're the one who wants the baby, Dani. You'll need to make the sacrifices.'

I glare at him. 'We always said that once we got married we'd have children.'

He nods. 'Yeah. We did. But at the time I hadn't really thought it through. My career's moved on. I don't want to jeopardise that. When we talked about it, it was just an idea, a fantasy. Since then, I've seen the reality. Lots of my friends have got children now. And it really is life-changing. I'm not sure if that's what I want.'

'You can't just change your mind. I… I married you thinking we'd have kids.'

Peter sighs. 'I'm just trying to be honest with you. Things have changed.'

'What things?'

'The barbecue, the fire. I… I'm not sure that we're cut out to be parents. I want to focus on my career, and I'm not sure motherhood would be right for you. Your temper…'

'That's rubbish! You've decided you don't want kids and now you're trying to pin it on me.'

'You know that's not true. Since we've got married… well, we've become closer, haven't we? I've seen that you're not as perfect as you like to come across.'

'No one is. Everyone has the occasional bad day, the occasional bad mood.'

'You know that's not what I'm talking about.'

I glare at him, feeling the rage building inside me. I need to leave the house before it explodes out of me, proves him right.

I go outside, get in the car and drive. I keep going for miles and miles down the dark streets, finding myself on the dual carriageway into London, the terraced houses rolling by. I need to think, process everything that Peter's said. It's not like it's a surprise. I'd suspected that he'd changed his mind about having kids. It just seems so unreasonable. I went into my marriage wholeheartedly. I remember the beginning, when I was falling in love, when I was desperate to see him all the time, desperate to hear his voice. I'd been drawn to him, couldn't leave him alone. Back then we'd worked in the same office and I used to keep making up excuses to go upstairs to the floor where he worked just to catch sight of him. We used to make time for each other, grabbing stolen moments at lunchtime. Now we hardly see each other.

I'd thought he was the one. I could hardly believe my luck. I'd planned out our lives together perfectly. But now he's saying he doesn't want children. I'm thirty. I know there's plenty of time to persuade him, but what if I don't manage it? What if he keeps saying maybe, but then we never get round to it?

Suddenly everything feels overwhelming. Like I need to make a decision as soon as possible. I've read the stats. Fertility's supposed to fall off a cliff at thirty-five. And I want three children. If Peter isn't right for me, then I don't have long to find the right man to have kids with.

For a moment I consider staying with Peter, living happily ever after but not having kids. I can't imagine it. There's nothing wrong with my life, but sometimes it's like I'm just waiting for something to happen. There's a part of me deep inside that feels empty and unfulfilled. I know kids will make me happy, that they're the missing part of me. But if Peter doesn't want them, then I can't see how he fits into the picture. I fight back tears. I love Peter and I'm desperate for a future with him. But I can't contemplate a future without children in it. If he's certain he doesn't want kids, then I'm going to have to make a decision.

Peter. Or the children I've always wanted.

CHAPTER 19

BETH

The swing goes higher and higher, Charlie stretching his feet out to the sky. It's a crisp Saturday morning and there's only a smattering of dads with their kids in the park, taking their turn at childcare. They make awkward conversation as their children run and shout and play.

It's so long since I've taken Charlie here. During the week I'm so busy with clients and looking after Charlie that I struggle to keep up with the housework and admin. I always end up spending Saturday mornings catching up while Charlie watches TV. But today I have the afternoon free to get all that done. Richard's taking Charlie to the new soft-play centre and then Charlie's staying over at his flat on the camp bed for the first time.

He's buzzing with excitement about staying at his dad's flat and hasn't stopped talking about it. I'm pleased he's adjusting so well to our split, but it hurts to think he won't miss me. I've never been apart from him overnight before and I'm not sure how I'll cope.

Charlie jumps down off the swing and heads to the climbing frame. He scales it confidently. I remember the days when he was learning to walk and I used to have to hold his hand as he toddled round the park, and help him up the steps to the slide. He doesn't need me anymore, and I feel like a spare part, just watching. A part of his childhood is already over, and I'm not at all ready.

'Look at me, Mum!' he shouts from the top.

I smile up and wave. 'Well done! You're so high up.'

'Take a photo of me!'

I wonder why he wants a picture of something he's done so many times before, but I get out my phone obligingly and snap the photo.

As he scrambles back down, I think about the bruises on his arm. Could he have got them from just playing? He says he doesn't remember how he got them and his teacher hasn't spotted any signs of bullying.

He's beside me now, grabbing at my phone.

'Can I see?' he asks.

I show him the photo and a grin spreads across his face. 'Can I show Dad when he comes round?'

My heart drops. So that's what this was about.

'Of course,' I say. I reach out to touch his arm, but he's already running off to the big slide at the other side of the playground.

As I follow him I think of this afternoon when he'll be at his father's. He'll be in a new place, a flat I've never seen, a part of Richard's life I've never known. Richard has said he will keep his place a bit longer, to give me time to see if I can find new clients to pay the mortgage on our house. If I can just do that then I'll be able to stay put, at least for a little while. I know that in the longer term I'll have to move out so he can get some of his money back to buy his own place. But I'm not thinking about that now. Right now all I want is some continuity and stability for Charlie. I just need to find the clients. Tonight, I'll have some time alone and I'm planning to email every other therapist I know, asking if they know of any clients they can't accommodate themselves.

I imagine the endless evening ahead of me, free time at last. I've craved time alone to get on with things, maybe read a book or watch a bit of TV. But now I'm faced with it, it seems unappealing, as if I'll just be waiting for my son to come back.

We leave the park and go back home to have lunch and get ready for Charlie to go to Richard's. He's shaking with excitement as we pack his pyjamas, his toothbrush and the soft toy penguin that he's gone to bed with since he was a baby. I must tell Richard to remember to bring it back. Charlie can't sleep without it.

Richard arrives while I'm helping Charlie put one final toy into his little suitcase, and then I watch from the window as my husband walks my son to his car and they drive away. When they're gone I get out my list of counselling contacts and email every single one, carefully crafting a personal message to each contact and asking if they have any potential clients they could pass on to me.

When I've finished, I pick up the picture of Nick from the sideboard. I miss him so much. I'd always thought he was the one, my soulmate. When I'd lost him I'd been devastated. I put photos of him up on every surface in my flat, so I'd always be surrounded by memories smiling out at me. It was only when I broke down and ended up in hospital that I started to realise that it was unhealthy to stay stuck in the past. I started rebuilding my life piece by piece, and I painstakingly packed away the remains of my life with Nick into my bedside drawer. But now my life has fallen apart again and it's Nick I turn to for comfort. It feels good to have his photo out on display. I'm acknowledging an important part of my past.

Over time, my memories of him have faded. The feel of his lips brushing my cheek, the strength of him as he lay on top of me, the connectedness we felt, his soothing voice. Sometimes the memories feel like they were just yesterday, but when I try to examine them in more detail, they take on the sepia quality of old photos and the closer I try to look, the more faded they become.

I look round the house at the washing-up, and the dusting and the vacuuming that needs doing. It's so quiet in here without Charlie, and the silence is overwhelming. I decide to ignore the housework and take a book I've been intending to read for ages off the shelf and settle down on the sofa with a glass of wine. It seems decadent to be drinking so early in the afternoon, but why not? It's so rare to have the chance.

I'm only a few pages into my book when my phone rings. I'm glad of the interruption, unable to focus and already missing Charlie.

It's Danielle. I hesitate before I answer. I wouldn't normally take calls from clients at the weekend, but she's never called me before and I remember what she said about feeling scared of Peter. I feel a twinge of worry as I answer the phone.

'Hello?'

'Beth – Beth – it's me.' She can hardly get her words out through her tears, and I'm suddenly alert, my heart thumping, scared to think what might have happened to her.

'Are you alright?'

'No… I—' Her sobs get louder. 'I – I've messed up. I was going to ask Peter to leave, to tell him it's over… but I'm scared… I'm scared about what he might do to me.'

'Has he threatened you? Do you want me to call the police?'

'No, he hasn't done anything, not yet. But he's going to be home soon. He's angry. I've texted him to tell him I've packed up his things.'

'OK,' I say, my mind spinning. I'm scared for her too. From what she's told me, Peter has a temper and can be unpredictable. And there might be other things she hasn't told me. It could be a lot worse than that.

'I can't undo it. He knows what I'm planning to do. I thought I was being so brave, finally accepting the relationship wasn't right, finally taking action. But I've really messed this up. My friend was supposed to be coming so I had someone with me in case he got angry, but her mother's just been admitted to hospital so she's had to go and see her instead. I don't want to be on my own when he gets back.' Her sobs are louder now, her words muffled by tears. 'I don't know what to do.'

My heart aches for her. I don't have any choice. I can't leave her to deal with this on her own. 'I'll come over, as soon as I can.'

Danielle lives in a detached house right at the end of a cul-de-sac of new build houses and flats. Her home is intimidatingly big, with roses growing up the walls and a sky-blue front door. There's a mat that says 'welcome', a carefully tended garden. It's like a child's fantasy of a house, an image of the perfect home from the storybooks I read Charlie.

I shouldn't have come here. It's a blurring of professional boundaries, acting against the code of ethics for counsellors. I think about turning round, phoning my supervisor, getting someone else involved. But I know that Danielle needs my help now. She could be in danger, and that's more important than any code of conduct. A knot twists in my stomach as I step up to the door and I hesitate for a moment. Is Peter already there?

I knock on the door tentatively.

When Danielle opens it her face is tear-stained. She's dressed casually, in jeans and a T-shirt. The scars on her face seem more prominent in the bright light of her hallway. 'Hello,' she says quietly. 'I'm so sorry to interrupt your day. Thanks for coming. Peter's not home yet, thank god. Please come in.'

She indicates the four huge suitcases by the door. 'I've packed up his stuff. I'm just waiting for him to come back.'

I stare down at the suitcases and wonder what triggered such drastic action. I hope he hasn't already hurt her.

'Are you OK?' I ask, although I can see she isn't.

'Holding up,' she says. 'Come through.'

As I step into the hallway, I notice the single white orchid in a pot on the windowsill and the clean wallpaper, unblemished by children's crayons. All the photos that cover the walls are of her and Peter: their wedding, their honeymoon, sunny holidays.

The couple pictured doesn't match how Danielle describes their relationship, but then whose happy wedding photos truly represent the ups and downs of marriage? My clients have shown me the underside of those seemingly happy partnerships.

Danielle sees me looking. 'I thought I finally had it figured out when Peter proposed,' she says. 'I didn't think it would end like this.'

'No one does. People make their vows in good faith.'

'I've opened a bottle of wine,' Danielle says, looking slightly embarrassed. 'Dutch courage for when Peter gets back. Would you like some?'

I think of my glass of wine at home, how I'd abandoned it to come here, how this is the only time I have no responsibility for Charlie. My only afternoon off. 'I'll have half a glass.'

She smiles and pours me a whole one. I don't object, pushing down the guilt that stirs inside me. 'When will Peter be back?' I ask.

She looks at her watch. 'About fifteen minutes, if he left when he said he would.' She paces up and down.

I stand and sip my wine.

'So, where's your son tonight?'

'With his father.'

'It must be hard,' she says, and I nod, feeling awkward.

Half an hour of stilted conversation later, I've finished my glass of wine and Danielle's topped me up, but Peter still isn't home. We've both talked about our relationships and our regrets, and it's nice to have someone listening to me for once. But I've tried not to say too much. Danielle is still a client.

She checks her phone. 'Oh my god, he's messaged me.'

'What is it?'

'He says he's not coming home tonight. He's going to stay at a friend's place.'

'That's good news, isn't it?' I smile. 'He's accepted that you've split up.'

'I suppose so.'

'I'd better go then,' I say, although the thought of my empty house is far from appealing.

I stand up, feeling a bit light-headed from the wine. I haven't had that much to drink, but I don't feel right. I shouldn't drive like this.

'Are you OK?' Danielle asks.

'Fine,' I smile. 'Just a bit tipsy.'

'You could stay for dinner if you like.'

'No, it's fine. I just need to wait until I'm a bit more sober, so I can drive. Or take a taxi home, I guess. That's probably better.'

'If you're taking a taxi home anyway, then why don't you have one more glass with me?'

I think about my huge empty house. I imagine sitting alone on the sofa, the whole evening stretching out endlessly ahead of me, thinking of Charlie and Richard having fun together without me.

One more glass of wine with Danielle can't hurt. 'Go on then,' I say.

CHAPTER 20

DANIELLE

Beth sinks onto the sofa and starts to gently snore. I persuaded her to have a couple more glasses and she seemed to relax. She's verbose when she drinks, and I was glad to get to know her better, to be her confidante the way she has been mine. Now I take the empty glass of wine from beside her on the coffee table and go to the sink, washing it out thoroughly before placing it on the draining board.

I call a taxi, waking her when it arrives.

'What?' she says groggily. 'Did I fall asleep? I'm so sorry.' She slurs her words and stumbles as she gets up from the sofa.

'Come on,' I say. 'Let's get you home.'

I take her arm. 'What happened?' she asks.

'You've just had a bit too much to drink, that's all.'

She blushes. 'I'm so sorry.'

'Don't be sorry. It happens to us all.' I guide her into the hallway, help her with her coat, pick up her bag and escort her out into the cold air. The night is bitter and we both shiver as we make slow progress towards the waiting taxi, its headlights glaring out into the empty street, the engine running. Beth needs my support and I hold her arm to steady her as she stumbles down the driveway towards the car.

'You might feel a bit rough in the morning,' I say.

The driver watches me as I manhandle her into the car. 'She's had a bit too much,' I explain.

'Not going to be sick, is she?'

'No, but I'm coming with her to drop her off. If she's sick, then I'll clear it up.'

He grunts and then drives us away into the night.

CHAPTER 21

BETH

When I open my eyes, harsh daylight beams through open curtains. I stare at the window uncomprehendingly. Why aren't I in my bedroom? What time is it? It takes me a moment to recognise the red curtains and off-white walls. I'd once spent ages agonising over that precise shade of paint. I'm at home. On the sofa in my living room.

My heart pounds as I'm suddenly overwhelmed by panic. Where's Charlie? But then I remember. He's at Richard's. He's probably having a brilliant time. My brain's foggy and slow as I try to think back to last night. Everything's hazy. I remember going to Danielle's, having a few glasses of wine with her. But then what?

I try to roll into a more comfortable position. My neck aches and my body feels heavy and dirty. My mouth's dry, my stomach's churning and beneath my clothes, I'm sweating alcohol. I push the blanket off me to try and cool down. It's an old one, kept upstairs in the hall cupboard. Had I gone up to look for it and then brought it downstairs to sleep with? That makes no sense.

Jumbled memories flash through my mind. Being helped into a taxi. Struggling to focus as the town rolled by outside the window. Feeling overwhelmingly tired. Stumbling into the hallway, the cold wall against my palm as I fought the zip of my ankle boots. Falling over as I forced them off. The kitchen tap spraying me when I turned it too far. Sitting on the kitchen floor and swallowing a whole glass of water in two gulps.

I ease myself off the sofa. My foot hits something hard, which rolls noisily over the wooden floor. I stare down in disbelief. An empty bottle of vodka. It's the one from the kitchen cupboard. Richard bought it from duty-free on our way back from a weekend in Spain years ago. It had been opened at the time and then quickly cast aside. I don't normally drink spirits, they make my throat burn. But there's a single tumbler beside me on the coffee table, half an inch of clear liquid in the bottom. Water? Or vodka? I lift it to my face, sniff it and then retch. Definitely vodka. I can't have drunk it all, can I? What happened?

With each tentative step I take across the living room, my head pounds. I drag myself up to bed to try and get more sleep, but I can't get comfortable, turning over the pillow again and again to find a bit that doesn't feel quite so lumpy. I think of Danielle. She can't possibly be a client now. I've completely messed up, overstepped a boundary by having a drink with her. I flush with embarrassment as I imagine what I might have said to her when I was drunk. I feel the nausea rise within me, and I try to stay completely still, praying I won't be sick.

I'll have to message her, tell her I can no longer be her therapist. I search around on my bedroom table for my phone, but realise it must be in my bag. I have no idea where I might have put it when I came in. I give up and fall into a fitful sleep.

I'm woken by the sound of banging on the door. Loud, insistent rapping. I roll over and pull the pillow over my head, wondering if I can ignore it.

'Beth! Beth!'

Oh, god. It's Richard. He must have brought Charlie back.

I grab a hairbrush, drag it through my hair and then run downstairs. Luckily I'm still dressed from yesterday.

I open the door, blinking back the pounding sunlight.

'Hi Beth,' Richard says, strolling through the door.

'Charlie!' I say, and hold my arms out to my son. 'How was it? Did you have a great time?' It takes every ounce of my energy to smile brightly.

Charlie hugs me reluctantly. 'You smell, Mum.'

I glance up at Richard and smile apologetically. He's staring back at me. 'Where were you last night?' he asks.

'Oh, umm… out… with a friend.'

'We tried to call you. Charlie was upset. He wanted to come home.'

'Oh, Charlie.' I get down to his level and ruffle his hair. 'I missed you too. Are you alright?'

He shrugs away from me, going to switch on the small TV in the kitchen. I'm too exhausted to tell him not to.

'He's been pretty grumpy. I think he was worried when we couldn't get hold of you. In the end I decided to bring him back here. I thought he'd be happier with you. But there was no answer when I knocked.'

'I'm sorry,' I say. 'I should have checked my phone. I was out.'

Richard looks down at the floor. 'Have you met someone new then?'

'No. I was just with a friend.'

'I suppose it's none of my business anyway.'

'No, it isn't.'

Suddenly my vision starts to blur. 'Beth, are you alright?'

'I'm fine,' I insist. But I stumble, reaching for the wall to steady myself.

Richard takes my arm and leads me into the living room.

He stops in the doorway.

I see what he sees.

The sofa that I've so clearly slept on. The empty bottle of vodka on the floor.

CHAPTER 22

DANIELLE

On Sunday, I wake up to an empty house. I felt wrung out last night, emotionally drained, but this morning I feel surprisingly well. I have a new lease of life. I thought I'd miss Peter's warm body beside me in bed and have trouble sleeping. But I didn't. The house felt peaceful without him.

It's still early and I can't sleep, so I walk up the road to the bakery and buy myself a pain au chocolat as a treat. I deserve it after last night. I think of Beth, how unwell she'd been after the wine, how I'd had to look after her. I hope she's feeling better this morning.

I eat the pastry on the move, wanting to enjoy the winter sunshine. During the day, the scars on my face must always be shielded from the sun by my wide-brimmed hat, but it feels good to see the bright sun reflecting off the winter frost. I keep walking and walking, trying to clear my head. It's forty-five minutes before I find myself back on the street I once knew so well, the street where I grew up. Subconsciously I must have known where I was going, but it's still a surprise to turn left under the railway bridge and find myself on the familiar pavement. I walk past the big detached houses I used to go by every day for years on my way to school. I recognise every lamp post, every electricity box. I remember walking down to the church on Sundays clutching my mother's hand and counting the trees by the side of the road. The smell of spice invades my senses as I go past the Indian restaurant.

Along the road, by the fish and chip shop, there's a waist-high wall I used to walk along the top of when I was little, holding my hands out for balance, my father catching me when I got to the end and jumped off.

I try to imagine what my father would look like if he was still alive. It's hard to imagine him older. He always kept himself in such good shape. I can't imagine him with grey hair or wrinkles. I wish he was here now, waiting in the house where I grew up, to welcome me back home. He'd open the door and hug me. I wish I'd been kinder to him before he died, wish I'd told him I loved him. But I'd been too busy arguing with him and Mum.

Years later, I walked these streets as a teenager, on my way to the Underground station to get the tube into London, or going to hang out in the local park. I hadn't spent so much time with my parents then, but I remember the stilted meals out in restaurants to celebrate birthdays and the occasional family trips to the cinema. What will I do with my mother when she's out of prison? Will we go out for meals? Will we have the kind of relationship where we can chat for hours? Somehow I can't imagine it. There's so much that's unsaid between us. And so many missing years. There's been no chance to repair the cracks. Up until now. Maybe it will truly be possible to start again. I've told the probation service she can move in with me. Now I just have to tell Peter.

I stop when I reach the park and wander inside. Sitting on a bench near the children's playground, I listen to the shouting and laughter and crying, watch the parents sighing and complaining. They don't know how lucky they are. I long to be in their position, to hold a small hand in mine, to push a child higher and higher on the swing. I imagine Beth there with Charlie and feel a twinge of jealousy.

Tears form in my eyes and I touch my belly. Perhaps I'm looking into my own future, but it feels more like I'm looking into my past.

The playground has been refurbished since I was a child, but I can clearly remember sliding down the slide, my mother's arms wide, ready to catch me at the bottom. I remember the bump when I fell off the climbing frame and scraped both knees, the sting of the baby wipe as my mother cleaned away the bits of grit from the wound. Later, on a bench in the wooded area, I smoked my first cigarette and met my first boyfriend.

I leave the park and continue to the place I've been heading towards all along, the house I was brought up in. I'm back again. From the opposite pavement I have a clear view of my childhood bedroom, where I sang, laughed and cried, where my mother read me stories and where I listened to my parents' raging arguments when I was supposed to be asleep. There'll be no trace of me there now. My childhood ended when my father died.

I'm not far from Beth's house, and I think about going over, checking she's OK. I felt sorry for her last night. She was so vulnerable. But I decide against it – I'm sure she just needs to sleep it off. Besides, I have so much work to do, and I want to spend the whole afternoon going through the files for the appeal. The weekends are my only real opportunity to work on my charity clients, and it's so important I get it right. My client was acting in self-defence and should never have been convicted. I'm determined to get him off on appeal.

But there's one other thing I need to do first. I can't put it off any longer. The small parade of shops at the end of the street still contains the same family-run pharmacy that was there when I was a child. I stand in front of the display for ages, picking up packet after packet to read the small print and check the statistics on accuracy. I don't want there to be any mistakes. Finally, heart thumping, I choose the most expensive pregnancy test and take it to the till.

CHAPTER 23

BETH

I'm just thinking about what to give Charlie for dinner when I hear the front door. For a moment, I consider not answering. I've been looking forward to a quiet evening ahead, and I don't want anything to interfere with it. But then I remember the set of screwdrivers I'd ordered online to fix the cupboard door in the hallway. Perhaps it's the delivery. I go to the door.

Richard.

I stare at him in confusion and then remember he's here to look after Charlie while I see Danielle. But I've cancelled her session. I left a message on her phone explaining that I can't be her therapist anymore. I crossed a line by getting drunk with her, and it would be unfair to continue to see her in a professional capacity. I hope she understands. I didn't mention I could be investigated and perhaps even struck off for going to her house and having a drink with her. She didn't ring me back like I asked, and it suddenly occurs to me that I might not have heard from her because something awful happened when Peter came back. I feel a shiver of guilt. I should have made more effort to contact her.

Richard nods as I explain I don't have any clients tonight. 'I can still stay,' he says. 'Help you with Charlie.' He holds up a paper bag. 'I bought takeaway from the deli for us to share.' I think of the leftovers I was planning to eat for dinner.

'Sounds great,' I reply.

*

Once we've all had dinner and Richard's put Charlie to bed, Richard and I sit down together in the living room.

'So what happened with your client?' he asks.

I'm about to make something up, but at the last moment I change my mind. Richard is a therapist himself and he understands me better than anyone else. 'I tried to help her. She called me in tears. She was asking her husband to leave and she thought he was going to hurt her. So I went round to her house…'

Richard sighs. 'You must have known that wasn't a good idea. You're her therapist, not her friend.'

'She didn't have anyone else. And she was scared.'

'You were always so determined to do the right thing.'

'I've been so stupid.'

He puts his hand on mine. 'You did it because you cared.'

'Do you think I should report it? Tell the governing body I made a mistake?'

He meets my eyes. 'No, don't do that. They might penalise you. You made a mistake, but at the end of the day you helped your client, didn't you? Was she grateful you intervened?'

I nod. 'She certainly seemed to be when I got there. Her husband didn't come home in the end anyway, so she didn't even need me.'

But I don't remember the whole evening. I can't bring myself to tell Richard that. He saw the bottle of vodka on Saturday morning, but he doesn't know that was the day I saw Danielle.

Richard pats my hand patronisingly. 'Well, it sounds like it worked out for the best then.'

'Yeah, I suppose so. I've lost a client though.' Just at the time when I need to earn more money.

'How are you getting on with finding more work? The mortgage is due this week.'

'It's too early, Richard. I've put up lots of adverts, contacted colleagues for referrals, but nothing's come to anything yet.'

'So no new clients?'

I shake my head. 'It takes time to build up a business.'

'It does, Beth. I know that. I've built my counselling practice over many years. And I had my teaching to supplement my income. In comparison you're just starting out.'

'I know.' I've only had one enquiry since I started advertising, and they've decided not to proceed because of the cost. And now I've lost Danielle as a client too.

'I didn't think you'd be able to pay the mortgage. And with the amount of stress you're under, maybe it's not a good idea to be taking on more clients for the moment.'

I know he's thinking of the empty vodka bottle by the sofa the other day. The one I don't even remember drinking.

'I'm not that stressed,' I say. Although I can't see any way I can find enough new clients.

'OK. Well, just make sure you keep an eye on your mental health. You know how vulnerable you are.'

I nod.

'Did you ever get to the bottom of how Charlie got those bruises?'

'No. He won't tell me anything.'

'I'll see if I can get anything out of him when we have some time together.'

'Thanks.'

Richard stands and I see him staring intently at the side table, at the row of photos. He goes over and picks one up. My heart stops. It's the picture of Nick. I want to tear it out of Richard's hands, stop him touching it. It's all I have left of him.

'Why have you put this up?' he asks.

'Why shouldn't I?'

He sighs. 'You know it's not good for you. To get stuck in the past.'

'Put it back,' I say, snatching it from his hands.

'Beth.' He puts his hand on my shoulder and I shrug it off. 'Is this why you were drinking the other night? Were you thinking of Nick?'

'No, I—' But I can't explain. I can't even remember.

'You get lost in grief when you think about him. I thought you'd got over it when you were my student. I thought you'd dealt with all that before you qualified as a therapist.'

'I don't think I'll ever get over Nick,' I say quietly.

'I was worried about you when I saw the empty bottle.'

'I'm fine, Richard.'

'Do you drink like that when you're looking after Charlie?'

'No, of course not. It was my one night off. It's not surprising I let my hair down a bit, is it? It's not like I get the chance every day.'

'No, I suppose not. You're OK, aren't you? Still taking your antidepressants?'

'It's none of your business, but yes, I am.'

'Remember, I know you, Beth. I know what you were like before. When you were obsessed with Nick. When you couldn't put his death behind you. It was unhealthy.'

'I wish he was still alive,' I say quietly. 'Maybe I'd still be with him now.'

He sighs. 'And we wouldn't have met? Our relationship wasn't a mistake, we just grew apart.'

I laugh bitterly. He's composed our split into a neat little narrative, an unfortunate but inevitable occurrence.

'We didn't grow apart! You cheated on me.'

'I don't think that was the problem. Just a symptom that things weren't right between us.'

'Save your therapy for your clients.'

'Are you seeing a therapist yourself, Beth? Perhaps you should think about it. It's a difficult time for you.' His voice is gentle, as if I'm an awkward client.

'Because of you!' I'm shouting now, and I feel guilty as I think of Charlie upstairs. 'It's difficult because of you. Because you left. And besides, I'm coping just fine. Me and Charlie are fine without you. In fact, I think we're both happier without you dragging us down.'

He nods, my words bouncing off him as if they don't mean a thing. He doesn't believe me; he knows he has hurt me. And I can see now that he doesn't care.

I put the picture back down, moving it until it's perfectly in line with the others. 'Nick was the one for me,' I say. 'I told you that when I first met you. You persuaded me that you could replace him. But the connection I had with Nick was special. No one could replace him.'

I can't read the expression on his face. At first I think he's jealous, as I intended, but then I realise that he just feels pity.

'I worry about you,' he says. 'That was one of the reasons I found it so hard to leave you. Because I thought you might fall apart.'

'What do you mean?' I reply, angrily. Had he been thinking about leaving me for ages?

'Even though everything was wrong, even though I knew there was no going back, I was scared about what would happen to you if I left. You broke down when you lost Nick, and I thought you might break down when you lost me.'

'Don't compare yourself to Nick. You're nothing like him. He wouldn't have done this to me. And besides, I can look after myself.'

'That's good to hear, Beth. Because I can't look after you anymore. I have to move on.'

'I don't need you to look after me.' I try to keep my voice level.

He looks relieved. 'I'm so glad you're feeling OK now. After Saturday, I was worried. I know how far you can spiral. I don't want you to end up back in the psychiatric hospital.'

*

Richard leaves, and I double-lock the door behind him. I don't want there to be any chance of Charlie escaping again. Another reason for Richard to think I'm not coping. When the doorbell rings ten minutes later, I'm still shaking from what Richard said, and I don't want to answer, but I know if it rings again, Charlie might wake up. It's probably just Richard coming back because he's forgotten something.

I rush to the door. On the other side of the frosted glass I can make out two figures. I hesitate for a moment.

I think about not opening the door. It's dark, I'm in the house on my own and I don't know who it is. But whoever it is has seen I'm in. I bend down to undo the bottom lock with my key. Then I open the door a crack. My mouth drops open.

It's Danielle. And standing beside her is the man from her wedding photos. Peter.

CHAPTER 24

DANIELLE

Beth takes ages to open the door for our counselling session. I notice her double take as she sees Peter. She must be surprised after the weekend. I rush to explain.

'I thought I'd bring Peter with me this time, work on the relationship together. We nearly split up at the weekend, but we've decided to make things work.'

Beth stares, dumbfounded. 'I wasn't expecting you. Either of you. Didn't you get my message?'

I shiver as a cold wind blows my hair around my face. 'What message?'

'I left you a message on your phone, saying we couldn't continue.'

'I didn't get anything through. Why can't we keep going?' I need to keep coming here. Especially now. I feel Peter's hand in mine, a united front.

'I felt we'd become too close.' She looks at Peter, and I wonder if she's going to tell him she came round to the house to help me break up with him. I pray she doesn't.

'Isn't that a good thing?' I ask. 'That we get on well?'

'Yes and no. I felt I'd overstepped a boundary.'

I smile. 'You just showed that you cared.' I try to close down the conversation, not daring to look at Peter.

She looks relieved, then nods. 'Well, if you're happy to continue, then we can go to the room.'

Once we're upstairs, Peter and I sit on the sofa opposite Beth and I start to relax. Peter seems tense, staring warily at the box of tissues and the candle on the table.

He turns to me. 'So this is where you've been coming every week?'

I nod. 'I find it really useful to talk things through.'

'I'm glad you've had the opportunity. I think it's helping you.'

'I *know* it is.' I look at Beth, who's staring intently at Peter, trying to figure him out. He must seem nicer than she expected. He can be charming.

'I'm pleased to hear that,' she says, settling into her chair. 'And it's nice to finally meet you, Peter. This is the first time you're here. Can I ask, why tonight? What's brought you to the session this time?'

'Well,' he says. 'We've been through a difficult time lately. We were on the verge of splitting up when—'

'We have news!' I interrupt suddenly, desperate to tell Beth. 'I'm pregnant.'

Emotions flicker across her face. Shock, then confusion. She looks from me to Peter, then back again. I realise she's not sure whether it's good news or bad news. I frown. She knows how much I wanted a baby. How can it be anything but good?

'We're delighted,' I say, taking Peter's hand in mine, squeezing it tightly. 'We literally can't wait.' According to the books, which I've devoured, it's too early in the pregnancy to be glowing and yet I feel full of warmth and light and love. Everything feels right with the world.

'It's lovely to see you so happy,' Beth says with a genuine smile. I beam back at her. Then she turns to Peter. 'This is big news for you both. And how do you feel about it, Peter?'

'I—' He hesitates and I squeeze his hand tighter. 'Well, I think we need to talk about it. Because we've been so close to splitting up lately. And like Danielle says, even at the weekend she was considering ending it. And I'm just not sure that a baby can change everything.'

I shake my head. 'But the pregnancy explains why I was erratic at the weekend. It must have been the hormones making me irrational. Everything's different now. So many of our arguments were about having a baby, and now I'm pregnant. So most of what we argued about just isn't an issue anymore.'

'I wouldn't say that,' Peter says.

'What do you mean by that?' Beth asks.

'Well, I don't think our problems will go away just because we have a baby. I think if anything they may get worse.'

I glare at him. I wish I hadn't brought him here. Wish he wasn't saying all these things to Beth.

'What problems are you referring to? I've heard things from Danielle's side over the last few weeks, but I'd love to hear your view.'

Anger bubbles inside me. I'd thought Beth cared about me, I thought she was on my side. But now she's listening to Peter, wanting to hear what he has to say. I feel like I'm losing control.

'Danielle has a temper,' Peter says. 'And I think she needs to try and manage it before we have a child.'

'I don't have a temper.' I try to say it softly, but it still comes out louder and angrier than I intended. I make myself sit completely still, to stop my hands from clenching into fists.

'You do,' Peter says. 'You know you do. And that's why I've hesitated before agreeing to have a baby. You know that. You know I don't think we're ready yet.'

'But now we have to be,' I say. 'Because I'm pregnant.'

Peter sighs. 'I have no idea how you got pregnant. I thought you were on the pill.'

'It must have failed. It's not completely reliable. I might have forgotten to take it a couple of times. I've been so busy with work.'

'How could you forget?'

'I don't know. I'm sorry. But that doesn't matter now. All that matters is that I'm pregnant and now we're having a baby. We can't change that.'

Peter frowns. I'd hoped that once I was pregnant he'd be just as excited as me about the baby, but he didn't react like that at all.

'We only got back together a couple of months ago. We said we'd wait before we had a baby. And now…'

'And now it's happened sooner than we thought. It's like fate… like there was a plan for us all along.'

'I don't think so. I think you wanted a baby and you made it happen. You always get what you want.'

I can't hide my smile. He's right about that. 'But it was an accident.'

'That's what you say. A lot of "accidents" seem to happen around you. Like you "accidentally" forgot to take the pill.'

'I didn't do it on purpose.'

'OK, then.'

'Look. We're lucky. We're having a baby. Lots of people never get that opportunity.'

'But we'd spoken about it and we'd decided to wait.'

'Things have changed.'

Peter looks directly at me. 'But what if I don't want them to change? What if I don't want the baby?'

CHAPTER 25

BETH

Despite rushing out of the house, I'm late dropping Charlie off at school and I have to go to the school office and sign him in.

'Third time this month,' the receptionist says. 'Don't let it happen again.'

'I won't.' It's harder to get Charlie ready on time without Richard here to help, and I'm always forgetting something. I feel like I'm only just about holding it together, that I'm letting Charlie down. The school rang me last week when he didn't have his lunch box. I didn't know how I'd forgotten it but then I saw it, all packed, on the kitchen counter. I just hadn't taken it in to the school. I'd cancelled my next client and rushed in, but I still missed the lunch break. I was racked with guilt, imagining him waiting on his own while the teachers scrambled round to find some food for him. I can't mess up again.

When I leave the school, I head for the tube station. I've arranged to meet Genevieve for coffee. It's the tail end of the morning rush hour and the tube is packed. I huddle by the door, trying to minimise body contact with other passengers. I think of Danielle. She commutes into London every morning. I wonder if she has one of those 'Baby on Board' badges now she's pregnant, and if she gets offered a seat. I remember how sick I was when I was carrying Charlie, the constant nausea and light-headedness. Danielle's pregnancy was almost as much of a shock as my own.

I usually pride myself on predicting my clients' behaviour, but I hadn't seen it coming.

It was interesting to finally meet Peter. From everything Danielle had said about him, I'd imagined someone manipulative and unreasonable. He was very direct telling her he wasn't sure he wanted the baby, to the point of cruelty. And yet I hadn't got the sense that he was doing anything other than telling it straight, that he wanted to confront their issues head-on. There's nothing I can put my finger on, but something about him just didn't match the way Danielle had portrayed him. He seemed so ordinary.

I wonder what they'll decide to do about the baby. My own pregnancy had been unexpected but once we'd got used to the idea, Richard and I had embraced it. Richard had even proposed to me, but I'd turned him down. I still missed Nick, and even though I was happy with Richard, a part of me still wished my future was with him. I couldn't marry Richard while I was thinking like that.

We'd had a small christening for Charlie. I'd lost touch with my friends by then, so ashamed of being struck off from teaching and my breakdown. So the christening was just me and Richard, his family and a couple of his friends who'd agreed to be godparents. There was a time when I'd have invited Genevieve to the christening; she might even have been a godparent. She'd looked out for me when I started at the school, taking me under her wing, and she'd become a bit like a mother to me. We'd been close friends, even though, as the head teacher, she'd been my boss. But our friendship had ended as soon as the investigation into my conduct started. Our last conversation had been when she fired me. I push away the memory. I don't want to think about that now.

I'm fraught with nerves as I enter the coffee shop she's chosen, wondering why she's got back in contact with me now, if she's still angry with me for damaging the reputation of her school.

The cafe is crowded with tourists, but Genevieve is already there, settled into a small table in the corner. She's let her trademark fiery red hair go grey, and she's dressed smartly in an aquamarine shift dress, with a matching silk scarf round her neck. She looks so different, so unlike the woman that the other teachers used to be afraid of. I must look different to her too.

She stands up to greet me, a huge smile on her face, and for a moment, I remember the good days when we used to chat for hours.

'Hi.' I smile back. 'How have you been?'

'I'm alright. Older, creakier, but otherwise the same. Two grandchildren now. They run me ragged, but I wouldn't have it any other way. And how are you?'

'I'm good,' I say. I realise she won't know about anything that's happened since I left her school. Nothing about my relationship with Richard. Or about Charlie. 'I have a kid now, myself.'

'Oh, I'm so glad to hear it. You were always so good with children. A natural teacher.' She reddens and I wince. She was the one who put an end to my career in teaching.

'I'm going to get a drink,' I say. 'Do you want anything?'

'I'm fine. Got my morning coffee.'

'OK then.'

In the queue for the counter, I try to clear my head. She's acting like nothing happened between us, like she didn't fire me and block me from her life completely.

I return to the table and sit down. 'I was so sorry to hear about Nathan,' I say, remembering her husband and reaching across to gently touch her arm.

She looks down at the floor. 'It was a long illness, so it was expected, but it was still hard.'

'It must have been.' I feel tears forming in my own eyes. Genevieve and Nathan had been married for over thirty years. I can't imagine what it would have been like for her when he died.

'Yes… But you've been there yourself, haven't you? I remember you talking about Nick. How much you missed him after he passed. I didn't understand at the time.'

'I still miss him.'

'You were going through all that when you started at the school, weren't you?'

I nod. I'd been struggling so much to hold everything together after losing Nick, but I'd still worked as hard as I could, trying to put my all into teaching.

'Do you think that contributed to your mistakes?'

So this is what she wants to talk about after all. I'm not sure I can face her judgement.

'The coffee's good here,' I say.

She looks me in the eye and takes a deep breath. 'I want to say I'm sorry for what happened to you. You were a good teacher. One of the best. You understood your students. I didn't want things to turn out the way they did.'

I stare into my coffee. Her words are a relief. 'I thought you hated me. I was so ashamed when I lost my job.'

She reaches out, touches my hand. 'I was angry, of course, when it happened. But even at the time I knew your heart was always in the right place.'

I think about how much her words would have meant to me if she'd just said them back then. 'Why didn't you tell me that at the time?'

'I couldn't. I had to keep the details of the investigation confidential. I couldn't maintain any kind of relationship with you. Not in my position. Teaching was my life's work.'

I nod. 'And mine. But you let me fall by the wayside.'

'You were young. I thought you could start again, doing something different. I was so upset when I heard what happened to you afterwards. Your breakdown. Your time in the hospital. I so desperately wanted to visit you, to try to help. But you know I couldn't. I had to cut ties for the school's sake.'

My only friends had been other teachers at the school. When I was under investigation they couldn't speak to me either. 'You knew I didn't have any close family and that I'd recently lost Nick. I didn't have anyone to watch out for me. Spending all that time on my own with my thoughts drove me mad. I even started to think I was being followed. But it was all in my head.'

I had no reason to get up in the morning, nothing to do, and I'd slowly become delusional, thinking everyone was out to get me. After a while I stopped leaving the house at all. Eventually I'd had a panic attack when a food delivery came, and lashed out at the delivery man. Oscillating between terror that I'd be attacked and fear I'd end up hurting someone else, I'd admitted myself to hospital and they'd treated me for my delusions, made me see they weren't real. I wince at the memory. I'd been so confused back then, and so afraid.

'I'm sorry. That's why I wanted to have coffee with you. Now I'm retired I'm not tied to the school anymore. I don't have to stay away from you. I thought maybe we could be friends again.'

'I'm not sure,' I reply. She hurt me, cast me adrift. But so much time has passed, and I do need a friend. After everything that happened I've been wary of people, relying on Richard and not forming my own friendships. 'But maybe we could meet up again,' I concede eventually.

'That would be great. You look really well. You've blossomed. I'm so glad to see it.'

'Thank you. I'm a therapist now.'

'Oh, that's brilliant. I can imagine you'd be an exceptional therapist. You were always so good at listening to the kids. You really helped them. Particularly the ones who were struggling.'

We say goodbye an hour later, and I feel weightless, as if the past has finally been put to rest. I'd felt so guilty about what happened to my teaching career, but all along Genevieve had known I did care about the kids, that I was a good teacher. I think about how scared I've been recently about my job, worried that I might be investigated again, just for going round to Danielle's house.

Maybe that's paranoia. After all, I'm convinced I did the right thing, trying to help her with Peter.

By the time I get home, I'm in a good mood. I take my key out of my handbag and unlock the door. As the door swings open, I stop still. I hear voices. Men's voices. Inside the house.

I'm suddenly aware of my vulnerability. I'm completely on my own. My heart races. What if I'm interrupting burglars? What if they feel threatened and attack me?

I creep into the house, grabbing an umbrella as a makeshift weapon. I shut the door quietly behind me. I don't shout out hello.

The voices are getting louder. They sound conversational, almost jovial. I hear the weather mentioned, the observation that snow might be coming.

Richard. One of the voices is Richard's. I let out a shaky breath.

I put down the umbrella. 'Hello?' I shout out.

Richard comes running over. 'Oh, Beth, hi. I didn't think you'd be back yet.'

A suited man appears beside him. 'Dave,' he says, holding out his hand. 'Nice to meet you.' He hands me a card and I read it. Dave Richards. Estate agent.

'My ex, Beth.' Richard says. His words sting. *Ex*. That's all I am to him now.

'What's he doing here?' I ask.

Richard looks sheepish. 'A valuation on the house.'

'Why?'

He sighs. 'I wanted to talk to you about this, but I know you've been having a tough time lately, so I was going to wait until I'd got a bit further in the process… I've found a house I want to buy and I've put in an offer. So I need to get moving on selling this house. You need to prepare yourself, Beth. You're going to need to move out.'

CHAPTER 26

DANIELLE

I struggle through my mid-morning Saturday yoga class, battling nausea and guilt. I was supposed to work on my client's appeal this morning, but instead I slept in. I dragged myself to yoga thinking it would make me feel better, but I wish I hadn't bothered. I feel like I want to lie down on the mat and nap, instead of doing the stretches.

When I get home Peter is settled on the sofa watching the rugby. I'm planning to go to the study and catch up with work on the appeal, but I need to speak to him first. We've hardly seen each other since the counselling session with Beth. I've felt like he's been avoiding me, making sure that we're never in the same room at the same time. If I'm cooking dinner, he makes sure he's in the living room. If I settle down in the living room to watch some late-night TV, he decides he needs to iron his shirts in the utility room. He doesn't want to talk about the baby, won't confront it. But we have to.

'Do you want a drink?' I ask, suddenly hesitant about opening up such a difficult conversation.

He grunts, not listening.

'Did you want a beer?' I hope the alcohol will improve his mood. He's been grumpy for days.

'Yeah, OK.'

I pour him the beer, place it beside him.

'We need to talk,' I say.

'Hmmm…' Peter stares intently at the TV.

'We need to plan for the baby.' I can hear the edge in my voice, hear my annoyance with him, although I'm desperately trying to contain it. My mood has been all over the place lately and I feel angry at the slightest thing.

'Can we talk about this after the rugby?'

'How long until it finishes?'

'Another hour.' He turns up the volume.

I move closer, grabbing the control out of his hand and turning the TV off. 'Peter, we have a lot to talk about.'

'Don't do that! How about we talk at half-time?' He reaches for the TV remote and turns it back on.

I sigh. 'OK, then.'

I get out my laptop and open my files on the appeal. But I can't concentrate. Not with the conversation I need to have with Peter hanging over me. I scroll through social media instead. An ad appears for a baby show in the centre of London, and I imagine wandering contentedly down aisles of buggies and cots, toys and clothes. I wonder if Peter will come with me. I'm not sure if his outburst with Beth the other day was just a sign of nerves or something more. I need to find out.

As soon as the whistle blows for half-time, I reach for the control and turn the TV off.

'What's wrong?' he asks.

'You know what's wrong. What you said about the baby. That you're not sure if you want it.'

He sighs. 'It can't be a surprise to you. I've always said I wasn't sure about a baby. That you need to sort yourself out first. Only a couple of months ago, we were on a break.' He looks at me, meets my eyes.

'But we got back together. Because we wanted to make things work. And now I'm pregnant, and everything's changed.'

'If we keep the baby, everything's changed. If we don't, it hasn't.'

'How can you say that? We're keeping it!' I put my hand over my stomach protectively, shocked that he would even consider it.

He laughs. 'Do you even know the baby's mine?'

I feel sick. 'Of course it's yours.'

'It's not from when we were on a break?'

'It's yours.'

'How do you know?'

'Peter, don't be like this. I just know. It must be yours. I… I used extra protection when we were on our break. And the timings work out.'

'Do they? You wanted a baby and you're having a baby. I'm not sure it's anything to do with me.'

He grabs the control and flicks the rugby back on.

'Don't ignore me!' I scream, snatching the control from him, losing it completely. 'We need to talk about this.'

He doesn't even look up, his eyes fixed on the screen.

I catch sight of the beer glass on the table, imagine pouring it all over him. Just to wake him up, to get him to engage with me, to talk to me. I'm pregnant and I can't deal with it alone.

'This isn't just about you.' I'm shouting. I don't like the sound of my voice, but I can't seem to calm down. 'It's not even about me. It's about our baby. We need to do what's best for it.' Already it feels like a real person to me, a little boy or girl that I'll push on the swings in the park, that I already love so intensely I can't imagine a future without.

'There isn't a baby yet,' Peter says softly. 'It's just a bundle of cells.'

I'm so angry I can hardly see or think. I pick up his pint glass, hardly aware of what I'm doing. I lift it, the beer sloshing round the glass and over the top. Then I throw it against the wall. Shards of glass spray across the room and pale liquid trickles down our carefully chosen paintwork.

CHAPTER 27

BETH

All week I've deliberated over whether or not to allow the therapy with Danielle and Peter to continue. Last week, I'd been caught off guard and allowed the session to go ahead, but since then I've been questioning whether it was the right thing to do. I've consulted the ethical framework for counselling, which expressly forbids friendships between clients and therapists. But Danielle and I aren't friends. I was just doing what was necessary to help her when she was in a tricky situation. I've also thought about what Genevieve said over coffee, how I'd really helped some of the kids, particularly the ones who were struggling. I think I can help Danielle too. Surely it's my duty to try to help, particularly now she has a baby on the way.

When we sit down in the counselling room my eyes are drawn to Danielle's brooch, the Victorian design with the jade stone, matching her delicate earrings. She's worn it once before. I remember because it's the kind of thing Richard used to buy me, from the little antique shops that he likes to frequent.

'I love your brooch,' I say.

'Thank you. I've been in court today. Didn't have time to get changed.' She looks professional in her suit, but the scars on her face still stand out, angry and loud. They must be the first thing anyone ever notices about her. I can't imagine how that makes her feel.

I smile at Danielle and then notice Peter's insolent expression, the way he's slouched against the sofa. I notice that Danielle's eyes are watery. 'So, shall we get started then? How have things been this week?'

'Not good,' Danielle says, holding back tears. 'Well, awful really.' She turns to Peter. 'I want to try and make things work between us for the baby's sake, but it feels like Peter's just not interested, like he's already checked out of our relationship.'

Peter stares at the carpet. 'I just can't see this all working out. It can only end badly.'

'End badly?'

'I don't think Danielle and I are going to be able to make our relationship work. And I worry about the baby. I don't think we're ready for one. I don't think we ever will be. It's just not meant to be.'

Danielle's face is wet with tears. 'How can you say that? How can you not even be willing to try?'

Peter sighs. 'You know why.'

'You still think that?'

I stare at them intently, unsure what's going on between them, what piece of the puzzle is missing.

'I'm sure of it,' Peter says.

'Of course it's yours.' She places her arm round her stomach protectively and the penny drops. My mind spins, trying to remember what Danielle said about other relationships. I'm sure she's never mentioned cheating on Peter. But she had mentioned that they'd had a break. That she'd seen someone else then. I'd been under the impression that their break-up had been quite a while ago. Not so recently that Danielle could be pregnant by another man.

'Maybe we should check. Do a DNA test,' Peter says.

'OK, sure. Whatever you want. Whatever I have to do to prove myself to you.'

Peter frowns. 'I can't bring up another man's child.'

'It's not like I cheated on you. We had broken up. And you slept with other people too,' Danielle continues. She turns to me. 'Don't you think this is an example of double standards?'

I can't take sides. 'I think you need to talk it through, work out what you both want.'

'I'm not the one who's pregnant,' Peter says. 'I'm really not sure if it's anything to do with me.' I feel the blow as if he's said the words to me, not Danielle.

'It takes two to get pregnant.'

Peter sneers. 'Yeah, you and him. Did you come back to me because he dumped you? Is that why?'

Danielle laughs. 'No, of course not. I wanted to be with you. I've always said that in here, haven't I?' She looks at me for confirmation, but I say nothing.

She turns to Peter pleadingly. 'Honestly, being with someone else convinced me that you were the one for me.'

'You liked him, didn't you? You said that he swept you off your feet, that he listened to you the way I never did.'

'I just said that to make you jealous.' She turns to me. 'He's talking about the man I told you about. I dated him on my break from Peter. He said I had Reese Witherspoon's energy and Kate Winslet's smile. A real charmer.'

I freeze. I remember her saying something about Reese Witherspoon's energy. But Kate Winslet's smile? That was exactly the line Richard used on me.

Danielle is looking directly at me. 'He got on my nerves in the end. And he behaved as if he was superior to me, talked to me about books and theatre shows as if he was the only one entitled to an opinion on them. He went on and on. The whole thing was a mistake.'

The man sounds just like Richard. Is it possible that she was the one he had the fling with? No, I tell myself. There are tons of men who talk down to women. And Kate Winslet is a well-known actress. I stare at the brooch she's wearing, so similar to the ones Richard bought me. My heart flips over in my chest.

CHAPTER 28

DANIELLE

I throw up bile into the toilet as soon as I get up. It's become a familiar part of my morning routine, and even though I feel grotty, it gives me a buzz of satisfaction to think of the baby growing inside me. I've read that morning sickness is a sign that the baby's developing well.

I find Peter downstairs, in his suit at the breakfast table, listening to Radio 4 as he reads the news on his phone.

He looks at me, sees my dressing gown. 'Still throwing up?' he asks.

'Yeah.'

'Not going into work today?'

'No, I have my midwife's appointment, remember?' I frown. I've had to make up an excuse about feeling ill, and I feel guilty about missing work. I'll have to catch up later, which will mean less time to work on my appeal case for the charity.

'Oh, yeah. Good luck.'

'Are you sure you don't want to come with me?'

'I can't. We've got the partner meeting about the intellectual property case.'

'OK, then.' He's been avoiding me ever since our last session with Beth. I know he's still not sure if the baby's his.

'We're going to have to talk about this properly at some point.'

'I know,' he sighs. 'Tonight?'

'Yeah, sure. I should get my due date confirmed today.' Then I should be able to prove the baby's Peter's.

'Great.'

'And remember I told you my mother's coming to stay?' I'd finally plucked up the courage to tell him last week, making up a story about suddenly wanting to reconnect with her now I'm pregnant. I couldn't bring myself to tell him that she's getting out of prison. I've lied to him all these years, telling him we're estranged because she had a breakdown and I had to go into foster care.

Peter sighs. 'Are you sure that's a good idea, with everything else that's going on?'

'She's flying all the way over from Sweden.' Another lie. 'I've promised her she can stay with us.'

'I don't have any problem with her staying. It's just that… well, our relationship is complicated at the moment. And I'm not sure that it's the right time to bring another person into our home. Especially your mother, who you haven't seen for years.'

'It's important to me to see her. And now the baby's on the way, it seems like a chance for a new beginning.' I've said she can live with me now. There's no going back. She hasn't got anywhere else to go.

'OK.' Peter stands up and strokes my hair in a rare display of tenderness. 'If you're sure. It's up to you. But I know she's hurt you in the past. You hated being in foster care. It won't be easy for you with her living in the house.'

'I can cope,' I say. But he's right; having her around will be difficult after all these years.

'OK. If you're sure, then I suppose it will be good to meet her at last. When's her flight arriving?'

'In three days.'

How long's she staying for?'

'I'm not sure, but it will be a while. I don't think she knows anyone else in the UK. She hasn't been back for years.'

Peter picks up his briefcase. 'Right. I'd better be off then. Good luck at the appointment.' He hesitates for a moment, then leans down and kisses me on the top of my head. 'Hope it goes well.'

I sit on the uncomfortable plastic chairs, waiting for my name to be called. Looking around the waiting room I see the happy couples, women sitting down while men stand behind them, a reassuring hand resting on their shoulders. That could have been Peter and me, if only things were different.

I get out my phone to check my work emails and find myself googling, heavy-hearted, how to be a good single mother. If Peter decides not to stick around, there are lots of role models out there. I'm sure I can do it. But then I think of my job. How will I manage that and a child on my own?

'Danielle Brown.' The sound of my name being called jolts me out of my thoughts.

I smile as I approach the midwife.

'Hi,' she says. 'Come on in.'

She goes through a detailed questionnaire about my health and Peter's health, and our families' medical histories. I don't know the answers to any of the family history questions. I haven't had anyone to ask for the last fifteen years. She asks me if there's any domestic abuse in my relationship and I say no. It's too hot in the consulting room, and my palms are sweating. I just want to know that the baby's Peter's. 'Will you be able to tell me when I conceived?'

She smiles over her glasses. 'We can work that out together. When was your last period?'

'Over a year ago. I haven't had periods since I've been on the mini-pill.'

She frowns. 'Well, that makes it very difficult to date the pregnancy. Do you have any idea yourself when you conceived? Did you miss any pills?'

'Yes, a couple. About two months ago, I think. I'd been going through a difficult time and I just forgot.'

'OK. So it will be most likely then. But we'll want to double-check.'

'OK.'

'Can you just get up onto the bed, so I can feel your belly?'

I do as she says. 'That's a nasty injury,' she says casually.

'Sorry?'

'Your face.'

'Oh.' The question takes me by surprise. For a moment I had forgotten about my scars. I feel the heat rise through my body, embarrassed.

'It's a burn. An accident.' The skin is darkening and thickening now, the scars becoming part of my complexion.

'They're healing nicely.'

I nod, unsure what to say.

'Watch out, cold hands,' she says as she places them on my skin. She presses hard and I wince.

'Was that painful?'

'Just uncomfortable.'

She moves her hands around, pressing and prodding, and then smiles at me. 'OK, you can get down now.'

'Can you tell how far along I am?' I need to know. I need to reassure Peter that the baby's his.

She shakes her head. 'No. You need to have a scan. Just in case you're further along than you think.'

CHAPTER 29

BETH

I sit across from my supervisor, Grace. It feels good to be sitting on her sofa in her therapy room, to be the one seeking guidance, to have someone listening to me for once. I meet her every month, but we missed the last session because she was in bed with a virus. I'd emailed her before our meeting today to let her know that Richard and I had split up.

'How are you?' she asks warmly.

'I've been better.'

'How are you coping without Richard?'

'Alright.' I don't really want to talk about the loneliness that wraps around me at night, the anxiety I've started to feel, the triple-checking that the doors are locked before I go to bed.

'How are you balancing the stress with seeing your clients? It can be difficult for a therapist when they have their own problems. It can make it harder to see their clients' issues as separate from their own.'

'I want to talk to you about one of my clients,' I say. I take a deep breath, realising how unlikely what I'm going to say sounds. 'I think she might be the woman Richard had an affair with.' Tears prick my eyes.

I've brought the photos of Richard and his mistress that I was sent in the post with me in my handbag. I've been studying them. The woman in the pictures has short blonde hair. A bit shorter than Danielle's… but suddenly I could see it, so clearly. Even though I couldn't see her face, I just knew. Danielle's hair's grown out a bit since then. But there was no doubt in my mind. The woman was Danielle.

Grace pushes over the box of tissues. 'You think Richard had an affair with your client?' she asks gently.

'Yes. Not while she's been my client. It was before.'

'I'm a little lost. So has Richard admitted this affair?'

'He's said he's cheated on me, but not who with.'

'So what makes you think it's her?'

I sigh. 'She's trying to fix her relationship with her husband. A few months ago, when they were on a break, they were both seeing other people. She was seeing a man who sounded exactly like Richard.'

'*Exactly* like him?'

I hear the doubt in her voice. 'He used the same line as Richard, told her she had a smile like Kate Winslet, just like Richard told me. And he talked down to her about books and theatre the way Richard talks down to people…' Now I'm saying it out loud it sounds vague.

Grace looks at me intently.

'And the brooch… she wears this jade brooch. It's quite a rare style. Richard collects them. He's bought them for me in the past, as presents. And she has the same type.'

I swallow, not sure if I can bring myself to say the rest. The thing that makes everything so much worse. I force it out. 'And now she's pregnant.' The full horror of it hits me once more, like a punch to the stomach. Richard having a baby with someone else, Charlie having a half-sibling. I reach for the tissues and dab my eyes.

'The baby…' I continue, unable to meet Grace's eyes. 'Her husband thinks the baby isn't his, that it might be another man's. Richard's.'

'Her husband says it might be Richard's?'

'No. He doesn't know who it was she slept with. He doesn't know she slept with my partner.'

'OK. So you don't know for certain whether this baby is Richard's. Or even that she was having an affair with him?' I sink into my seat, suddenly unsure.

'No,' I say. I haven't found the courage to confront Richard. My mind's been like a pendulum, swinging from one extreme to the other. One moment I'm certain he's been sleeping with Danielle; the next, I lose my confidence, wondering if I'm imagining the whole thing. I don't want to look like a fool in front of him, to give him a reason to think I'm not coping.

'If this is true, Beth…' Grace pauses, and I can see she is choosing her words carefully. 'If this is true, then you won't be able to continue to see her in a professional capacity. There would be a conflict of interest.'

I nod. I'm not sure I can face sitting opposite Danielle, advising her on her marriage, when she was responsible for breaking up my relationship.

'She was the reason Richard left,' I say.

Grace raises her eyebrows. 'I thought you said she was seeing you with her husband for marriage counselling?'

'She is. But Richard wouldn't have left me if it hadn't been for her. His affair… I think it made him decide that he was unhappy, and then that our relationship wasn't worth saving.' My tears come faster now. I miss Richard so much. I was prepared to give it another try, to give him a second chance. It was him who wanted out.

A thought occurs to me out of nowhere. 'Do you think Danielle knew I was married to Richard when she started therapy?'

'What do you mean?'

'She started therapy just after I found out that Richard had had an affair. Maybe she knew I was his partner. That's why she chose me.'

'Why would she do that?'

'I don't know.' I scan my mind, trying to remember each session, if there were any hints. But I can't think of anything that suggests she already knew who I was.

'I think you need to speak to Richard. And then take it from there.'

'Do you think I'm right, then? That they were seeing each other?'

'I don't know. The evidence you have; the Kate Winslet line, talking down to women, the brooch… it does seem suspicious in some ways. But it's all circumstantial. There's no way you can really know without asking.'

'OK,' I say. But I'm not sure I'm ready to hear the truth. Danielle might be having Richard's baby. If that's true, I'm not sure I can cope.

Suddenly I remember the photos in my bag. 'There's something else,' I say triumphantly. 'I have photos of them together.'

I take out the photos and lay them on the table.

'What are these?' Grace asks.

'The photos I got in the post, the ones that someone sent to me to show me that Richard was having an affair. That's her.' I stab at Danielle's head in the photo. 'Right there. That's Danielle.'

Grace leans over the photos and studies them. She stares intently at the one I was pointing at, of Richard outside the university.

Then she looks up at me. 'These are all of the back of someone's head,' she says softly.

'I know. But I recognise her.'

Grace reaches out and touches my hand. 'I'm sorry, but there's no way you could recognise someone from these. There's no way anyone could.'

'But it's her,' I insist. 'Her hair's slightly longer now, but it's that exact shade of blonde.'

Grace looks at the clock on the wall. 'Beth, we'll be coming to the end of our session soon. I'd like to explore your feelings about this in more detail. Maybe we should book another session in as soon as we can?'

I frown. Grace and I see each other once a month. That's the way it's always been. 'Why?' I ask.

'I'm worried about you. You know that as your supervisor, my role is to help you manage your caseload, to talk through any issues you're having with your clients. And I think in this case, your own life is clouding your judgement on Danielle.'

'What do you mean?'

'You're looking for someone to blame for your split from Richard. And you think it could be your client he cheated with. But a lot of things don't make sense. For a start, why would she have chosen you as her marriage counsellor to fix her own marriage if she'd slept with your partner?'

'I don't know.'

'And do you have any evidence that Richard and Danielle have even met? Apart from the photos?'

I shake my head. 'No.'

'So what you've got to ask yourself is why you've become so fixated on Danielle. Whether this is really about her at all, or if it's about you. I think you're struggling to process losing Richard and you're looking for someone to blame. Danielle just happens to be there.'

CHAPTER 30

DANIELLE

Peter's agreed to come with me to the hospital for my scan. He's spoken to his boss and told him he has an urgent medical appointment so he could get time off work at the last minute. I'm so glad he's prioritising this appointment, and I feel a kernel of hope forming inside me. Is he coming round to the idea of the baby? I don't know what I'm going to do if I have to bring it up on my own. My mother will be living with me by then, but I'm not sure how involved I want her to be.

I haven't been able to sleep lately, unable to get comfortable, or stop the thoughts swirling around my mind. And every time I roll over I feel a fresh wave of nausea. It doesn't help that work has been really busy. I'm struggling to keep up with the pace. I feel like I have constant flu, but I dread telling work about the baby. I've seen how women who have had children have been forced out of the office, on spurious grounds of redundancy, when it's really because they can no longer work late every night. I'm sure that as soon as I tell the partners at the law firm, I'll start to be sidelined. I'm already worried about all the time I'll miss for antenatal appointments.

I reach for Peter's hand as we sit in the hospital waiting room. I really hope he'll stand by me. I'm praying this baby is his. It has to be. I was so careful with the other man.

I watch the pregnant women being called in for their scans one by one. Some of them clutch their backs as they walk to the consulting room, struggling under the weight of their bumps. I can't imagine my body expanding so much. I touch my stomach, which is still showing no signs of a bump. It's hard to believe there's really a baby growing inside me. The constant nausea is the only thing that reminds me I'm pregnant. But just months from now I will be as big as those women.

I'm called through and Peter and I walk into the small consulting room. The sonographer smiles as I climb up onto the bed. When she rubs cold gel on my belly, Peter reaches for my hand and squeezes it. It feels good to have him beside me. The probe touches my stomach and the sonographer presses harder than I expect.

There's a rushing sound on the screen, but no picture, only darkness. The sonographer keeps moving the probe, pressing harder. I feel a stab of fear. What if the baby's not there? Eventually she finds something. The flicker of a white line. And then more. Our baby.

'There it is,' she says, smiling.

'Wow,' Peter says, staring at the screen. And I can see that he's forgotten his doubts entirely.

'Can you tell when it was conceived?' I ask quickly.

'Let me just run some checks and take some measurements, and then I'll have a better idea.'

Peter and I watch in silence as the sonographer works, staring intently at the screen. I feel Peter squeeze my hand tightly. I can hardly believe this is real. My baby. On the screen. Growing inside me.

'OK,' the sonographer says. 'This looks like a healthy baby. Congratulations. Now I can't give you an exact date of conception. But from the measurements, I'd say this foetus is about nine weeks old. You have to take two weeks away to get the date of conception, so you would have conceived seven weeks ago.'

I smile at Peter. I can see he's thinking what I'm thinking, because he can't help beaming back at me. The baby was conceived just after we got back together.

CHAPTER 31

BETH

I sit on the sofa with my laptop, browsing through houses on Rightmove. Charlie is staying at his father's tonight. When Richard came round to collect him, I nearly asked him about Danielle, but something stopped me. I remembered what Grace said about me just looking for someone to blame. Can that be true? Is this all in my head? I glance over at the photo of Nick on the sideboard. I wish he was here to talk to. He always saw things so clearly, always gave me the best advice.

I go back to looking at houses. I think of how hard I've worked over the last month, trying to find new clients, advertising and building up my website. But it's not enough. I haven't managed to acquire any more clients, and Richard's made it very clear that he's going to sell the house. I've been looking up more information about beneficial interest and I intend to ensure I get my fair share of the proceeds from the house, but in the meantime I still need to find somewhere to live. Richard said he wants the equity from our home to buy a place of his own. A bigger place, where he has enough space.

Enough space for what? A baby? Danielle's baby?

No, that can't be right. I'm just being paranoid, jumping to conclusions, like Grace said. There must be other people who compare their partners to Kate Winslet, other men who talk down to women. But the brooch…

Taking the steps two at a time, I go upstairs and take out my jewellery box. I've always saved the brooches Richard bought me for special occasions, which is why most of the time they stay out of sight. I pick one out now, turn it over in my hand. It's not identical to the one Danielle has, but it's similar enough. This style of jade brooch is so uncommon. Richard always used to seek them out, looking for them in tiny antique shops, delighted when he found one. It can't be a coincidence.

I think of how I liked Danielle from the first time I met her, how much I'd admired her empathy for her charity clients, how determined she was to fight for the under-represented. She reminded me of myself, my reasons for training to be a therapist. She'd said she'd thought of being a counsellor too. I remember how Richard and I got together at the pub after my course ended. I hadn't been the first student he'd got together with in that way, as soon as the course had finished and he was no longer their teacher. I think about how the pictures I'd been posted showed him with the woman outside the university. Danielle could easily have been one of his students.

I abandon Rightmove and go to the study and open the filing cabinet Richard uses to store notes for his teaching. I've never felt the need to look in it before and I'm pleased to find it unlocked. I go through the top drawer, but find only printed PowerPoint slides annotated in his small, neat handwriting.

The second drawer is divided into the different courses he teaches. And in each section there's a list of students for the course. I scan through them one by one, reading through the lists of unfamiliar names. After ten minutes I've found Danielle's name. I clutch the piece of paper, staring at it in shock, my palms sweating. She attended a course on 'careers in counselling'. I look at the date. It was two months ago.

It all makes sense. Danielle attended a course with Richard. They probably all went to the pub afterwards, the way Richard always did with his students. And then they must have started their affair.

There's no doubt in my mind now. Danielle was sleeping with Richard. She's the reason my relationship broke up. And now she might be carrying his baby.

Back at the computer, I scroll through the rental listings on Rightmove. There's a house listed on my street, but the rent is way more than I can afford. I need a house with a room for Charlie, a room for me and another for my counselling. If I don't have a therapy room, I won't be able to work. But the three-bed houses are far beyond my price range. So are the two-beds around here.

I curse. If Richard hadn't cheated on me, then I wouldn't be in this position. This is all Danielle's fault. How dare she come and ask me for help with her marriage when she's torn my relationship apart? Does she really not know who I am? Richard and I have different surnames, so it's possible. But it still seems like too much of a coincidence. What does she want from me?

I remember the night I went round to her house. I hadn't got the sense she was hiding anything. But then it was odd that after her panicked phone call saying she was leaving Peter, she decided to get back with him after all. Because of the baby.

I change my search terms on the website to the area where Danielle lives and select 'any price'. I know I could never afford to live there. The listings are full of huge homes with big gardens and double garages. There's one on Danielle's street.

I stare at it for a moment. Then I think about it. I'll have to cancel Danielle's therapy sessions. I want her to know why, that I'm cancelling because she slept with my partner when he was in a relationship with me. I should go to her house and confront her, in front of Peter. I should tell him that she was sleeping with Richard, that the baby might be his. I will hurt her the way she's hurt me.

When I arrive, I park outside her house and stare up at it, rage seething inside me. She's got her huge house and her cushy career, and I'm about to lose everything because of her. Richard has already gone and soon my house will follow. I won't be able to afford anywhere big enough to include a room for therapy. My career will go too. I hate her. Her casual fling has destroyed my life.

The lights are on in her living room, but there's no movement inside. I wonder if both of them are at home. As I sit, a car pulls into the street. I slouch as the headlights swing over me, unable to think of a good reason why I'm here. A man gets out and waves to me and I manage a small wave back. He must think I'm a neighbour.

I get out of the car and walk towards Danielle's house, my stomach twisting with nerves. I haven't planned what I'm going to say. I need to check they're both in, so that Peter hears everything. I go round the side of the house. The blinds are open and I can see them through their bifold doors. Danielle's sitting at the island in the centre of the kitchen on her laptop, a glass of water beside her. Peter walks in, wraps his arms around her and she tilts her head to accept his kiss. I dig my nails into my palm, begrudging them this moment of happiness, when she has stolen my happiness from me. Suddenly she seems to sense my stare, and she pulls away from Peter, turning towards the window. Instinctively, I dart to the side, behind a garden chair.

As I stare at the scene of domestic bliss in front of me, I think of the confrontation ahead. What will happen when I knock on her door and accuse her of sleeping with Richard? Will she just deny it?

I haven't thought this through. I'm not sure if it's a good idea anymore, not sure how she or Peter will react. As soon as I've spoken to her, the moment will be over. If Peter doesn't believe me, then she'll continue her life just as before. It was a bad idea to come here.

Suddenly, I have a realisation. I don't need to come to Danielle's home to hurt her. She comes to me for therapy every week and sits opposite me, telling me her secrets. I can undermine her confidence, take her words and twist them to hurt her. I can damage her from the inside.

I watch Peter smile as he reaches out to touch Danielle's belly, and I feel a wave of bitterness. She doesn't deserve happiness. I keep watching until Danielle comes over to the expansive bifold doors that lead to the garden. For a second her gaze seems to rest on me, her eyes almost meeting mine. But it's an illusion. The dark night conceals me. She is the one who's lit up and exposed by her kitchen spotlights. I am safe.

CHAPTER 32

DANIELLE

My mother is leaving prison today. I busy myself with preparing the house, dusting the tops of the doors and the skirting boards, cleaning every nook and cranny. I know this home can never match the one I grew up in, with its sprawling gardens and huge bedrooms, but I hope she'll approve.

I put the couple of pictures that I'd managed to salvage of Mum and me on the mantelpiece, and add one of Dad, holding back tears as I think of everything I've lost. I don't know if she'll want to remember him, or if it will be too painful. In all the photos we're beaming at the camera, but my childhood wasn't always like that. I frown at the memories and try to push them aside. I should feel happy today, but my stomach knots with anxiety. I don't know what the future holds for my relationship with my mother. Everything's about to change. I put my hand to my stomach, wondering when it will start to fill out, become a noticeable bump.

I look at myself in the mirror before I leave. My dress is a bit too tight, slightly too much cleavage showing. I remember my mother criticising me once when I was fourteen, telling me my top was too low-cut for the pub. I was furious at the time, but I suppose she must have been looking out for me.

As I drive over to the prison in my two-seater soft-top, I think about how I've lied to everyone about Mum. I told most of my friends that she was dead. I didn't want them to find out she was in prison, and it stopped them asking too many questions. I worry now she's back that I won't be able to introduce her to any of them without admitting that I lied. Luckily I told Peter we were just estranged, that she lived in Sweden. But how long are we both going to be able to keep that up? How long before he discovers who she really is? Peter's just coming round to the idea of the baby. I don't want to drop the bombshell that I've been lying to him for years.

It's difficult to find a place to park the car, but I'm an hour early so I have plenty of time. I end up in a side street of run-down terraces and I reapply my make-up in the car, surveying my face in my compact. I'm fifteen years older than when Mum and I were last together outside the prison. I've lived a whole life she only knows about from the tiny snippets I've told her during visits. I don't really know who she is anymore either. We're practically strangers.

As I walk slowly to the prison, my heels catch on the uneven paving. I pass an old mattress strewn across a driveway and a rusted car in front of a garage. When I arrive outside the gate, I feel small and lost, like a child. Like the teenager I was when my mother was locked up. Gradually a small crowd forms, each watching the gate, each waiting patiently for someone to come out.

Finally my mother appears, dressed in jeans and a huge black coat, a holdall slung over her shoulder. 'Sophie.' She puts the bag down and wraps her arms around me. I sink into her embrace. It's everything I didn't know I'd been missing and tears of relief run down my face. But my mother doesn't feel the way I remember. Her bones stick out of her clothes; she's all angles. Her greasy hair brushes my face. I search for the scent of Chanel No. 5, but there's only a generic rose water smell that doesn't seem like her at all.

'You don't know how long I've spent imagining doing that,' my mother sighs. 'Hugging my own daughter.'

My emotions get too much and I start to sob. I try to pull away from her, to pull away from all the feelings, but she just grips me harder.

'I love you,' she says. 'I love you so much. You'll always be my daughter, no matter what.'

I can't speak through the tears.

She releases her grip slightly and looks at me. My vision is blurred, but I see my own face looking back at me, twenty years older. We are the same height, with the same short blonde hair. She started dyeing hers a couple of years ago, as she got closer to the end of her time in prison.

She seems so thin and fragile in my arms.

'You've lost weight,' I say.

'Think of all the years I spent doing Weight Watchers. Who knew that a prison diet was the answer?'

We begin the walk to the car, side by side in silence. Mum keeps stopping to touch things: a brick wall, a lamp post, an electricity box. 'I can't believe I'm out,' she whispers. She stares at a daisy growing between the concrete paving stones. 'Amazing, isn't it?' she says. 'How things find a way to survive, to continue growing whatever their circumstances. A bit like you, Sophie. You succeeded against the odds.'

When we get to my car, I put the soft top down. I'm ready to speed away from here, leave the prison behind forever. I think of the baby growing inside me. The future. I have no idea how my mother will react when I tell her.

'You'll feel the wind in your hair in a minute. You'll love it.'

She smiles. 'We're in this together, aren't we?'

'We always have been, Mum.'

'You know your father always wanted a soft-top sports car. He'd love this one.' I swallow down my sadness. I won't let myself think of my father now, won't let myself feel that toxic mix of emotions that come up when I remember his death.

'I still miss him,' she continues. 'If only we could have worked things out.'

I won't let myself think about that. Not now. Things could have been so different.

I rev the engine and speed off. My mother keeps speaking, but the wind drowns out the words.

We stop for lunch at a service station. Cheese and ham paninis in a roadside Starbucks. She wolfs hers down along with a hot chocolate, watching people come and go as if they are completely foreign to her.

'No one without a mobile phone in their hand,' she observes, and I glance up from mine. I was checking my work emails. I put my phone down guiltily.

I take a deep breath, and shift uncomfortably in my seat. I have to tell her before she meets Peter. 'There've been changes in my life.'

'Really?'

'People know me as Danielle now. Danielle Brown.'

'Oh, I see,' she replies. 'Was it because of the case?'

'Yeah, it was. And you know I always liked my middle name better than Sophie, anyway. It seemed a good time to change it.'

'And the surname?'

'I got married.'

She has tears in her eyes now. 'You got married? When?'

'Four years ago.'

'Why didn't you tell me?'

'I didn't know how to. I knew you wouldn't be able to be at the wedding. It would only have upset you.' Mum had cried and cried with guilt when she'd missed my graduation. I couldn't tell her about getting married too. It would have broken her heart.

Tears are streaming down her face now. 'But no one from our side of the family would have been there. No one to represent you.'

'It was a small wedding. We had lots of friends there.' I remember how we had to tell people from Peter's family to sit on 'my side' of the aisle to fill it up. I hadn't invited my aunts and uncles. I'd hardly spoken to them since I went into foster care. I remember the well of sadness I'd felt when I walked down the aisle without anyone in my family there to see it.

'I'm so sorry I wasn't there.'

'Don't worry, Mum. It was a happy day.' It had been one of the happiest days of my life, but there was no one there who'd known me from when I'd been born, no father of the bride to give a speech about what I was like as a little girl. I'd missed my father so intensely that I'd felt a tightness in my chest, and I could barely take the first step down the aisle on my own.

I think of telling Mum about the baby now, but then I look at her tear-streaked face and realise that it's not the right time. My marriage is enough for her to take in.

'And what's he like? Your husband.'

I don't know what to say. How can you explain someone you love to another person? All the little pieces of Peter that add up to make him special. 'You'll meet him soon.'

'I can't wait to see your wedding photos.'

'I'll show you them, Mum. All of them.'

'I'm so looking forward to it.' She reaches out and grips my hand across the table. 'I know it's four years too late, but congratulations. I'll have to buy you a wedding present.'

'You don't have to.' I blink back tears. Peter's parents had bought us everything we needed for our new home when we got married, but I'd still felt like I was somehow missing out, a blank emptiness inside me when I realised that I hadn't received even a token present from anyone on my side of the family.

'I want to.'

'Mum—' I pause, thinking how best to say this. 'Peter doesn't know about you... well, he knows, but he doesn't know you were in prison. He thought we were estranged.' I feel a surge of guilt and I can't look at her.

'He thought we'd fallen out?' Mum looks devastated. 'But you know I'd never do anything to hurt you.'

'I know. I suppose I was… embarrassed to tell him you were in prison.'

She nods. 'I understand. But I'm here now, and I can't wait to meet him.'

'I've told him you've been living abroad.'

'Haven't got much of a tan, have I?' she says with a smile.

'I said you were living in Sweden.'

'Why Sweden?'

'I don't know. It was the first place that came to mind.'

'What was I supposed to be doing there?'

'I said you had a new husband there, a new family.'

'Sophie!' She looks heartbroken. 'You know I'd never do that. You're my only family.'

'I had to say something. To explain why I'd gone into foster care. Why you weren't around. Why Peter couldn't ever meet you. Can you play along with it?'

She nods sadly. 'Of course. You know I'd do anything for you.'

CHAPTER 33

BETH

Charlie snuggles into my arms on the sofa and I wrap myself around him. He's been off school sick today and I've cancelled my clients. I think he's coming down with flu, he's so lethargic. I'm glad to have spent the day just holding him, watching children's TV and switching my mind off. Thankfully he managed a few bites of dinner, and now he's back on the sofa with me. The cold's locked outside the window, Charlie's still in his dressing gown, and the warmth of his little body comforts me as much as my cuddles comfort him.

I feel run-down and defeated. Run-down by looking after Charlie by myself most of the time, plus all the extra marketing in my attempt to attract new clients. And defeated by Richard, and Danielle, and the fact that I'll have to move out soon. I'm fighting as hard as I can against my circumstances, but I can't seem to keep my head above water.

I run my fingers through Charlie's curly hair. I think about the bruises on his arm. No matter how many times I ask him about them he clams up, becomes irritable and refuses my hugs. He hasn't seemed himself lately, quieter and more subdued than usual.

I hold him tighter as I think of what's ahead of him. Us moving house. A half-sibling possibly. I wonder how he'll cope. When I look down at him, I see he's fallen asleep in my arms, his chest rising and falling gently. I ease off the sofa and carefully place the blanket over him. I start moving around quietly, tidying up. Nick grins at me from his picture on the side table and I take it down to look. I wonder what he'd think of me now, now my life is falling apart.

I remember when I used to tell him my worries. I talked to him about the ex who used to hit me and tell me I was worthless. I confided in him that the other teachers at school thought I was too close to the kids, that I didn't keep an appropriate professional distance. He'd listen to me, and then take me in his arms and make everything better, his kind eyes locking with mine.

We met at the local squash group. I was lonely in suburban London, filled with couples and coffee shops and people who didn't say hello in the street. I'd taken up squash to meet new people. Nick had taken me under his wing, teaching me how to hold the racquet and patiently knocking the ball back to me so I could practise my shots. One session, I'd burst into tears. My boyfriend had been angry that morning because I'd been too long in the shower. He'd hit me, not hard but hard enough. I'd thought I might have deserved it. Instead of playing, Nick and I had just stood on the court and talked. Afterwards he took me to a local pub and bought me a glass of wine, made me laugh, forget everything. He told me that no one should be allowed to treat me that way. That he'd help me leave him, help me with a place to stay. After I left, it wasn't long before Nick and I were together ourselves. It was a whirlwind romance. Invigorating and intoxicating. He made me feel special. I haven't felt the same way again since.

I pour myself some wine and raise the glass to the photo, then return it to the sideboard. I sink onto the sofa next to Charlie. An hour and a half later, he's still in a deep sleep and I've polished off a second large glass of wine. I decide to carry him upstairs and put him straight to bed. I place him down gently, pulling his covers over him. His toys have fallen off the bed and rolled underneath. I pick up the penguin that he's had since he was a baby. And then

I catch sight of something else. A white plastic bottle. My pills. It's rolled all the way under his bed. How did it get there?

Charlie's always curious when he sees me taking my pills, but he can't reach the bathroom cabinet. I go to the bathroom and look around. How did he get into the cabinet? It doesn't make any sense.

Then I catch sight of Charlie's blue step in the corner of the room. He uses it every night to climb in and out of the bath and to reach the sink. I take a sharp breath, overcome by guilt. He must have used the step to climb up onto the edge of the bath and reach the cabinet. At least the pill bottle has a child-safe lid, thank goodness. There's no way he'd be able to open it.

Back in Charlie's room, I lie on my front to reach under the bed. My head aches and I feel stressed. I need to stop drinking for tonight, have something to eat. I shuffle underneath the bed until I can reach the pills. As I grab the bottle, the lid falls off. It was open. I swallow. That can't be right. How would he have opened it? Could he have taken any of the pills? I stare at the bottle, horrified.

CHAPTER 34

DANIELLE

When we get out of the car, my mother stops to look up at the house.

'It's lovely, Soph— Danielle.'

Her face is tear-stained, and I reach out to her. She leans into me and I tentatively place my arm around her. She smells unfamiliar, a musty scent only partly concealed by the rose water shampoo. 'Thank you,' she says.

We're side by side in the cold, shivering and staring at the house. Suddenly it seems foreign to me, like it's not mine at all.

I wonder if my mother's thinking the same thing as me. That everything about this moment is wrong. It's the wrong time, fifteen years too late, and the wrong house. Everything was taken away from us. We'll never get the years back, never be a mother and daughter in the same way again.

I remember when we all used to be together, my mother, my father and I. His absence weighs heavily between us. I wonder if she feels as guilty as I do, that we're alive, when he isn't.

All those years ago when Mum and I had left our family home, we hadn't realised it was for the last time. There hadn't been a moment like this to pause and take it all in. I think about all the things I lost: the furniture, my toys, family photos, postcards from family days out. Everything that gave me comfort. I had only been able to take a few things when I went into foster care, and later my aunts had arranged the sale of the house to pay Mum's legal fees. Mum must have agreed to the sale as she owned the house, but no one thought to consult me. I didn't find out it had happened until later. Someone must have had to clear it out, going through my teenage room, throwing away my books, my clothes and make-up, the posters on the walls, photos of friends and family. Stealing my memories.

I notice the light on in the living room. Peter's home. I'd planned it like this, but now I look at my mother in her dated clothes, tears running down her face, and I wonder if tonight is the right time to introduce them. But what choice do I have?

My mother is completely still, as if she's afraid. 'Let's go inside,' I say, taking her arm and guiding her towards the house. I fumble for my key and push the door open. 'Hi,' I call out.

Peter appears in the corridor.

'Hi, I'm Ginnie,' my mother says, her voice faltering.

'Hi, nice to meet you,' he says, throwing his strong arms around her. I see her involuntarily flinch, the flash of fear that passes through her eyes. What has prison done to her?

'Shall I get your suitcase from the car?' Peter asks.

I think of my mother's paltry belongings, thrown together in the prison-issue holdall. Peter thinks I've collected her from the airport.

'No, thanks,' I say, feeling heat rise to my face. 'I'll bring it in later.'

Mum bends awkwardly to take her shoes off.

'Can I get you a drink?' Peter asks. He's on his best behaviour because he wants to impress my mother. I feel a flicker of hope for our relationship, for our future together. I touch my stomach lightly and think of the baby.

'A coffee, please.' My mother smiles.

'Sure. Coming right up. How about you, Dani?'

'I'm OK,' I say. I turn to my mother. 'Do you want to see the rest of the house?' I want to show her how much I've achieved, how I've managed to succeed despite her not being here, despite everything.

'I think I just want to sit down.' She looks pale, her eyes wide, and I realise that this whole experience must be completely overwhelming for her. 'Then maybe a shower,' she says hopefully.

Peter comes in with the coffee which she takes gratefully. 'Long flight?' he asks. 'You must be tired.'

'Yes…' she replies.

There's a silence as she sips her drink.

'Do you want anything to eat? I could make you a sandwich, if you like?'

'No, thank you. We stopped for lunch on the way.'

'So what is it you do in Sweden?'

She looks at me uncertainly. 'Oh, this and that. I keep myself busy.'

'Right,' Peter says, leaning forward, waiting for more.

My mother stares vacantly into the distance, as if looking for inspiration for conversation. I see her glance at our wedding photo on the mantelpiece.

'So, how did you two meet?' she asks.

'At work. About six years ago.'

'Where did you get married?'

I relax as her questions about our wedding come thick and fast. I answer, telling her about the registry office, my dress, the small reception we had at the pub. I pick our wedding album off the shelf and take her through the pictures, trying to imagine that she was there, and that this is just an ordinary mother-and-daughter moment, remembering the day together. As she exclaims over my dress, I close my eyes and pretend things are normal.

Peter suggests he goes to the shops to get us something for dinner and I turn to Mum to ask her what she wants. She used to love Indian food. We'd get takeaway on Friday nights when Dad was away. He used to be away a lot at weekends, doing up the flat my parents owned in central London that was supposed to be mine once I left university.

'You can have anything you like,' I say to Mum, thinking of how limited her diet must have been in prison. But my words sound patronising.

'No decent food in Sweden, then?' Peter quips.

Mum smiles thinly. 'Not as much as you would think. Not much lamb. Do you think you could get lamb chops for dinner? I've really missed them.'

Peter nods. 'Sure. I'll get a nice bottle of wine too.'

After he's gone I get some fresh towels out of the cupboard, handing them to her so she can shower. She stands for a moment, just breathing in their scent, feeling how soft they are. 'These are lovely,' she says, and it brings home just how much she went without in prison. I feel a wave of pity.

'I'll get your bag from the car and leave it in your room,' I say, pointing to the spare bedroom with its crisp white sheets on the bed and view over the garden.

She nods, going into the bathroom with the towels and locking the door. I hear her turn the water on immediately. She seems desperate to be on her own. I feel a sense of unease at the pit of my stomach. I've missed her so much over the years, but now she's back it feels overwhelming.

When my mother comes down half an hour later, I notice her hair is still wet and unbrushed. 'Do you want to borrow a hairbrush?' I ask.

'Yes, please. I'm sorry to have to ask you for everything. I'll get myself sorted soon. I'll find myself a job, start paying rent.'

'No rush,' I say awkwardly, aware of our role reversal. I've missed her so much, but now it feels more like I'm the mother to her.

We go upstairs together and Mum brushes her hair in front of my mirror.

'I remember doing your hair when you were little,' Mum says wistfully. I think back, recalling the feel of the brush as she pulled it through my tangled hair. Once, when she wasn't looking, I'd pretended to be grown up, putting on her lipstick and shoes. I feel nostalgic, longing for the past, when everything was simple.

'Do you think you'll have children? With Peter?' she asks suddenly.

I smile to myself, thinking of the life already growing inside me, cells multiplying, limbs forming. 'I hope so.'

'I found it difficult sometimes. Looking after you could be very wearing, particularly when you were a teenager and we clashed all the time. I'm sorry if I lost my temper occasionally. I always loved you, though. With all my heart.'

'It's OK,' I say, fighting back tears. 'I love you too.' I never imagined she'd apologise for the way she was back then, and my heart aches with gratitude. We should have had this conversation years ago. But our relationship was stunted by her time in prison.

'Children can test your patience, that's all. I suppose you'll discover that for yourself eventually.'

'I'm sure I'll be fine, Mum.'

She stands, handing me back the hairbrush. 'Just make sure you've sorted yourself out first,' she says. 'You need to face the past before you're ready for a child.'

CHAPTER 35

BETH

I pull myself out from under the bed, heart thudding, and stare at the pill bottle in my hand. It's definitely mine. My name's printed on the front. There are no tablets left in the bottle. I try and recall how many were left yesterday. I have no idea. My brain feels fuzzy.

Has Charlie taken them? My heart pounds even faster. What if that's why he's exhausted and ill? What have I done?

'Charlie!' I shake him awake and he looks at me woozily. 'Charlie, did you get my pills out of the bathroom? Have you eaten any?'

He lifts his head slightly and stares at me groggily, then flops his head back down on the pillow.

'Charlie – answer me! Have you had any of these pills?'

He shakes his head no, then falls back to sleep.

I pace back and forth. He's been ill all day. Tired and sleepy. What if he took them in the morning? It could be poisoning.

I pick up the phone and ring the NHS helpline, my palms sweating as I dial. Guilt burns inside me as I explain that he might have taken my antidepressants and I don't know how many. They say they're sending an ambulance and my heart pounds, every inch of my body trembling with dread. This is all my fault.

I look down at Charlie, who's barely moving. I don't know if it's because he's tired or something far more serious, but I feel instinctively that I should try and keep him awake. I wrap his tiny body in my arms, repeating to him over and over again that everything will be fine.

Half an hour later the ambulance still hasn't arrived. I can't control my panic now. What if he's taken the whole bottle of pills? The drugs are strong. An overdose could easily kill an adult. I can't wait any longer. Charlie needs to be in the hospital. I'd drive him myself, but I can't. I've had too much to drink.

I phone Richard.

'How could you let that happen?' he shouts. I feel like curling up into a ball as his words cut into me.

'I'm so sorry.'

'There's no time to argue. I'm coming over.'

He hangs up the phone and within fifteen minutes he's driving us to the hospital.

We sit on hard plastic chairs in A&E, a sleepy Charlie between us. We've both asked him several times if he's taken the pills but he says he hasn't. He seems a bit better now, leaning against me and insisting on playing games on my phone. I run my hand through his hair. I'm so lucky to have him. How could I have let him down so badly? I feel sick with nerves.

We're soon triaged by the nurse, but then we're left waiting. A couple of hours pass by hazily. We must be low priority, which relieves me. My palms are sweating, but I can breathe properly now, and I know that things are likely to turn out alright. Richard waits for Charlie to fall asleep curled up against him, before he starts to question me.

'How on earth did this happen?' Richard whispers to me, over Charlie's head. I feel myself shrink into the chair as he glares at me. I feel so guilty, because I can't answer the simple question. I just don't know how it happened. I must be an awful mother. Surely any mum should be able to stop her son getting hold of her medicine. Any mum except me.

'I – I have no idea how it happened. The pills were in the bathroom cabinet where they've always been. He must have used his step to get them.'

'I thought he couldn't reach.'

'So did I.'

'Are you sure you didn't leave them out?'

'I'm positive. I always put them back.'

'But you've been drinking. You could have forgotten.'

Could I have forgotten? Could I have left them out somewhere where Charlie had found them?

'I don't think so.'

'You shouldn't be drinking on those pills anyway.'

'You always said one wouldn't hurt.'

'It's a bit different when I'm not there, though, isn't it? You're the only one responsible for Charlie.'

'Whose fault is that?' I mumble. I think of Danielle then, how between them they've wrecked my life. He doesn't know I know about her. I can't tell him because if he realises I see her for therapy, I know he'll say I can't be her therapist anymore. I wonder if he knows about the baby she's expecting, that it could be his.

Richard ignores the comment. 'You've got to pull yourself together, Beth. This is the second major thing that's happened with Charlie since I've left. First he tried to get out of the house when you weren't looking. Now he might have taken your antidepressants. Your carelessness is putting him in danger.'

Charlie stirs in Richard's arms and I feel a surge of guilt. Is Richard right? Am I a danger to my own child?

CHAPTER 36

DANIELLE

Peter takes the chicken out of the oven and starts to dish it up. It's just me and him this evening, and he's made the effort to get home from work at a reasonable time. My mother's gone to an open evening about adult education at the local college, and Peter's cooked me a light meal of chicken and rice that I'm hoping I'll be able to keep down.

'You seem more relaxed without your mum around,' he comments, as he hands me my plate.

'I am.' I love my mother, but it's been so long since she's been in my life that sometimes she feels like a stranger. I'm not ready to tell her I'm pregnant yet, but I'm worried that she will have guessed. I'm sure she hears me being sick every morning, and she can't have failed to noticed the bags under my eyes and how I wander around the house half-asleep.

'I wish someone had let me know how hard pregnancy would be,' I say. It's difficult to keep up the pace at work when I feel like I'm going to collapse from exhaustion any moment.

'Yeah, I had no idea. Mandy in my office just seemed to breeze through it. She didn't take a single day off.'

'I don't know how she did it.' It's only 8 p.m. Usually I'd still be in the office now, but I can't take the pace anymore. Even this conversation seems exhausting. I'd rather be in bed.

'I'm sorry,' Peter says. 'That was insensitive. I can see how tired you are.'

I stare at the grilled chicken, pushing it round the plate. I've lost my appetite.

'I wanted to speak to you,' Peter says, 'about the baby.'

I freeze. He takes my hand and I prepare for the worst. Him breaking up with me. Saying I'll have to bring the baby up on my own.

'I wanted to say I'm sorry,' he says. 'For questioning whether the baby is mine. Even if I thought that, there was no reason to be so nasty to you.'

'Oh,' I say, relief coursing through me. 'Thank you.'

'I can see how difficult things have been for you. You know I worry about your anger. But I'm glad we're having therapy, trying to address it. I think we can do this. I think we can have this baby together. Be good parents to it.'

My heart sings. I've wanted to hear this more than anything else in the world.

'It's so important the baby has a father,' I say. 'I was close to mine, growing up.'

'Were you? You don't talk about him much.'

Tears sting my eyes. I remember him holding my hand when I was a little girl, remember him pushing me on the swing, cuddling me when I cried.

'It's been hard,' I reply, my voice thick with tears. 'In foster care, I had to keep it together just to survive. So I tried not to think about him, tried to forget.'

'I didn't think you got on with your parents.'

I sigh. 'Not when I was a teenager. Things got complicated then. They fought all the time. Once my mother smashed everything in the kitchen. Every plate. Every glass.'

'Why?' His eyes widen in shock.

'I'm not sure. I think it was because of something my father had done. He'd had an affair, but I didn't know that at the time.' I remember sitting in bed upstairs, trying to read a book and ignore the sound of the kitchen being destroyed. When I'd gone downstairs to check Mum was alright, I'd seen the river of sparkling glass in the kitchen, seen my mother's bare feet bleeding from where she'd cut herself. Her blind rage as she took another glass from the cupboard and smashed it against the wall. I ran back up the stairs as fast as I could.

'That's crazy.'

'I know,' I say. 'I think she needed to release her anger. By the next morning she had swept it all up and was pretending to be cheerful again.'

'Wow,' Peter says. He frowns and strokes my hair. 'No wonder you sometimes get angry yourself,' he says. 'It can't have been easy growing up in an environment like that.'

'It wasn't.'

He frowns. 'Do you think she'll be safe around the baby?'

'Of course she'll be. That was just a one-off.' Even as I say the words, they sound wrong, as if I'm not sure I believe them myself.

Later, I lie in bed trying to sleep, wondering about my mother in the room two doors down from me. I place my hand on my stomach, thinking of the baby. I feel an unexpected shiver of fear. Who is my mother really? The loving woman who brought me up and attended every school assembly? The woman who went into a violent rage and smashed everything up? Or someone else entirely? Prison must have changed her, but I don't know how. Do I want her to be so close to our baby?

CHAPTER 37

BETH

The morning after the trip to the hospital Charlie is back to his usual self. When I wake him up he smiles brightly, and my worry yesterday seems like it was from another life, a figment of my imagination. The doctors had told me to keep an eye on him, in case he'd taken the pills, and I'd checked on him every half-hour through the night, unable to sleep myself.

I get him up and dressed and then, on autopilot, open the bathroom cabinet and reach for my antidepressants. I stare into the cupboard in disbelief. They're still there. I open the bottle and knock one back. There's a few days' supply left.

Where had Charlie got the other bottle from? It must have been an old one, an empty one. And then realisation hits. Sometimes we do craft projects, making robots out of cardboard boxes and whatever recycling we've got. He must have taken an old pill bottle from there. I almost laugh with relief.

Later, I light the candle to cleanse the air in my counselling room in preparation for my therapy session with Danielle. I've managed to avoid telling Richard that I know her. I don't want him to realise there's a connection between us and stop me seeing her.

Everything has changed now. I want to use the session to get under her skin. I don't want to help her or guide her. I want to punish her for what she did to me. I can't let her get away with taking Richard from me.

Tension fills the room as Danielle and Peter sit down. In the last session he was so convinced the baby wasn't his. I thought he might leave Danielle, that I might never see him again. But here he is, sitting nervously on the sofa, tapping his fingers against the armrest.

'How are you feeling, Danielle?' I ask as she sinks onto the sofa. She's not showing yet, but she looks pale, with shadows under her eyes.

'Tired. I just don't seem to have the energy I used to. Really I'd just love to lie down and go to sleep.'

I smile warmly at her. 'I remember feeling like that. Your body is just preparing you for having the baby. This is the easy part. You'll know what exhaustion really feels like once it's born and it's screaming all night.'

'I've been telling her to get more rest, but she's still working too many hours.' I hear a note of concern in Peter's voice, and wonder if he's changed his mind about the baby.

'Have you had the chance to talk about what we discussed last week?' I look at Peter, who stares at me blankly. 'Last week you expressed concerns that the baby might not be yours,' I confirm.

Peter flushes. 'I should never have said that. I know it's mine.' He reaches for Danielle's hand and entwines his fingers with hers. Jealousy burns inside me. He still loves her, despite everything.

'How do you know?' I want to find out more, to figure out what's changed since last week, but my words sound too challenging, not gentle, not how I normally sound in these sessions.

'Because of the dates. The midwife said we must have conceived seven weeks ago. We were back together then.' He looks at Danielle, a smile stretching over his face.

Seven weeks ago. I count back in my head. That was just before I got the photos of Danielle with Richard. I try to keep a relaxed posture, but I can't stop my jaw from clenching. I clasp my hands together and dig my nails into my palm as hard as I can. The pain distracts me and I manage to keep quiet, to stop myself laying into Danielle.

If either of them looked up at me they'd see that something wasn't right. But they're not looking at me. They're too busy staring into each other's eyes.

'We're both excited now, about the baby,' Danielle says. 'Although we haven't had much time to talk about it.'

'It's been difficult to find a moment. Her mother's come to stay with us.'

'Your mother?' I try to hide my surprise. Danielle had said both her parents were dead. A car accident.

'Yeah.' Danielle meets my eyes for a second, as she realises her lie has been exposed. 'I used to tell people she was dead. But we were estranged.'

'You told me she was dead too,' I say gently. 'You could have trusted me. I would have understood.' It's a big thing to lie about. I'm convinced she's lying to Peter about the baby too. I feel a shiver of unease run through me. I'm usually so good at reading body language, identifying when people are lying. But I hadn't picked up that she wasn't telling the truth about her mother. What else has she been lying about? Suddenly it seems too much of a coincidence that she's chosen me as a counsellor.

'I wasn't ready to tell you. Not then,' Danielle says quietly. 'But I am now. My mother and I are trying to rebuild our relationship.'

'How's that going?' I say. 'It can't be easy.'

'OK, so far. I mean… it's difficult, with her living with me after so many years. And being pregnant makes me reflect on my own childhood, how much I missed out on, growing up in care.'

'OK.'

'I don't want the baby to go through what I went through. I want it to have a happy family.'

'Danielle had a difficult childhood. Her mother… had a temper,' Peter says.

'A temper?'

'Yeah,' Danielle says. 'But she's changed now. And she was never that bad.'

'But I think that's the cause of so many of your problems,' Peter says. 'You've got so much repressed emotion that it escapes in fits of anger.'

I look at him, surprised at his insight.

Danielle looks at the floor. 'I don't want to be so angry,' she says. 'But sometimes my emotions get the better of me.'

'You know mental health issues run in families?' I say gently. 'If your mother struggled, then it's likely you will too. Even if you haven't suffered before, having a baby changes everything. You've already mentioned that it's making you think of your own childhood. Sometimes people find they're dredging up all their baggage from the past and realise they just can't deal with it. You won't be sleeping, and you'll be hormonal. All your emotions will be elevated. In these situations of extreme stress, sometimes people with difficult backgrounds like yours just can't cope.' I watch her face, to see if I've managed to get under her skin, to worry her.

'Really?' Danielle looks at me with fear in her eyes.

'Don't worry,' I say, trying not to smile. I can see in her eyes that she still trusts me, that she's looking to me to help her. 'You can talk through any concerns here. You're safe here.'

CHAPTER 38

DANIELLE

I'm finishing dinner with my mother, trying to keep down the rich lamb stew she's cooked, when Peter comes into the house, the door slamming behind him. My stomach clenches with nerves. Today we're going to tell Mum about the baby. I think back to what she said about me not being ready to have children yet. I hope she doesn't react badly.

'Hi,' Peter calls out.

'In here. Have you eaten? Mum's made lamb stew.'

'I've already eaten, I'm afraid. But it smells lovely.'

'It tasted good too,' I say, although I've only managed a few bites.

'Is everything alright?' my mother asks, looking at how much is left on my plate.

Peter sits down opposite us, raising his eyebrows at me. I nod.

'Actually, we've got something to tell you,' I say. My leg shakes under the table.

My mother's eyes flick back and forth between us. 'Is everything OK?'

'Yes, yes, it's fine. It's good news. I'm… I'm pregnant.'

I watch her face go through the emotions, from shock to worry to elation.

'Wow,' she says finally. 'Congratulations.' She gets up from her chair and we embrace. Relief floods through me. I'm so glad she's happy for me.

'My daughter. Having a baby. I'm going to be a grandmother.' I smile at that, but I feel tears forming at the backs of my eyes. I wish my father was here too, that he'd had the opportunity to become a grandfather.

'Yes,' Peter says. 'It's quite a shock, but we're delighted.'

'I bet you are.' She turns to me. 'Is that why you've been getting sick so often? I thought you were ill.'

I smile. 'Nope, just pregnant.'

'Do you know if it's a boy or a girl?'

'No. It's still early days. Too early to find out.' I smile. Whatever gender the baby is, my love for it already feels overwhelming.

'You'll have to look after yourself, make sure you're eating right.'

'At the moment I eat whatever I can keep down,' I reply with a wry smile.

'That will pass. I was horribly sick with you at the beginning, but it got better.'

'We need to minimise stress for her too,' Peter says.

'Yes, of course,' she says, turning to me. 'You should work less hard. You put in too many hours at the office.'

'I keep telling her that.'

'This is so exciting.' My mother grins as she digests the news. 'Is there anything I can do to help?'

'I don't think so, not yet.' I put my hand on my stomach, feeling protective of the life growing inside me. A whole load of complicated emotions swirl around my head. I'd like my mother to be the kind of grandmother I've seen some of my friends' mothers become. Grandmothers who help out with the babies, who want to spend as much time as possible with their grandchildren. But I'm not sure I can trust her.

'I suppose you'll need more help once the baby's born. I can be your live-in babysitter.' She smiles.

Peter looks at me. I feel slightly sick at the thought of her staying long-term. And I'd given him the impression that my mother would be going back to Sweden when her stay ended.

'We might need to make a few changes once the baby's born,' he says.

'Yes, of course. Baby-proof the house, that kind of thing. I really can't wait to be a grandmother.' She claps her hands together suddenly. 'This is the kind of news we need to celebrate. We should have champagne, toast the baby.'

'Good idea, Mum.' The house is starting to feel oppressive. 'Shall I pop to the shops and get some?'

I feel better as soon as I'm out of the door and in the fresh air. My body seems to be constantly overheating at the moment, and the chill of the winter air soothes me. I walk slowly out of the cul-de-sac, enjoying the relief that my mother's happy about the baby.

The road is dark, the street lamps spaced far apart. As I ease by a car parked on the pavement, right next to the hedge, I get the sense that someone is behind me. I turn round to look, but only see someone on the other side of the road. It's dark, and in their winter coat they are little more than a shadow against the brick wall. They bow their head, stopping to root around in their bag. I hear the sound of keys jingling. They must be coming home from work.

I keep walking, wondering why the hairs on the back of my neck are still standing on end, as if my body senses that something is wrong. I wonder if this is a symptom of pregnancy, a kind of mother's instinct. A hyper-awareness and hyper-vigilance – my body preparing me to protect my baby.

I've felt this a lot lately. Leaving work at night, I've noticed every person walking down the street, risk-assessing them and trying to work out if they are a danger to me. Usually I'd walk to the tube oblivious to everything around me, but now I feel a stab of fear whenever I'm alone. I thought I was being watched, but it's not that; it's paranoia. I think about what Beth said about mental health problems running in families. I hope this isn't the start of something more. I hope this feeling I have, this fear, will begin to fade as my pregnancy progresses and I get used to the idea of having a child.

I think about all the people I've helped in my charity work. I've appealed on behalf of people who've been convicted of fraud, serious assaults, gang stabbings. A lot of them were released afterwards. What if their victims want revenge? What if they target me, their lawyer, rather than the perpetrator? I can't believe I've never thought of it before, but isn't it possible there's someone out there seeking to hurt me?

I shiver, and try to put the thoughts out of my head. I'm pleased to see the bright lights of the supermarket, the line of trolleys outside under the fluorescent lighting, people milling around. I grab a trolley and the automatic doors open for me, drawing me into the warmth. It's good to have people around me, even if it's just strangers wandering down supermarket aisles.

I decide to pick up a few other bits while I'm here, to delay going back out into the cold night. I'm trying to find Peter's favourite brand of granola when I see her. At least I think it's her, her trolley drifting past the end of the aisle. Beth. I jump and my face flushes. Everything she said at our last session rushes back to me. She'd questioned whether I'd be able to cope as a mother, made me feel unsure of myself. I've been trying not to think about what she said about her fears for my mental health. I wasn't expecting to see her here, to be reminded of my worries. Not in the place where I pop in for a pint of milk or a loaf of bread. Not in a place where I feel secure.

I wait a couple of minutes, pretending to study the back of a cereal box before I move on. I turn left at the top of the aisle, the opposite way to the way she went. I can leave the other shopping, just pick up the alcohol and get out of here. I find the wine aisle and I'm searching for the champagne when, out of the corner of my eye, I think I see her again. I glance up. It is her. She's browsing at the end of the aisle. I pretend I'm deep in concentration, looking at the wines. She moves away into another aisle. Has she seen me? And what is she doing here? I think about how I've felt like I'm being watched lately. But I must be projecting my worries onto her. She hasn't even seen me.

I want to get out quickly. I'm overheating and I'm not sure if it's nerves or pregnancy or both. I abandon the trolley, bow my head and rush out into the fresh air. Outside, I struggle to catch my breath. I can't believe I reacted like that. I should have just said hello. I wonder if it's my hormones making me feel so fearful or if it's something more. I remember the feeling of being watched as I walked to the supermarket. Perhaps that's why I'm so on edge. What if someone had been following me?

CHAPTER 39

BETH

I stand in the corner of the kitchen sipping my wine as I watch the couples touring my house, casually dismissing the kitchen we remodelled just before Charlie was born.

'We could rip this out,' a tall man says to his pregnant girlfriend, indicating the kitchen cupboards that I'd painted myself when money had been tight. 'And knock that wall down, open up the space.'

David, the estate agent, appears behind them. 'This house has so much potential,' he says. 'You can really put your own mark on it.'

'We need a bigger place for the little one,' the man says, glowing with pride, as he looks admiringly at his girlfriend.

David doesn't miss a beat. 'This place is perfect for a family. Three good-sized bedrooms upstairs. And the seller's very motivated. He's found somewhere else already. So he might consider offers under the asking price if you were interested.'

I take a gulp of wine as I spot a woman looking at my photo collage on the wall. It's been there so long I'd almost forgotten it was there. Richard and me on holiday in Spain before we had children; cocktails in the sunshine, lying by the pool, standing outside churches and museums. She's staring at the pictures so intently that I feel like going over and pulling her away. Perhaps I should have taken it down. It's the house that she's thinking of buying, not my whole life.

Beside me I hear a cupboard door open. A man holds the door, revealing my rows of crystal glasses.

I cough. 'What are you doing?'

He frowns at me, irritated at the interruption. 'Just checking for damp. You never know what might be lurking in the backs of the cupboards.'

The pregnant woman comes back in and asks to get past me to turn the kitchen taps on. 'I want to check the water pressure,' she explains. I nod. Something about her manner and her assertiveness reminds me of Danielle. I tense at the thought of her. I no longer think of her as my client; I think of her as the woman who took Richard from me. I'll see her tonight in therapy. I grip my wine glass tighter, my knuckles white, as I watch the couple drift through my house. This is all her fault.

Later, when the hordes have left and Richard has returned from the park with Charlie, I sit in my therapy room opposite Danielle and Peter.

Danielle is wearing the brooch again, the jade one so like the ones Richard used to buy me. Richard must have bought it for her. I wonder why she'd wear it now she's trying so desperately to make her relationship with Peter work. Perhaps she hasn't completely left Richard behind.

Danielle shifts position on the sofa, trying to get comfortable. She runs her fingers through her hair.

'You seem very anxious,' I say.

'I am anxious,' she admits, her deep brown eyes boring into mine.

'Last week we talked about mental health.' I look pointedly at her hand resting on her stomach. 'It's very common for children to inherit their mother's anxieties. Maybe that's something we should address in this session.'

'You mean, the baby could pick it up from me?'

'Yes. Even in the womb. Your stress causes the baby stress. And as the child grows, your genetics will play a part too. Mental health problems run in families.'

Peter looks across at me. 'Does anger run in families too?'

'What do you mean?' I ask.

'I said before – Danielle gets angry, really angry. And I know her mother used to be the same. I – I just don't want what happened before to happen again.'

'What happened before?'

'The fire. Did she tell you about the fire? How she burnt her face?'

Danielle shifts awkwardly in her seat. She places a hand on Peter's leg and I'm not sure if it's to comfort him or to tell him to stop talking.

'She did,' I say, and I remember how once, before I'd met him, I'd thought that Peter might have started the fire on purpose, that he might be abusive. Since I've met him and seen the dynamic between them, I'm not so sure.

'There was an accident—' I start.

'An accident?' Peter looks incredulous and I feel a flicker of confusion. Is he admitting that he did it on purpose?

'You had a barbecue,' I continue.

Danielle interrupts. 'Please,' she says. 'Don't go on. We all know what happened. I don't want to relive it again.'

'No,' Peter says firmly. He puts his hand on Danielle now, taking back control. He looks at me. 'I want to hear what she's told you. If she's told you the whole story.'

The whole story? Does he mean he had some kind of reason for starting the fire, some kind of extenuating circumstances? It's amazing the excuses clients sometimes come up with for their own behaviour.

'Danielle – I think it would be good to address this. It feels like a big issue in your relationship,' I say, curiosity overcoming me.

She touches the scars on her face. 'It changed my life,' she says darkly. 'You both know that. Let's just leave it alone.'

'Have you and Peter ever talked about it?'

They look at each other, and neither of them answers.

'OK,' I say. 'Let's recap the facts. The barbecue wouldn't light. Peter threw petrol on it to help it along and it got out of control.'

Danielle cries out at the memory.

I stare at Peter, watching his reaction. Danielle had made me think it wasn't entirely an accident, that he'd lost his temper.

'Is that what you said to her?' He leans towards Danielle, and suddenly she seems small beside him. I haven't seen any sign of his temper in our sessions, but his anger's coming out now. He wouldn't be the first man who was an expert at hiding it. I've learnt that it's the polished professionals you've got to watch out for. They're often the ones who go undetected the longest. They can hurt their partners behind closed doors without anyone suspecting anything.

'I—' Danielle looks terrified next to him.

'Peter,' I say sharply. 'Your body language seems threatening.'

He looks up at me, surprised, as if he'd forgotten I was there, and retreats back to his side of the sofa.

'What's bothering you?' I ask him.

'What she's said is completely wrong.' I sit up, lean closer. Is he just covering his tracks? Maybe he's worried I'll report him.

'It wasn't me who threw the petrol,' Peter says. He must be lying. He doesn't want to admit his mistake to me. Won't admit Danielle's scars are his fault.

'It was Danielle,' he continues. My eyes widen and I stare at him in shock, unable to maintain my usually neutral face. 'She was in a rage. We'd just argued about something small. Whether we'd be ready on time for the guests. And she just lost it and grabbed the can of petrol. I was screaming at her not to. But she didn't listen. She threw it on the fire. The barbecue went up in an instant. Her hair caught fire. She caused her injuries herself.'

CHAPTER 40

DANIELLE

I'm working late and the office is empty. I'm the only one still here. The combination of the artificial lights above me and the buzz of my computer is giving me a headache, but I'm nearly finished for the evening. I look at the time on my phone. Ten p.m. I'm completely exhausted. I haven't worked this late since I found out I was pregnant, but tonight I had to stay just to keep on top of things.

I used to always be the last to leave, the one to lock up and turn the lights off, feeling the satisfaction of a hard day's work. Now I'm more likely to leave at seven to go home, have a small dinner and then sleep for hours on end.

I shut down my computer and gather up my papers, grabbing my black corporate rucksack and making my way out past the empty meeting rooms and unoccupied desks, towards the light switches. Tomorrow this office will be buzzing again with life. But for now it's devoid of people and chatter, of whirring printers and shouts from the partners, of the bell that rings when we win a case.

There's raucous laughter from outside the office window. I jump. But it will just be people on the way back from the pub.

It's too quiet in here.

I reach the light switches and flick them all off. The office is dark and gloomy, the rows and rows of empty desks casting shadows on the dark blue flooring. With the computers no longer humming the office seems deathly silent, the only noise the rumble of traffic and conversation outside.

My heels click-clack on the tiles as I make my way to the lifts, the sound echoing round the office. A fleeting, unwelcome thought passes through my mind. I should have worn more sensible shoes. I couldn't run away fast in these heels.

My eyes flit from the meeting rooms to the spaces under every desk. It's never occurred to me before but there are so many places you could hide in this office. I can't help thinking of a man I'd defended recently, who'd been accused of assaulting his colleague in a meeting room after hours. I'd managed to get him released. Not enough evidence. What if he'd done it?

I reach the door, feeling the relief of the cold metal against my skin. I look round the office one final time and then go and press the button for the lifts. The bell dings and the doors of the nearest lift glide open. I'm about to step inside when I see a movement out of the corner of my eye. I turn my head to see a huge black machine. A hoover. A woman in overalls with headphones is slowly wheeling it out of the other lift. I should have realised. The cleaners come in every evening around this time.

I nod at the woman but she hasn't even noticed me, distracted by whatever is playing through her headphones. In my lift, I watch the doors slowly close and I start to breathe again.

Then I see the reflection in the mirror and I gasp. I'm not alone.

The man smiles. 'Getting home early for once?' He's just making a joke, but it implies he knows my routine. I recognise him from somewhere, perhaps a Christmas party or after-work drinks. He's the kind of man I'd smile at if I wasn't alone at night in a lift with him, if I wasn't so paranoid.

I don't reply, wishing the lift would move faster.

'Do you want me to walk you to the station?' the man asks. I wish I could remember his name. And how does he know I got the tube in? I tell myself to calm down. Everyone gets the tube into work except the partners. They're the only ones with parking spaces.

'No, thanks,' I say.

When we get downstairs and out of the building, I hold my breath as I wait for him to set off. Once he's striding away down the street I turn and head in the other direction, even though the tube is the way he's walking. I circle the block and double back on myself once I'm sure he's gone.

There's no one about, and the street lights cast an eerie glow. I pick up my pace, eyes scanning ahead, looking for alleyways, doorways, anywhere someone could jump out at me from. I decide to walk close to the parked cars.

I'm nearly at the end of the street when one of the cars' headlights suddenly come on. I jump out of my skin.

I'd been walking up the road towards it and hadn't seen anyone else. No one had got in or out of the car. They must have been sitting there. Waiting. But for what?

I don't want to get any closer. My whole body's on alert. Standing still, I watch as the car manoeuvres out of the space and then speeds past me.

Then I recognise the person in the driver's seat.

Beth.

CHAPTER 41

BETH

The lavender scent of the candle fills the room as I take the photos out of the envelope and lay them on the coffee table, lining them up neatly: Danielle and Richard walking side by side along the street. Him hugging her. The two of them kissing outside the university.

I've dressed carefully in my favourite casual blue and white striped dress, accessorised with the delicate silver teardrop earrings that Richard bought me for our fifth anniversary. I want Danielle to really see me, realise that I'm a real person too, not just someone who listens to her talk about her life every week. That I'm also someone with a life and hopes and dreams. I want her to see that she broke up my relationship, heartlessly caused my life to fall apart.

All week I've been thinking of the best way to confront her. I thought about going to her home, or embarrassing her in front of her colleagues. But here, in this tiny room, with Peter, will be perfect. I can't wait to see his expression when he sees the photos. The shock. I imagine the embarrassment on Danielle's face, the flush of shame.

I'm looking forward to telling him that I don't think it's his baby. I looked up the course Danielle went on with Richard. The timings fit. He was teaching her a few weeks before she's meant to have conceived.

Charlie's staying at Richard's flat tonight, so I have the house completely to myself. I don't want him to overhear if things get heated.

At 8 p.m., I'm pacing up and down the hallway, waiting for them to arrive, preparing my smile. Usually they arrive on time, so when it gets to ten past eight I start to get nervous. Perhaps they aren't coming. I feel a shiver of disappointment.

And then the doorbell goes.

Glancing at myself in the hallway mirror as I go to the door, I smile at my reflection. I am ready.

I see the shadow in the frosted glass and pull the door open, stretching my face into a smile.

But it falls from my face when I see who it is. Just Peter, his bulky frame filling the doorway.

'Where's Danielle?' I ask.

His eyes flash. 'She's not coming. She's not coming back here ever again. I won't let her have anything to do with you.'

I stare at him, shocked.

He steps over the threshold into the house before I can react, towering over me.

'She told me you'd been following her,' he says.

'I haven't—'

'She saw you. In your car outside her office. She was afraid.'

'I was just passing by.'

'What do you want from her? Are you obsessed with her? Is that it?'

'No – I—' I think about telling him that she stole Richard, taking him upstairs and showing him the photos. But I don't think he'll believe me.

'What kind of therapist are you? You know Danielle's vulnerable. She's pregnant. And you do this.'

'I – I wanted to help her. I wanted to help you both.'

'No, you didn't. I can see right through you. The questions you ask. Making her doubt herself. Telling her she'll have mental health problems like her mother. You're no good for her at all.'

He looks me up and down as if I'm completely pathetic. His face is too close to me, his breath on my cheek. I remember how the boyfriend I was seeing before Nick used to hold me up against the wall, use me as a punchbag. Suddenly I'm aware that I'm in the house on my own with him. I glance at the door, which he must have closed behind him. It's only a few paces away, but with him blocking my path it seems like miles.

'I'm sorry if you feel like that,' I say quickly. 'But I think it's best if you leave.'

He doesn't move. 'You've got problems. Serious problems.' I think about my phone on the side in the kitchen. If only I could reach it and call for help. A tear trickles down my cheek.

'You're pathetic. Stay away from me and Danielle or I'll go to the police. Consider that a warning.' And then he thumps his hand into the wall, strides to the front door and lets himself out.

CHAPTER 42

DANIELLE

On my drive back from work, I think about Beth. I haven't seen her this week. Not at my office, not outside my house, not at the supermarket. I'm always looking over my shoulder, whenever I see a shadow or sense someone behind me. But she's not there. The police didn't help when I called them. But Peter has. He went to see her and I haven't heard anything from her since. I smile. My rescuer. I imagine having his baby, a smiling, happy family of three. Things are looking up. Beth was the one I'd paid to help me, but it was my own husband who I could depend on all along.

When I pull into my driveway it's already 11 p.m. and I doubt anyone will be up. I've had another long day at work and I'm exhausted. But there's a light on in the living room. I hope it's Peter, not my mother.

'Hi,' I call out tentatively as I open the door.

'Hello.' Peter appears in the doorway of the living room.

'About to go to bed?' I ask him as I take off my shoes.

'Not yet. We need to talk.'

'Is this about Beth?' I go into the kitchen and pour myself a glass of water and he comes with me. I think Beth's stopped following me. I look at him and see the troubled expression in his eyes. Does he know something I don't?

'No, it's not about Beth—'

'If it's about me working too hard, then I promise I'll have more time after the appeal's been heard. You know how important it is that we prove my client's innocence. He only has us to help him. He has no family at all over here. Once the appeal's over then I'll relax a bit more. Make sure I'm fighting fit for the baby.' I put my hand on my stomach.

'That's what you always say. But there's always another case. More work. Another wrongful conviction. Plus your day job too. You can't keep going on like this.'

I nod. I know he's right. 'Can we discuss this another time? I'm exhausted.'

'We can talk about that later. I wanted to talk about your mother.'

'What about her?'

'She can't answer a straight question. A bit like you. You're both hiding something.'

I swallow. 'Let's not argue now,' I say wearily, hoping we can leave this conversation for another day, when I'm more prepared for it.

'Were you ever going to tell me, Dani?'

'Tell you what?'

'She's not who you say she is. There was a letter to her, in the post. To Virginia Loughton.'

'Oh.' I feel light-headed, tiny specks dancing in front of my eyes, and I grip the kitchen counter to steady myself. It feels like all the troubles in my past are chasing me down, determined to ruin the life I've built for myself.

'At first I thought it was to the wrong address. I put it on the side to post it back to the sender later. But when I came back downstairs, it had been opened. She was reading it.'

'I can explain—'

'The name had sounded familiar but at first I couldn't think why. But then I remembered the case. It was when I was training.

It was all over the papers. I thought I recognised her face from somewhere, but I just assumed it was because she had a familiar-looking face. But that wasn't it. She's Virginia Loughton. She hasn't been in Sweden, she's been in prison.'

My hands grip the work surface. 'You're right,' I say. 'I'm sorry.'

Peter's face falls. 'But you said she had a breakdown and she left you in foster care. You said you were estranged.'

'As good as. We were estranged because she was in prison.' I've dreaded this moment for years, dreaded him finding out. But I've held the secret tight for so long that it feels a relief to get it out.

Peter paces up and down. 'So you're Sophie Loughton? We've been together for six years and you never thought to tell me?'

'I couldn't. I'd changed my name to get away from it all. It was such a huge case. My name was leaked at the time and the press still tried to find me, even years later, every anniversary. When we started dating I didn't know we'd end up married. We were just work colleagues back then, and I didn't want anyone at work to know. You know how it is in the firm. Any sign of weakness and someone takes advantage. Imagine what they'd have thought of me if they'd known my mother was in prison. I never told my friends either. I wanted to forget. Put it behind me.'

He stares at me. 'Do you have any idea what you've done?' he says. 'You're letting her live in our house. She's dangerous. She murdered your father.'

CHAPTER 43

BETH

I get back from dropping Charlie off at school, unlock the front door and peer into the empty house. It's strange how something which once gave me comfort can now make me feel so alone. There's post on the doormat and I flick through it listlessly. Bank statement. Junk mail. And an official-looking letter in a brown envelope. I remember when the photos of Danielle and Richard were posted through my door and feel a sense of unease at the unfamiliar letter. I brace myself and study the envelope. The address is typed and the letter is too thin to contain photos. I ease it open.

When I see the logo of the professional body that monitors my counselling practice on the letterhead, I wonder if I've forgotten to renew my membership. It could have easily slipped my mind with everything else that's going on.

But then I read the letter. I'm being investigated for malpractice. A client has reported me for inappropriate behaviour. I stare at the words in disbelief. The letter doesn't state the name of the client, but it's clear from the accusations who it is. I've been reported for developing a friendship with a female client and for 'stalking'. It must be Danielle and Peter. I see my career, that I've spent so long building, crumbling before my eyes.

*

I cancel my clients for the rest of the day. There's no way I can see them with this hanging over me. I don't know what to do. I wish Nick was here to guide me. I wish I could see his face just one more time, wish he could hold me and comfort me. I go over to the side table, looking for his picture. But the photo's not there. It's gone. Someone must have taken it.

I think of the people roaming through my house during the viewings. It must have been one of them. My heart fills with anger and my body shakes. How could they? Pictures are all I have left of him.

But what's the point in talking to Nick's photo anyway? He's gone; he's never coming back. I wish I had someone else to talk to. A friend. I look at my phone, remember Genevieve, how she said she wanted to meet up again. I think about calling her. But I can't tell her about the complaint against me. It will remind her of how I was fired from teaching. She'll think I keep making the same mistakes. Tears form in my eyes. I can't ring her in this state. Instead I drop her a text, suggesting we meet up. It will be good to see someone, even if I'll never be able to tell Genevieve what's really going on in my life.

I pace up and down. I need to speak to Richard. I need to let him know what Danielle's really like. Someone who's not only had an affair with a man already in a relationship, but also someone who's willing to report her therapist, to try and get me struck off.

I hadn't told Richard that Danielle was my client before because I didn't want to alert her to the fact that I was his wife. Not while I was still seeing her for counselling. But now it doesn't make a difference. And it's time Richard knew what she was really like.

It's his day off today. I find the address of his new flat in my emails and drive over.

He answers the buzzer immediately, sounding surprised it's me.

'You should have told me you were coming,' he says, as he shows me into the flat. 'I would have tidied up.'

But aside from the pile of marking on the sofa, the flat is neat and tidy. There's no sign of Danielle here. But then there wouldn't be. She's back with Peter.

'Do you want a drink?' he asks me. 'Tea? Coffee?'

'No, thank you.'

He moves his laptop and the pile of essays off the sofa onto the coffee table. 'Do you want to sit down?'

I ease into the seat. 'Nice to see where you live.'

'It's a bit cramped, but I won't be here for much longer. I suppose you've heard I got an offer on the house? Is that what you've come about?'

'I've met your girlfriend,' I say abruptly.

'Beth, I've told you, I'm not seeing anyone anymore. It was just a fling.'

'Well, I've met the person you had a "fling" with, in that case.'

'That hardly matters now, does it?'

'She's pregnant, Richard.'

The colour drains from his face.

'Pregnant?'

'Yes. She hasn't told you, has she? She's keeping the baby. She's planning to stay with her husband, pretending it's his.'

'How do you know this?' Richard says urgently. 'How did you find out who she was?'

'I got those photos in the post, remember? Of you and her. They were taken outside the university. So I knew she was your student. And she started seeing me in therapy. She talked about you there. Danielle asked me what she should do about your baby.'

'Danielle?' The colour returns to Richard's face. 'I think you're confused. Her name wasn't Danielle. I don't even know anyone called Danielle.'

'What do you mean? She was on your course. I found the course list in your filing cabinet.'

Richard shakes his head. 'I don't remember teaching anyone called Danielle.'

'It was only a couple of months ago. You must remember. She was on your Careers in Counselling course.'

Richard sits down on the sofa beside me and reaches out to touch my arm. 'I know you've been stressed lately. But really, I don't remember her. Careers in Counselling is only a day course. It's a low-cost introduction to try to get students to sign up for the more intensive courses. A lot of students don't turn up. I don't remember anyone called Danielle. And even if she did turn up I wouldn't necessarily remember her from just one day.'

'You'd remember her,' I say quietly. What Richard's saying is starting to sink in. 'She has severe facial scars. She was in a fire.'

Richard shakes his head. 'I haven't taught anyone with noticeable facial scars. You've got the wrong idea. This Danielle – I have no idea who she is.'

My head spins and I sink onto the sofa. I look into his eyes. They crinkle round the edges, concerned. I don't think he's lying.

I feel sick… In that case, I've been trying to get into her head, following her, all for nothing. I've got Danielle completely wrong.

CHAPTER 44

DANIELLE

'Your mother murdered your father,' Peter repeats.

I realise that Peter only knows what he's read in the press. The papers had painted her as a monster.

'She didn't,' I say. 'She didn't do it. She just couldn't prove it in court.'

'Really? You believe that?'

I go over to the door to the hallway and shut it. Mum's upstairs. I don't want her to overhear.

'I know it. I know her. Know what she was like. She had a temper, but she would never have killed him. She was just in the wrong place at the wrong time.'

'In the wrong place at the wrong time? Her husband was cheating on her and she set fire to the flat with him inside it. That's premeditated, Dani. You know that. His body was barely recognisable afterwards.'

I shake my head, the memories of the smoke flooding my senses. 'You're talking about my father.'

'I'm sorry,' Peter says. 'You're right. I can't imagine what that was like. It must have been awful for you.'

I remember the thick, acrid smoke, the bright flames. I can still hear the screams. Desperate. The world starts to spin.

Peter grabs my arm. 'Sit down,' he says. 'You look pale.'

I collapse onto a dining chair and think of the baby. I know stress is bad for it.

'She didn't do it.'

'I know you want to believe that, Dani. But how can you? She was convicted in court.'

'This is different. She's my mother. I know her. I believe her.'

'And you know the court system. There has to be a whole heap of evidence to go down for murder. There are many more criminals walking free than innocent people who are wrongly convicted.'

'But there are some who are wrongly convicted, aren't there? I work on their cases every day.'

'Some. Not many. Maybe your work is clouding your judgement. You only see the cases where the verdict's in question.'

I stare down at the dining table, feeling defeated. 'I work on appeal cases because of my mother,' I explain. 'Because she was wrongly convicted but was never able to appeal. I couldn't help her. I was too young back then. But I wanted to help people like her.'

Peter looks at me and takes my hand. 'I know you think she's innocent,' he says. 'But at the end of the day, she's a convicted murderer.'

I feel tears running down my face and I try to stem my emotions, to stay calm for the baby. 'I know she didn't do it,' I say again.

'You may well believe that. But I can't have a convicted murderer living in my house with my child. She has to go.'

CHAPTER 45

BETH

I fumble around in my handbag for my keys and pull them out, unlocking the door quickly. There's a woman standing at the bus stop down the road, wearing dark glasses and a long winter coat, her scarf wrapped round her face. I see a flash of blonde hair underneath. I'm sure it's Danielle. I'm sure she's watching me, trying to scare me the way I scared her.

I hurry inside the house and lock the door behind me straight away, a habit I've got into ever since Charlie got out on his own. Once I'm inside my heart rate starts to slow as I calm down. Perhaps it wasn't Danielle at all. Perhaps I imagined it. I couldn't even see the woman's face.

I feel a horrible sense of déjà vu. I'm becoming increasingly isolated, just like before. I take Charlie to school and collect him, but spend the rest of the day in the house. I feel the same way as I did when I was struck off from teaching, ashamed of my mistakes, like I don't want to see anyone. I feel like I've been judged and found wanting, like there's something fundamentally wrong with me. I'd become convinced that someone was watching me back then too. But it was all in my head. Looking back, I can now see I was delusional. It was the beginning of my breakdown. Is it all in my head now? Or did I really see Danielle at the bus stop?

I'm just tidying up the breakfast things when my phone rings. 'Hello?'

'Hi, is that Beth?'

'Speaking.' I don't recognise the voice. For a terrible second I think it might be someone from Charlie's school, telling me he's had an accident. But I have the school's number stored on my phone. I would have recognised it.

'Hi, Beth. Richard's asked me to get in touch. My name's Lisa. I'm from social services.'

'Oh,' I say. Why is she calling me? What's Richard said to her?

'Now I want you to know that you're not in any trouble. I work with Richard sometimes, and there've been some concerns raised, so I offered to call, to see if you needed any support.'

'What concerns?' My heart thumps in my chest, thinking of all the things that have gone wrong recently.

'Well, Richard has told me that Charlie got his hands on some antidepressants and you thought he'd taken them.'

'He hadn't, though. It was fine.' A knot of worry forms in my stomach. I'm furious with Richard for speaking to social services without talking to me first.

'And that he managed to let himself out of your house.' I'd told Richard he tried to get out, not that he succeeded. He must have realised I was playing it down.

'Yes. Since then I've been double-locking the door when he's inside. It won't happen again.'

'And he has bruises on his upper arm that you can't explain.'

'I think he's being bullied at school.'

'None of these things would be a cause for concern in isolation, but Richard just wanted us to check on you, check you're coping OK, especially given your previous mental health problems.'

I swallow. I don't want social services to know about when I admitted myself to the psychiatric hospital. What if they use it against me?

'He also said that things were tough generally. You'd had a difficult break-up and were moving house.'

'Because of *him*,' I mutter, furious.

'So I just wanted to check whether you need any support with Charlie.'

'No, Charlie's fine.'

'OK, that all sounds good, Beth. I'm going to give you the number of some local groups that may be able to help you if you're struggling.'

'I don't need them,' I say, offended.

'If you're sure—'

I hang up the phone, shaking with anger, and then call Richard.

'Beth?' His voice is monotone as if he's not surprised to hear from me.

'How could you call social services?'

'I didn't call them. They called me. There'd been some kind of complaint about you. Saying you weren't caring for Charlie properly. Lisa knows me, so she called me first to get to the bottom of it.'

My mind spins. Someone's reported me. Who? Could it be the school? I'd been in to see them to ask if they knew if Charlie was being bullied, confessed I didn't know how he got the bruises on his arm. 'I would never hurt him. You know that.'

'I do know that. I vouched for you. But they had to do something to investigate the complaint. Lisa said she'd call you, just check everything was alright. I told her I'd been worried about how you were coping since our split.'

'Well, thanks for that, Richard.'

'Look, I *am* worried about you, Beth. You don't seem yourself lately. It reminds me of when you had your breakdown.'

My heart stops. 'You shouldn't have mentioned my mental health. They'll use it against me. And besides, it's all in the past.'

'Look, all we want is what's best for Charlie. And if you're finding things difficult, well, I need to know. I can always take Charlie for a few days or weeks if you need some time to yourself.'

As much as I long for some help with looking after Charlie, I can't accept his offer. He'll see it as me admitting I'm not coping. 'I'm fine.'

'Do you know where you're going to move to? I'm planning to complete the house sale in about a month. You won't have time to buy somewhere before then. It might be best if you rent. I could help you look for somewhere, if you like. Maybe we could find somewhere near my new place. I've seen a few nice two-bed flats on the market.'

I shake my head, feeling trapped. 'What about my clients? Where would I see them in a flat?'

'You'd need to look at renting a room elsewhere for your work.'

'Right.'

'And maybe you should be thinking of cutting down on client hours if you're feeling stressed. It can be difficult giving therapy when you're struggling yourself.' I remember Grace saying the same thing, that it was challenging to be a therapist when you had your own problems. She'd also said I should stop seeing Danielle. I should have listened. Maybe it's the stress that's caused me to behave so out of character towards Danielle. I can't believe I followed her when she'd done nothing wrong. Richard didn't even know her. I'm so unsure of my own thoughts. I can't distinguish the truth from lies. And now Danielle's put in a complaint about me. Maybe Richard's right. Maybe I can't manage everything. But I'm not going to admit that to him.

'I'm not struggling.'

'OK, well, just let me know if you need any help with anything. And like I say, I can always look after Charlie for any length of time if you need a break.'

What if Richard uses me needing a break from Charlie as justification for asking for full custody? I imagine a future without my house, without any clients, without my son. It's unthinkable.

'Don't worry about me,' I say quickly. Then I hang up the phone and burst into tears. I've already lost Richard. I can't risk losing Charlie too.

CHAPTER 46

DANIELLE

I get home late as usual. We're in the final weeks of preparing for the appeal and I'm struggling to balance my charity work with my corporate job, so I've had to stay in the office longer to catch up. Peter is out for work drinks tonight, avoiding my mother and the tense atmosphere in the house, heavy with unspoken words. I know Peter doesn't trust her, that he wants her to move out. But I can't possibly ask her to do that.

My mother is sitting on the sofa, a glass of red wine cupped in her hands.

'Do you want a drink?' she asks.

I hesitate, a part of me wanting to retreat to my room and be on my own, avoid any conflict. But then I feel guilty. I should spend time with her. 'Sure,' I say. 'I'll get myself a water.'

'No, you sit down. I'll get it.' She goes to the kitchen and returns with a large glass which she hands to me, before sitting down beside me. Soon we're chatting easily about my work on the appeal, and I wonder if it might really be possible to make up for lost time and recover our relationship. But then I remember what Peter said.

Midway through the conversation, she goes over to the mantelpiece and looks at the photos. There are pictures of me and Peter, plus the ones I've added more recently of her and Dad. One of us all as a family and individual shots of the two of them. She looks pensive in hers, whereas my father looks happy.

She picks up the photograph of Dad, studying it. 'He looks young here,' she says.

'It was shortly before he died,' I say. 'He wasn't that young.'

'I suppose he'll never age now. Sometimes I just wish I could rewind to a year before he died. Stop everything from happening.'

'Yeah,' I say, fighting back tears. I've tried for so many years to block out my memories, to forget.

'I still can't get the sounds out of my head,' she says softly. 'I heard him screaming. Before he died.'

I close my eyes and all I can see are the flames in the windows. My body flushes with heat and I start to sweat, as if I'm there now, in the flat, with him.

'Oh.' I can't make myself say anymore.

'I was trying to get into the flat. Trying to save him. I knew he was in there. We were supposed to be meeting there to talk about our marriage.'

They'd said that in the court too. That she'd gone to meet him. They'd said she'd set fire to the place in a fit of rage.

'It must have been awful for you.' I take a gulp of water, trying to distract myself from the feelings rising up inside me.

'When I got to the building the flat was already in flames. But I went inside to try to rescue him. I still loved him. But that was why they thought I set fire to the place. I was in the wrong place at the wrong time.'

'I know. I'm sorry, Mum.'

'It wasn't your fault.' She looks down at the photo. 'He looks happy here.'

I smile. 'He does.' It's nice to remember him like that, instead of all the arguments. That's why I like the photo.

'But I don't remember this being taken.' Mum frowns and peers more closely at the photo. 'He's wearing the watch I bought him for his last birthday. Six months before he died.' She brings the picture over to show me. 'Where is this?' she asks. 'I can see something in the distance. A pier.'

'I'm not sure…' I reply, my heart beating faster.

She looks closer. 'Oh, yes. It's Brighton.' She looks at me. 'We never went to Brighton that year.'

'Oh.'

'You got it from her, didn't you?'

'From who?'

'From Beth.'

I freeze. How does she know about Beth?

'I—'

'I've seen you with her.'

'What do you mean?'

'I've been watching you. You've been to her house.'

'Oh, I—' I struggle to think of an explanation.

'You've become friends, haven't you? You always looked up to her. Do you think she can replace me? Is that your plan? To replace your mother?'

CHAPTER 47

BETH

After I drop Charlie off at school, I walk down to a local coffee shop, where I'm meeting Genevieve. I nearly cancelled at the last minute, unsure if I could go through with it. I've been holed up in the house, barely daring to go out. Even little tasks are starting to feel insurmountable. It takes a huge mental effort just to force myself out to buy milk from the shop. I can feel myself spiralling. I remember the last time I felt like this, when I stopped getting dressed in the morning, stopped washing. It seemed like there was no point. Locked in my tiny flat, with the windows and the blinds shut, the air had grown stale and fetid as my mind whirred.

I don't want to get like that again. I can't get like that again. So I drag myself to the cafe, see Genevieve in the queue ahead of me and force a smile. 'Hello.'

'You don't look well,' she says when we've found a table. 'Are you OK?'

I stir my coffee and nod. 'Just tired. You know how it is.'

'How old did you say your son was?'

'Four.'

'I remember those days. Well, just about, it's all a bit hazy. I was rushed off my feet.'

I nod.

'And you're working too. It must be exhausting.'

I stare down at my coffee. *Not for much longer. Not if I'm struck off.*

'Are you sure you're alright?'

'Yeah.' I dab my eyes with the napkin, thinking about the call from social services, the need to find a new place to live.

'Is it about your ex?'

I look up at her, see the concern in her eyes, remember how I used to confide in her.

'I just feel like everything's getting on top of me. I have to move house because Richard is selling the one I'm living in. And a client complained about me. It's being investigated.' I swallow, wondering how I've ended up blurting it out so easily.

She reaches out to touch my arm. 'I'm so sorry.'

'I feel like I'm constantly messing up. I lost my teaching job because of a complaint, and now it could happen again.'

'I really hope it doesn't. I'm sure you're a great therapist. You've always been the kind of person everyone trusts.'

'Thanks. What you said last time we met – about me being a good teacher. Did you mean it?'

'I wouldn't have said it if I didn't. Look, I really didn't want to lose you from my teaching staff. But you wouldn't admit your mistakes. I think if you had just said why you didn't follow the procedure you could probably have got away with just a warning. But you didn't.'

The original complaint had been about how I'd handled a fight that I'd broken up between two girls. The fight had happened while I was on duty at the end of the school day, helping kids onto the school buses home. I should have followed procedures and reported it, but I hadn't because I knew the girls well, I knew it was a one-off and I didn't want to get them into any more trouble. When I'd been questioned about the fight, I'd played down what had happened, insisting it hadn't needed reporting.

'So if I'd come clean about not reporting the fight, then I'd have been fine?'

'I think so. It was the investigation that followed that got you dismissed. We found out you were regularly ignoring the safeguarding policy and taking the students' welfare into your own hands without any consultation with other staff.'

I sigh. I'd only done what I thought was best for my students. Some of them were going through really tough things at home, and I'd let them come and sit in my classroom and chat it through with me when they were supposed to be in other lessons.

'You had one-to-ones with students without telling anyone or leaving the door open. You let students miss classes without reporting them. They even came to see you instead of going to other lessons. You were in complete contravention of the safeguarding policy. I knew your heart was in the right place, that in reality those students probably depended on you, but you repeatedly hadn't followed the guidelines and we had no choice but to ask you to leave and refer your case on.'

I wince as I remember the day I was told I no longer had a job. I hadn't been expecting it, and it had tipped me over the edge.

'Look,' she says, 'I'm sure it will work out for you. Just try and be honest about everything.'

I nod. For a moment I consider admitting my mistakes and apologising to Danielle. But it feels like it's all already gone too far.

'The whole thing's really affecting my health,' I admit. 'I feel like I'm heading the same way as I was before, like I'm going crazy.'

'You don't seem crazy to me.'

'I'm getting the same symptoms. Paranoia. Delusions. I've even started to think someone's following me. That's what happened before. After I lost my job, I imagined someone was following me. That was one of the reasons I ended up in the psychiatric hospital. No one was following me. It was all in my head.'

She reaches out and lightly touches my wrist. 'What makes you think you're being followed now?'

'I've seen a woman around. Hovering near my house. She stands at the bus stop down the road, but she never seems to get the bus.'

'What makes you think she's watching you?'

'I don't know, it's just a feeling. When you can feel someone's eyes on you. You just know, don't you? Or maybe you don't. Maybe I'm imagining it.'

'We often had people hanging around outside the school. It was difficult to do anything about them when they were outside the school grounds, but we did get the police involved in some cases. Most were men, two were arrested for flashing at one point. But there was the occasional woman. With women it took us longer to notice, because we'd assume they were parents at first.'

'Oh.'

'I'm sure there was one around the time you were there, used to hang around the gates when the kids got on the buses.' Genevieve stirs her coffee absent-mindedly.

'An estranged parent?' I say. If Richard ever got full custody of Charlie, I could imagine doing the same, hanging around outside the school gates, waiting for a chance to speak to him.

'We never got to the bottom of it. But she just stopped turning up one day. It must have been around the time you were working at the school. Do you remember her?'

I shake my head. 'No. I used to work late most days, so I left later. I was only around the gates when the children were leaving if I was doing bus duty.'

All of a sudden Genevieve stops stirring her coffee.

'We never knew who reported that fight at the bus stop,' she says. 'It was really odd. They gave a false name, said they were "a concerned member of the public". They said they saw you break up that fight, mentioned your name specifically, said they were worried by your behaviour. You were too rough with the girls.

That was proven to be false as soon as we spoke to them. We thought at the time it must have been one of their parents that complained. But it wasn't.'

I lean towards her, heart pumping. I had always thought one of the other students reported me.

'I'm wondering now,' Genevieve says slowly, 'if it was the woman hanging around outside the school who reported you. I hadn't connected the two things before, but she stopped appearing around the same time as you were being investigated.'

'So…' My mind whirs. 'Are you saying you think she was watching me? Waiting for me to slip up?'

'At the time we thought she was connected to one of the students. But perhaps she was connected to you. Perhaps she was following you. And when you left the school she didn't need to be there anymore. Maybe she continued to follow you.'

'So you don't think I was imagining it?' I can hardly believe what she's saying. I'd thought I was delusional when I went to the hospital. The psychologists had believed that I'd imagined being followed, that it had just been a symptom of my paranoia.

'I don't know,' Genevieve says, shaking her head. 'I'm just saying it's possible you were being followed back then.'

I nod, a shiver of fear running through me. Because if Genevieve is right, and someone was really following me back then, what if the same person is following me now?

CHAPTER 48

DANIELLE

I look at Mum. She's still holding the picture of Dad in her hands. I see the anger in her eyes. She thinks that after everything, I'd be friends with Beth.

'I do know Beth,' I admit. 'But I'm not her friend.'

'Why would you have anything to do with her? Why would you even want to live in the same town?'

'You know where she lives?'

'Of course I do. Don't you think that's the first thing I'd do when I got out? I've been keeping an eye on her.'

I tense. Watching Beth is the last thing my mother should be doing.

'She was my therapist,' I say.

'Your therapist?' My mother laughs incredulously.

'It's not like that. I chose her as my therapist because—'

'Hello?' Peter comes into the kitchen and we both fall silent. I look at my mother, trying to indicate that we'll finish this conversation later.

'Good day at work?' I ask.

Out of the corner of my eye, I can see my mother pacing up and down, feel her anger bouncing around the room.

'Yeah, fine.' He nods his head towards my mother. 'Is she alright?'

'She's OK. We were just talking.'

'Have you spoken to her about moving out?' He deliberately says it loud enough for her to overhear, but she's so lost in her own thoughts that she's not listening.

I pull Peter into the hallway, out of earshot. 'Not yet. And I'm not sure it's a good idea. She needs some time to get back on her feet.'

'She's had some time. I don't feel comfortable with her living here.'

'She'll move out before the baby's born. She'll be ready by then.'

'It's not about when she's ready. It's about us. Our future. I can't live here with her.'

I frown, caught between the two of them. I can't ask her to leave. I owe her too much.

'What are you two doing in the hallway?' My mother asks, sickly-sweet. She looks at Peter. 'Danielle and I were in the middle of a conversation.' I need to explain what's going on with Beth before Mum gets the wrong idea.

I turn to Peter. 'I do need to talk to her.'

He sighs. 'And so do I. We all need to talk. Virginia, I know who you are.'

She pales, reaching out for the wall, and then looks at me, fear in her eyes.

'You told him? I thought you didn't want him to know.'

'He found out.'

She turns to him. 'So you think I'm a murderer?'

'You were tried and convicted.'

I glare at Peter. He knows she's not a murderer. I've told him she was innocent.

'And I suppose you don't want a mother-in-law like me?' Her face is expressionless now, but I sense the fury simmering underneath.

'I think it would be best if you moved out of our house, found your own place to live.'

'I've served my time.'

'You have. But it doesn't mean I have to welcome you into my home.'

'Peter—'

'No, Dani. It's time to stop defending her. She's your mother and you love her, I get that. But I also see the corrosive impact she has on you, the impact of your childhood. Your own anger. You need to break free of her.'

My mother squeezes past me in the hallway.

'Mum, where are you going?'

I see the tears in her eyes as she walks up the stairs. 'I'm going to pack a case. I don't want to hold you back, Sophie. That's the last thing I'd want to do. I'll move out tonight.'

CHAPTER 49

BETH

When the doorbell rings, I peer out of the upstairs curtains and try to make out who it is. I've just put Charlie to bed, and I'm expecting Richard, but I want to be sure it's him before I open the door. I've been thinking about what Genevieve said. Recently, I've started to see the same person again and again. Her hood's always up, her face covered with a scarf. She's always around. At the bus stop down the road, at the shop near Charlie's school. I'd thought it was Danielle. But I'm not so sure anymore. Perhaps it's someone else. Someone from the past.

I go downstairs, unlock and open the door.

'Hi,' Richard says. 'Is everything alright?'

'Of course. Why wouldn't it be?' I think about how isolated I feel, how I might lose my career because of the way I behaved towards Danielle.

'You took ages to come to the door.'

He steps over the piles of shoes and coats in the hallway and into the house.

'I have a moving date for you,' he says.

'When is it?'

'Two weeks today. End of half-term. Do you think you can manage it?'

I panic. I was supposed to be looking at houses, finding somewhere to live, but I've been so worried about the investigation, so sure someone is following me, that I've hardly thought about it.

'I haven't found anywhere to move into yet.'

'I know. I've found somewhere near me you could live in temporarily. I can show you the pictures if you like. I can put the deposit down for you and Charlie.'

'You don't need to do that.'

'I'm worried about you, Beth. I think it would be best if you lived close to me. Just in case.'

'Just in case what?'

'You're vulnerable at the moment. I need to look out for you and Charlie. I spoke to Lisa from social services again. And she said the team had had further correspondence in the post about Charlie, more evidence.'

'What evidence?'

'She didn't say. Just said they were looking into it. Do you have any idea who might have reported you?'

I shake my head. I thought it might have been the school, but surely they wouldn't have had anything more to report recently. I've got Charlie in on time every day and there haven't been any more bruises.

'I think you need more support,' Richard continues. 'If you're closer to me, I can help more. And wouldn't it be nice for Charlie to be close to both of us?'

I sigh, defeated. This seems like the easiest option. Richard will pay the deposit and everything will be sorted for me. 'OK,' I say.

'Great. You'll earn a bit from the house sale too. Even though it's in my name, I'll give you a share of the increase in value. Just to give you a head start.'

I'm getting a headache. From what I'd read I was entitled to a share, as I had a beneficial interest in the house. 'Shouldn't we do this through lawyers?'

'I don't think we need to. It will only cost us a fortune in fees. We're both on the same side. I've stuck up for you with social services. I'm not planning to fight for custody of Charlie. I'm playing fair with you, so please play fair with me.'

I can't afford a lawyer anyway. And I don't want him to change his mind about custody of Charlie. 'OK, then,' I say reluctantly.

'Will you need any help packing up the house?'

He indicates the mess and I think of all the memories I've made here, how I want to consider each of them in turn before I pack them away.

'I'd prefer to do it on my own.'

When Richard leaves, I sink down onto the sofa and turn on some music. He's left the contract for me to look at, so I can see how much he's selling the house for and the date I need to move out. It's not signed yet, the precise details are being finalised, but he expects it to be sorted in the next couple of days.

I pick it up, my eyes widening when I see the price. It's more money than I'll probably ever see in my life. I'm never going to be able to afford to live anywhere near this nice again. I'll go back to being dependent on the whims of landlords, never feeling completely secure.

I turn the page of the contract and see the two names at the bottom.

I have to read them three times before I'm sure I'm not hallucinating.

Richard Murray.

Danielle Brown.

I stare at it in disbelief. Richard is selling the house to Danielle.

CHAPTER 50

DANIELLE

I run the iron over my shirt, back and forth, back and forth, until the material is smooth and creaseless. I have to appear in court this week, and I need to look my best. Luckily the worst of my morning sickness seems to be over, but I'm not sure how well I'm going to cope on my feet most of the day.

I try to iron away my anger, smooth over my thoughts. I can't believe Peter made my mother leave, that she just left without a fuss. I'd begged her to stay, but she wasn't having it. I know it's about Beth. I didn't have the chance to tell her why I went to therapy, that it was about getting close to Beth, that there was a good reason. Now my mother hates me. She's not answering her phone.

It's all Peter's fault. He hasn't tried to understand what happened, hasn't listened to me. I push the iron harder into my shirt, run it roughly over the material. I can't believe this is happening. After waiting for so long to be reunited with my mother, I've already lost her.

Steam rises from the iron in a hiss and as I lift it off my favourite orange shirt, the lucky one I always win my cases in, I see a triangle-shaped burn in the centre.

The rage builds inside me, and for a moment there's no escape from it, no release. I do it without thinking, holding the iron to my wrist and clenching my jaw through the pain, waiting for the smell of singed hair to penetrate my nostrils before I pull the iron away, revealing the raw wound.

'Dani – what happened?' Peter's in the room beside me before I know it.

'An accident,' I say softly. I bite my lip to cope with the searing pain from my wrist.

'Really? With the iron? Did your hand slip?'

I stare down at the seeping wound. It will definitely scar. Another one. To match the others.

'Yeah, my hand slipped. I'm tired. I wrecked my shirt too.' I look down at the burn across the orange material.

'Maybe you shouldn't be ironing when you're so exhausted. What if your hand had slipped and you somehow hurt the baby?'

'I'd never hurt the baby.' I stare at him. I've said too much, and I can see in his eyes that he understands it wasn't an accident.

'I'll get some antiseptic wipes and dressing,' he says.

'Bathroom cabinet. Left-hand side.' Peter nods and dashes up the stairs.

I don't know how much dressing I have left. Life's been stressful lately.

Peter sits me down on the sofa and bandages up my wrist. He's so gentle that I wonder why I haven't let him do this before, haven't told him how I hurt myself. Maybe he would have understood all along.

'Are you worried about appearing in court?' he asks. The illusion is shattered. He doesn't understand me at all.

'No. I'm upset because you made my mother leave our home.'

'Surely you understand why?'

'She had nowhere to go.'

'I didn't ask her to leave immediately. She made that decision herself.'

'How can you be so heartless?' I think of Mum all alone, wandering the streets. She doesn't deserve any of this.

'I don't understand you. She killed your father. Why don't you hate her?'

I feel the emotions building up inside me, spinning through my mind and swirling round my stomach. I should tell Peter the truth. We're going to have a baby together. He has to know what really happened.

'She didn't kill him,' I say softly. I look Peter in the eyes. What I'm about to say next could end our relationship. But I can't keep the secret inside me anymore. It's wearing me down; the guilt's eating away at me.

'I killed my father.'

CHAPTER 51

BETH

I stare at the names next to each other on the contract. Richard Murray. Danielle Brown. He's selling the house to her. Why would he do that? Bile rises in my throat. I must have got it wrong. When Richard told me he didn't know who Danielle was, I'd believed him. But he must have been lying to me. Are they planning to move into the house together once they've got me out of the way? Has Danielle split up with Peter?

I ring Richard.

'Beth? I've just got back home. Is everything alright?'

'I've read the contract. Why are you selling the house to her?'

'To who?'

'To Danielle.'

'Danielle? The buyer's called Danielle, but I've never met her. I don't know her. She put in a cash offer for the full asking price the day after the viewings. What are you saying? She's the same Danielle who you were talking about the other day?'

'How can you keep lying to me, Richard? Danielle was my client. And she's the woman you slept with. Are you all going to move into my house and live your life here? The life I was supposed to be living with you and Charlie?'

'Look, I told you I didn't remember her.'

'She was on your course.' I rush to the filing cabinet and root around for the piece of paper with his course list. Here it is. I pull it out. Suddenly I feel sick. What if I imagined seeing her name on the piece of paper? What if it's a symptom of my paranoia? But then I see her name. In the middle of the sheet. Danielle Brown.

'Are you sure it's the same person? It's a common name.'

'She's been coming to me for counselling. And she looks like the person in the photos.'

'It was just a fling, Beth. I've told you before, I told you so many times. If you must know, the person I slept with was called Antonia.'

'But why were there photos of you with her outside the university?'

I hear his sigh reverberate down the phone. 'Antonia was a student too. I'm sorry, but I lied to you about meeting her in a bar. I didn't want to tell you she was a student, because I thought it would hurt you. It was so similar to the way we got together and I didn't want you to feel replaced.'

'Not Danielle?' My hands grip my phone tighter. Another one of his students. I imagine him in the bar, flirting with her, then taking her to a hotel. The same way he did with me.

'No, not Danielle. I've told you, I don't remember her. She may not have even turned up for the course. We always have a few who don't turn up for day courses. And you said she had facial scars, didn't you? I'm sure I'd remember if I'd met her.'

My mind spins, still thinking about his betrayal. Another student. It was a different student he'd been kissing outside the university.

'Beth, are you OK?'

'Yeah, I'm fine. Look, I've got to go,' I say, as I press the button to end the call. But I don't feel fine. Danielle may not have slept with Richard, but it's clear she's trying to hurt me. I'm likely to lose my job because she's reported me for misconduct. She's buying my house, taking away my home with Charlie. I feel a shiver of fear and think how often I've sat across from her in therapy, her eyes meeting mine. Why was she there really? And what does she want from me?

CHAPTER 52

DANIELLE

Peter stares at me incredulously. 'What do you mean, you killed your father?'

I stare at the burn on my wrist. I want to pull away the dressing, to suffer the punishment I deserve.

'I started the fire. In the flat.'

'But all the evidence pointed to your mother.'

'I know. She was there that day to meet my father. They were supposed to be talking about their relationship. But I didn't know that. I was feeling down and I went to the flat we owned in central London, just to escape the house. My parents had told me that the flat had been bought as an investment, for me when I was older. The idea was that I'd live in it after university, and I already thought of it as mine.'

I swallow, remembering how excited I was to see it. My father had been spending every weekend there, decorating it, for months. He'd told us he wanted to wait until it was completely finished before we saw it. I'd thought he was doing it all for me.

'But when I got there it was clear that the decorating had been finished long before and that someone lived there. I realised that my father had been having an affair, that his mistress was living in the flat.' My hands clench into fists as I remember my anger, the unfairness of the whole situation. 'The police arrested my mother early on and all the evidence pointed to her. She made sure it did. To protect me.'

'What exactly happened?'

I start to shake and I sink down onto the sofa, remembering. I've tried so hard not to think about it for so many years.

'There were lots of candles in the flat. She – the other woman – seemed to love them. I didn't think anyone was there. So I lit one. I don't know why. Maybe just to mark out my space, to let her know I'd been there. I was trying to digest what was going on, that my father was having an affair. Every weekend when he'd said he was doing up the flat he'd really been seeing her. Her books were on the shelves, there were magazines on the coffee table, coats and shoes by the door. And there were his things there too. His shoes next to hers, an old coat that he never wore at home. But still a part of me didn't want to believe what I was seeing. I told myself he was just renting it out to someone else, a friend of his maybe. Then I went into the bedroom. I saw a pack of condoms on the bedside table, and a red dress hanging on the wardrobe door. And I felt sick. I took the candle and I threw it into the middle of the duvet. I had expected it to just go out. But the fire took hold in the bed. And then it spread. I watched it. I should have put it out. But for some reason I couldn't. I just watched.' I remember watching the flames spread, how free I felt. Just for a moment.

'But you killed him…' Peter looks at me like he doesn't know me at all.

'I didn't mean to.' My voice cracks and I put my hands to my face, gripping my temples, trying to get the images of flames, the sounds of screaming, the smell of smoke, out of my head.

'I didn't realise he was in the flat. He was in the study with the door shut. He must have had headphones in. He can't have heard me come in. By the time I heard his screams, the fire had already taken hold and I was in the corridor, away from him.' I'm sobbing now, rocking back and forth on the sofa. How could I have just run away? Why hadn't I tried to save him?

'Why didn't you admit it?'

'I was fifteen. I was scared. My mother said not to tell anyone, that she'd cover for me. She'd come to the flat just after I left. I hadn't seen her. She'd come up in the lift and I was already on the stairs down. She was supposed to be meeting Dad at the flat to discuss their marriage. She found it on fire. She tried to save him, but couldn't get past the smoke. People in the block saw her running out and they gave evidence in court that she'd done it.'

'It was a miscarriage of justice?'

'She made it look like she did it because she didn't want them to find out it was me. I could hardly live with myself.' I run my fingers over the scars on my wrists. The work of razor blades, shards of glass, whatever I could find. Ever since it happened, I've been punishing myself.

'I didn't understand at the time, why she covered for me.' I stare down at my stomach, thinking of the life inside me, thinking about how I'd do anything for my baby. 'I understand now. It's just because she loved me. I owe her so much.'

CHAPTER 53

BETH

I'm in the living room putting Charlie's toys into a huge suitcase, tears running down my face. Richard has taken Charlie to stay with him for half-term, and I'm packing away our lives, dismantling our relationship item by item, slowly and steadily pulling it apart. I pick up one of Charlie's teddies. I really should dispose of it; it's not like he needs it anymore. But I can't bring myself to throw away the memories.

I take another gulp of wine. It's just me here on my own tonight, clearing out the house in a scruffy white T-shirt. It won't matter if I drink the whole bottle. I smile sadly, wondering if I should have let Richard help me, rather than doing it all on my own. I've got Nina Simone blaring out from my speaker. I'd hoped the music would help my mood, but it's not. Instead I just feel nostalgic, lost in my memories.

I've finished with the toys downstairs now. Maybe I should put the ones from Charlie's room into the same case, so that they're all in one place when I get to our new flat. I lug the suitcase upstairs, then go back for my glass of wine. I carry it into Charlie's room and then start shoving the remainder of his toys into the suitcase. It's already nearly full. They won't fit. I'll have to put the rest in a box. The music is fainter now, and I decide to bring up the mini speaker at the same time as I fetch a box.

I take a sip of wine and then go into the hallway, still clutching my glass. I hear a clicking noise and I hesitate at the top of the stairs. Then another sound. A kind of shuffling. I think it came from my therapy room. It's probably just the branches of the tree brushing against the window, but I feel an urge to check. I open the door of the room with one hand, holding my wine in the other.

I scream. Someone's in here.

She turns.

Danielle.

CHAPTER 54

DANIELLE

I wait for Beth to stop screaming and see it's me. She looks terrified, her skin pale, her knuckles white as she clutches her wine glass. She clearly wasn't expecting to see anyone; her hair's scraped back clumsily into a ponytail and she's wearing a stained white T-shirt emblazoned with the logo of a brand I don't recognise.

'Hi,' I say brightly. 'I'm sorry to scare you. I didn't think anyone was in.'

'But the music…'

She's right. The music playing downstairs is a giveaway that someone's home. 'I thought you might have gone out and left it on. I shouted out but there was no answer.'

I can tell she doesn't believe me. She still looks nervous, afraid of me.

'Why – why are you here?' she asks.

'Oh, I'm sorry, I thought you knew. I'm buying your house. The estate agent gave me a set of keys so I could measure up, work out where to put my furniture.' I hold up the tape measure in my hand.

'Now's not a good time,' she says curtly. She steps towards me and her red wine sloshes over the glass, dripping onto the cream carpet, leaving dark blots, but she doesn't seem to notice. She's drunk. 'No one let me know you were coming.' Her eyes seem to go in and out of focus as she carefully articulates each word. 'The estate agent shouldn't have given you keys. I'm moving out in a few days. You can measure up then.'

'Don't worry. I've nearly finished anyway. I was about to leave.'

'Why are you buying my house? You never mentioned you were looking for somewhere.' She steps towards me, more confident now. She seems to have got over the shock of finding me here.

'It's close to where I grew up,' I reply, watching for her reaction, to see if she senses what's going on, if she realises who I am. 'And why not? It's a lovely house. The perfect place to bring up a baby.'

She winces and draws away from me. 'Like I said, it's not a good time. So could you leave, please?'

I nod. 'Of course. I'm sorry for interrupting. I'd assumed the estate agent would have let you know.' I walk over to the door, as if I'm about to leave. I move round Beth and she sways a little as I brush by her. I'm clutching the key to the room in my hand. It feels solid beneath my fingers. When I get to the door, I slam it shut, then push the key into the keyhole and turn it, locking us both in the room.

CHAPTER 55

BETH

'What are you doing?' I ask, my blood running cold. When I'd first opened the door I'd been shocked to see Danielle, but relieved that she wasn't an intruder. But now she's locked me in this room and I realise that that's exactly what she is. An intruder in my home, in my life.

My own key for this room is downstairs. I won't get out unless she lets me out.

'I didn't only come to measure up,' she says. 'I've been missing you. Missing our therapy sessions.'

'You have?' I look at her warily, gripping my glass tighter. I feel dizzy, as if nothing makes sense. Wasn't she the one who reported me to my professional body?

'I thought if I rang you and asked for another session you might not speak to me. But I've needed to talk to you for a while.'

Fear pricks my skin. 'We don't need to do this now. Why don't we do it another time? We can have a session when I'm more prepared.' If I can just persuade her to unlock the door, to leave the house, then I can work out what to do about her later. My mind's too fuzzy to think straight at the moment.

She shakes her head. 'I want to talk to someone now. And you're the only one I can confide in.' Tears start to slide down her cheeks, and for a moment I feel sorry for her.

'Why me?' I ask.

'I trust you. I've always trusted you.'

'Look, just unlock the door. We can book in a session for another time. I promise.'

'Please, Beth, just hear me out. I've been having a tough time lately. My mother's gone missing and I don't know who to turn to.'

'Your mother?' I remember her saying she'd come to live with her. They'd been estranged.

'It reminded me of the old times when she used to disappear sometimes, when she was angry with my father. But she always used to come back.' Danielle eases herself down into my therapy chair, where I usually sit. I can see she's not going anywhere. I sit opposite her on the sofa reserved for my clients and try to focus, my vision blurry from alcohol. Our roles are reversed now. It's Danielle who holds the power.

'It reminds you of your childhood?' I struggle to take control of the conversation, repeating her words back to her, forcing myself into therapist mode, despite my mind being a jumble of confused thoughts.

'Yeah. I longed for help then too.'

'Did you have anyone to talk to about it, back then?'

'Just one person.' She looks at me shyly.

'A friend?'

'Well, I thought so. But she wasn't really. She wasn't a school friend. More like a concerned adult. Someone who cared about me. Someone who looked out for me. Someone who I could tell everything to. You see, even before my father died, I was unhappy. My parents were fighting constantly and I needed someone to help me. She did. She just listened to me. Like you're doing now.'

Something stirs inside me, a memory from long ago. Before I had my breakdown, long before. But I can't grasp it.

'I'm so glad you had someone back then,' I say, but I feel horribly uncomfortable, my stomach churning. Maybe I'm drunker than I thought. Maybe I need to be sick. The four walls of the room seem to be caving in on me, the space getting smaller and smaller. Sweat pools on my back. The intensity of Danielle's gaze is too much for me. I try to take deep breaths.

'It was a teacher who helped me,' she says. My breathing stops completely. 'An art teacher. She was kind to me.'

I can hardly focus now. I can hardly think at all. It's *her*.

'Sophie?' I ask.

'Yes,' she nods.

I stare at her. I'm the teacher she's talking about.

She continues. 'When Peter and I were having problems with our marriage, I saw your name on a list of counsellors. At first I thought it couldn't possibly be you. There must be so many Beth Evanses in the world.'

Lots, I think. *And that's why I hoped your mother would never find me.*

'But then I came to the first session and it *was* you. I was so pleased.'

'You were pleased?' I stare at her in shock.

'Of course. You were so important to me when I was a teenager. You looked out for me when I had no one. You always took the time to listen to me. I wanted to thank you.'

'So why didn't you?' I say, confused. My mind's racing. Did she really just want to thank me? Does this mean she doesn't know what I did?

'I should have told you who I was at the beginning. I changed my name after the court case so I could start again, so no one knew who I was. I thought you might recognise me when you saw me, but you didn't.'

'Your scars…' I whisper. 'I couldn't see who you were underneath.' She'd had long, dark hair back then, so unlike the blonde bob she has now.

'I should have told you. Thanked you for helping me then, and asked you to help me now. But I was afraid you'd turn me away, you might refuse to give me therapy. And I needed help.'

I let out my breath. I can't think straight. There are too many things flooding through my mind and the alcohol is mixing up my thoughts. About her. Her father. Everything. Perhaps she really doesn't know. Perhaps she did just want to say thank you. She'd been fifteen at the time; she was at school when her mother's trial was happening. She must have known her father had had an affair. That much was in the papers. She just didn't know it was with me.

I think of her father for a moment. Nick. He'd come into my life when I needed him most, and I'd never felt so loved and accepted. He had rescued me. And then he'd been taken away. Burnt to death by his wife.

CHAPTER 56

DANIELLE

I had idolised Beth once. She'd been the teacher that everyone liked. She must have been in her twenties at the time, only recently qualified, and she'd seemed like one of us. We called her Beth instead of Miss Evans and she'd listened to our problems, running evening 'group drama' sessions after school, which were an excuse to talk about our teenage angst. She ran them like group therapy and we all sat in a circle. I could tell even then that she liked the power of it all, the control, the ability to change the direction of our lives. We all looked up to her, wanting to be liked by her. And looking back, I can see how she was desperate to be liked by us too.

She had time for everyone, but particularly for me. I confided in her about what was going on at home, about my parents' fights, how my mother was so angry all the time. She said if it ever got really bad I could move in with her. But she hadn't meant it at all.

After my father died and my mother was arrested for his murder, I'd tried to find her at school. I needed to talk to her more than ever. She was off sick for a while, and I'd prowled the corridors looking for her. My case worker had told me to stay home the week after my mother had been arrested, but I'd insisted on going in to school. I couldn't bear to be at home without Mum there, couldn't bear to accept my new life.

I started to worry about Beth when she was off sick. Really worry. Since my father had died the ground beneath my feet had shifted and I became irrationally worried that she was seriously ill. I couldn't face losing someone else.

When she returned and I saw her in the corridor, I was so relieved that I wrapped her in a hug there and then. She was the only person I didn't want to push away. I needed her.

I saw her eyes widen as soon as she saw me. But I didn't register her averting her gaze, trying to step out of my way, until my arms were wrapped tightly around her. I felt her body stiffen, and it scared me. I gripped her harder.

'Sophie,' she said. 'Sophie,' she repeated urgently. 'You know the school has rules about physical contact.'

I laughed for half a moment, thinking she must be joking. She was the one who always flouted those rules, who was willing to give us a hug, or jokingly ruffle our carefully styled hair.

But she wasn't joking. I felt it in the way she extracted my arms from around me, saw the irritation in her frown.

Dark circles underlined her eyes and she looked like she'd been crying. Her face was bare of make-up. The only time I'd ever seen her like that.

I wondered once more if she had a serious illness. If that's why she'd been off school. Was that why she was being so cold to me?

'I need to talk to you,' I said.

'I don't think that's a good idea.'

I thought that she couldn't possibly know what had happened to me, couldn't know my father had died. She must have been off sick for longer than I thought. She must have been off when it happened.

She turned to walk away.

'Please' I said, grabbing her arm.

'Don't make a scene,' she hissed.

Students were already staring at us curiously. They all knew who I was. The girl whose father died in a fire. The girl whose mother was accused of his murder.

I'd already got used to their stares, but they clearly alarmed her.

'Come with me,' she said, pulling me into an empty classroom.

We stood opposite each other and I thought of all the times I'd confided in her, all the times I'd confessed to her.

I was about to blurt it out, ask to move in with her when she started to cry.

'I'm so sorry about what happened to your father,' she said. 'I'm so, so sorry.'

I watched her tears falling down her face, mesmerised. I hadn't been able to cry myself. I'd felt numb, as if I was operating in some kind of parallel universe, as if it was all just a dream. Or perhaps my previous life was the dream and this nightmare was reality.

'Thank you,' I said blankly. My heart filled. She really cared about me.

'How are you holding up?' She reached for my hand.

'Not great. I don't know where they're going to put me. My aunt's staying with me at the moment, but they're talking about foster families. My own family won't take me.' I stared down at my feet, thinking of all the excuses my relatives had made about being too busy with work.

I expected her to butt in and say I didn't need to go to a foster family, that I could move in with her. To say what she always used to say to me when I told her about my parents' fights. She'd want to take me in now, to help me.

But she didn't say anything. I wondered if it was because of her health.

'Can I move in with you?' I blurted out. 'Like we talked about.'

She pulled her hand away from me. 'No, no you can't. I'm sorry.'

'Why not?' I could hardly believe what she was saying.

'I don't have the space.'

'But you must do. You offered before.'

'You don't understand. Before, well… I was expecting to move into a big house where there'd be space for all of us.'

'For all of us?'

'Yes…' She looked at me, her eyes searching mine. 'I mean, my boyfriend too. But that hasn't worked out.' She started crying again, loud, angry sobs.

I'd never seen her like this.

'I can sleep anywhere,' I said. 'On a sofa, wherever.'

'I just can't take you in. I'm sorry, but I can't. I have a lot of stuff going on myself. In my family. And it's just not the right time. I'm sorry.'

Afterwards, she went into the staff toilets. I stood outside, listening to her sob. I hadn't cried when I heard my father had died. I hadn't cried when my mother was arrested. But now the tears came and I couldn't stop.

CHAPTER 57

BETH

I stare at Danielle. If she's really Sophie, like she says she is, then it was her mother who murdered Nick, the love of my life.

'What happened to your mother?' I ask Danielle, remembering what she said about her mother coming to live with her. She couldn't have meant Virginia, could she?

'She was in jail for fifteen years. She's just been let out.'

I stare at her in shock. Virginia's sentence had been for life. I remember reading something once about life not really meaning life. But fifteen years? Surely that was too short. And surely someone should have let me know she was being released. But I've moved house so often since then. I never thought to give the probation service an updated address. I'd thought it would be years before she was out.

'And now she's living with you?' I say, my voice wavering. I feel sick with fear. All this time she's been so close by.

'She was until recently.'

My whole body stiffens. On the stand Virginia had said the fire was my fault, that it would never have happened if I hadn't been sleeping with her husband. She blamed me.

But she hadn't understood. Hadn't understood how much in love we were. Nick and I were meant to be together.

'I'm sorry for everything you went through back then,' I say, trying to ease the tension that fills the room. 'It must have been so tough.'

'I really wanted to move in with you,' she says. 'Why did you say no?'

'I was in a difficult place in my personal life.' I can't tell her more, can't explain that I had been living in the flat that was burnt down when her father died, that I was the woman who was sleeping with her father. That I couldn't take her in without him.

'In what way?' Danielle asks.

'It... it was just... I'm tired. I don't want to talk about it.'

'Because your lover had died?' she asks. 'My father.' And then I see the rage burning in her, the rage that's been there all along.

'You knew?'

'I've known for a long time.'

CHAPTER 58

DANIELLE

At first I hadn't wanted to go to my mother's trial. I didn't want to watch her in the dock, shrunken by the position she found herself in, accused of murder. And I didn't want to remember the fire. I didn't want to think of Dad, dead and buried in the ground. Didn't want to think how things might have been different.

But one day, instead of going to school, I went to the courtroom. I was surprised when I had to queue for a seat in the public gallery, when I found myself squeezed in between two strangers. The court was full of journalists and law students with notebooks, sitting alongside voyeurs, drawn in by someone else's trauma. Who were all these people who suddenly had the right to know all the details of our lives? It made me feel sick, our lives laid bare for everyone to pore over, for everyone to have an opinion on.

My mother looked small but stoic in the dock. She stood perfectly still as the police officer who'd been first on the scene gave evidence. When he described my father's body, I couldn't stop the tears from cascading down my face. I wiped them away with the back of my hand and sniffed. The courtroom was silent, collectively holding its breath as it listened to the witness testimony.

My mother didn't react. She was dosed up on antidepressants, drowning out all her emotions. Eyes staring expressionless as if she was just listening to the news. Even I could see that she looked guilty, that her lack of emotion wasn't going to play out well in the court. What kind of woman wasn't sad when her husband died? Of all the people in that room, only she and I knew who'd really started the fire. I wished so hard that I hadn't gone to the flat that day, that none of it had happened. All I wanted was to be back home with her, listening to her shout at me to tidy my room and unload the dishwasher.

I looked at the jury, some of them shaking their heads, moved by what the police officer was saying. I wanted to catch my mother's eye, to communicate to her that she needed to look sadder, play the part of the grieving widow. Otherwise she was going to prison. I'd be left on my own. But she never looked up, never saw I was there.

And then the next witness was called to the stand. I didn't catch the name. I was so caught up in what the police officer had said. It was inconclusive. My mother might not be found guilty. My heart was racing with hope. My mother might come home to me.

But then I saw her take the stand. Beth.

She took the oath as I stared at her in shock. She was introduced and then the lawyers hit her with the first question.

'How long had you and Nicholas Loughton been in a relationship?'

CHAPTER 59

BETH

'You know about the relationship I had with your father?' I ask.

She nods, her gaze never shifting from me. I see the hatred in her eyes.

'You understand, don't you?' I say, desperate to explain. 'He was everything to me. We were in love. And your mother killed him. She thought if she couldn't have him then no one could.' Virginia wasn't supposed to be with Nick. She wasn't good for him.

'It wasn't like that. It was her flat, hers and my father's. It was supposed to be mine once I finished university. But instead he let you live there. His girlfriend. And all the time you were befriending me at school.'

She knows everything.

'All I did was love your father. You know how unhappy your parents were. You used to tell me about it.'

Nick had told me their relationship hadn't been working for a long time. They weren't sleeping together anymore and he'd wanted to get out, to be with me.

'If you hadn't tried to take him from my mother, he wouldn't be dead.'

'Their relationship was as good as over. You know what your mother was like.' Nick had told me how controlling she was, how when he'd tried to talk to her about me, she'd smashed up their kitchen. I had thought I could rescue them both, Nick and Sophie. That we'd all be able to live together happily. That was why I'd told Sophie I could take her in, get her away from her mother.

'So that's your explanation, is it? That you were in love?'

Danielle glares at me and my stomach contracts as I think about how much I loved Nick, how much I still love him. It feels like a piece of my heart will forever be missing.

'We were. We were in love. Why are you here, Sophie? To get some kind of revenge?'

'I just want to talk. Just want you to explain yourself.'

'There's nothing to explain. I loved him. I wanted us all to live together. You, me and Nick.'

Danielle laughs incredulously. 'That was never going to happen. Not after your affair.'

'Nick didn't do anything other than look out for me and you. He loved you. Your mother wasn't right for him.' She'd needed to let him go, let them both be free of their volatile relationship. It would have all worked out in the end, if she'd only let go of him. Nick and I could have started again, Sophie would have been free of her parents' arguments, and Virginia would have been out of a relationship that was making her unhappy.

Danielle laughs. 'I don't know how you can be a marriage counsellor, sit there all day telling people how to fix their relationships, when the truth is you destroy marriages.'

'What do you want from me? Do you want to punish me? Is that it?'

'Something like that.'

'You were the one who complained about my counselling, weren't you?'

'You deserved it. You were following me. But even before that, you paid no attention to any of the professional guidelines. You jumped at the chance to come to my house and help me ask Peter to leave, even though you knew you were breaking the rules.'

'Because I felt sorry for you.' She had been manipulating me, even back then. I realise that I don't know what happened between her and Peter after that night. The next time I'd seen them, she'd been pregnant and our session had been focused on that. 'What was that night about? Did you really ask Peter to leave?'

She grins smugly, taps her fingers on my desk. 'No. He was already staying with a friend that night.'

'So why did you call me over?'

'I wanted to see how much it would take to get you to break the rules. It turned out to be easy. And I wanted to get you drunk, to find out more about your life. I learnt a lot that evening. About your break-up with Richard. How you were probably going to have to move house.'

I remember that night. How ill I'd felt after just a few glasses of wine.

'I wasn't drunk, was I? You drugged me.'

'I needed you to lose control.'

'Why?'

'So I could take photos of you, passed out drunk. They've all been helping in the case against you. Going to a client's house and getting drunk hardly looks good, does it?'

'But that wasn't what happened.'

'We'll see what the investigators believe, shall we? I've got my diary to back up what I say. I've been keeping the diary that you suggested I start in our first session. Recording every moment of your incompetence. How you tried to persuade me I wouldn't be a fit mother. How you started following me.'

I shrink down into my seat, ashamed.

'Were you were always planning to get me struck off? From the beginning?'

'I wanted you to lose everything. Your home. Your family. Your job.'

'My family?' I whisper. I remember what I'd thought about her and Richard, how she'd told me her ex had said she had Kate Winslet's smile, just like Richard used to say to me. How she had a Victorian jade brooch, like the type Richard liked to buy me. How would she have found out that about him? She'd first worn the brooch before I'd gone to her house. 'Did you have a relationship with my husband?' I ask.

She grimaces. 'No. I wouldn't sink so low. Even to hurt you. But I did send you the pictures. Of Richard with his younger girlfriend. It was funny, I'd planned to find Richard, figure out a way to break up your relationship. I'd even signed up for one of his courses, so I could befriend him, find out what made him tick, work out how to get to him. But I didn't need to do any of the hard work. He'd already done it himself. When I started watching him, saw him going to the pub with his students, it was easy to see he was already cheating on you. All I had to do was befriend her, which wasn't too difficult, but it did take a few months. I found out she went to a weekly Pilates class in the evenings and I started going too. I told Peter I was working late. Antonia and I started going out for drinks after Pilates. And then after a while she confided in me about Richard.'

I stare at her incredulously. I hadn't even met Danielle then, and she went to all that effort to find out about Richard. Just so she could taunt me.

'I understand why you sent me the photos. But why wear the brooch to therapy?'

'I was playing with you, Beth. I wanted you to think it might be me who was sleeping with your partner. I wanted you to really question yourself, to wonder if you were going crazy again. Before I came to counselling I dyed my dark hair blonde. I wanted to look like her. I wanted you to think that I might be the person Richard had been sleeping with.'

'You're the one who's crazy,' I say. I'm starting to realise just how far she's gone to hurt me. I feel a cold fist of fear around my heart. She wants to destroy me. How will this end?

'I planned everything so carefully.' She smiles at me, as if she's expecting me to congratulate her. I want to scream at her for destroying my life, but I need to get her onside. She wants validation.

'I never even guessed,' I say. 'You completely fooled me.'

She smiles gleefully. 'You're so easy to fool.'

'But why involve Richard? Why not just target me?'

'Richard made you happy. And you didn't deserve a happy family. It was so frustrating when I'd gone to all that effort befriending Antonia and sending the photos, that you just forgave him. But then I had to find another way to get to you. That was when I started therapy. I needed to get close to you. Get close to Charlie.'

A shiver runs down my spine. Charlie's with Richard now. At least, I think he is. 'What do you mean, get close to Charlie?'

And then I remember. The bruises on Charlie's arm. How they had appeared after she'd found him when he'd let himself out of the house onto the street. 'Did you hurt him? When you found him in the street? Did you hurt him to get at me?'

'Maybe a little. But not on purpose, that wasn't part of the plan. It was difficult to get him to come back to the house. Once I'd given him a taste of freedom, he didn't want to come back to you at all. Just wanted to find his dad. I had to drag him along a bit to get him to cooperate.' She shrugs. 'It wouldn't have hurt him that much. It wasn't a big deal.'

'What do you mean, you gave him a taste of freedom?' My eyes are wide, realisation dawning. 'Was it you who let him out of the house?' I remember how I'd been distracted that evening, how I'd been rushing to answer the phone.

She nods. 'I called your landline to distract you so you were out of the way. Then all I had to do was tell him that his daddy was outside and wanted to see him. It was easy. He practically ran out of the house. He was just outside when you came back to say goodbye to me.'

My mind races. So that's why he said he'd been looking for his dad. Danielle had told him that Richard was outside.

Fury rises inside me. I jump out of my chair, lunge at her. 'How could you do that?' But my words slur and she ducks out of the way. I land with a thud on the floor. 'He nearly got hit by a car. Because you let him out.'

Danielle shakes her head. 'I made that bit up. Just to scare you.'

'But why? Why did you let him out in the first place?'

'It was all part of my evidence base,' she says calmly. 'Evidence that you were an unfit mother. Like the prescription pills you thought he swallowed.'

'What?'

'I put your bottle of pills underneath Charlie's bed. When you finally found it and Charlie had to go to hospital – well, it all added to the evidence for social services.'

'Social services? It was you who reported me. Is that why you planted my pills? So Charlie would get ill and you could report me to social services? You didn't care about Charlie at all?'

'Nothing happened to him, Beth. The bottle was empty. It was there over a week before you even found it. All that happened to Charlie was that he was taken away from you. And that will be good for him. He'll be happier, living with Richard.'

She thinks that Charlie's been taken away from me, that that's why he's not been in the house the last few days.

'He's not living with Richard. He's just staying with him for half-term.'

'Maybe for now. But I think you'll find he'll be living with him soon enough. I've sent everything to social services. The photos of you passed out drunk on your sofa after drinking at my house.

Details of how you left the door unlocked and he got outside onto the street on his own. Information about the bruises on Charlie's arm. How Charlie nearly swallowed your prescription pills. There's no way they'll let you keep him.'

CHAPTER 60

DANIELLE

Beth leaps at me again and I move away. I smile at her anger. This is what I wanted all along, and it feels good to finally see her upset, to see how much I have hurt her. It's what she deserves.

'I want you to leave, now.' She stands over me, her face red, slurring her words, indicating the door.

'No. I haven't finished.' There is so much more to say, so much more to tell her. I've been the puppetmaster of her life for years, manipulating everything. And she hadn't even noticed.

'What do you mean?'

'Can't you guess, Beth? Or are you too stupid?' I'm enjoying this, but not as much as I thought I would. I thought she'd be more impressed that I'd made her think I'd slept with Richard, that I'd orchestrated social services' involvement in her life. It had taken a lot of effort, a lot of planning. But she's too drunk to realise the extent of it, just how clever I've really been.

'Get out of my house,' she repeats.

I shake my head.

She speaks slowly, as if she's struggling to form the words. 'What else have you done? Is it you who's been following me?'

I laugh. 'The way *you* followed me? No, that's not me. At least, not now. It's my mother.' My mother told me she'd been watching Beth since she got out of prison, that she'd seen me come here for therapy.

'Is she the reason you want revenge now? Are you doing all this for her? She doesn't even love you. She never did.'

I recoil. That's not true. My mother sacrificed everything for me. 'She did. She always did.'

'How could she kill your father if she loved you? How could she do that to you?' Beth is shouting now.

'She didn't,' I say quietly. Suddenly the room feels airless and I feel like I can't breathe. I've said it out loud. The truth. But Beth isn't listening.

'She's put you up to this, hasn't she? She's a hateful person, she always has been. That's why your father wanted to leave her. Can't you see that?'

'She hasn't put me up to this. It was all me.' I hate that she's making this about my mother. 'It started long before she came out of prison.'

'What did?'

'How did you lose your teaching job, Beth?' I smile now, enjoying this once more. 'I expect you deserved that.'

'It was a mistake,' she starts and then stops, looking at me, tears in her eyes. 'Was that you too? Were you the member of the public who reported the fight and cost me my job?'

I smile. She's starting to get it now, starting to understand. When I was out of foster care and at university, I'd looked Beth up. I couldn't believe that she was carrying on with her life as normal, that she was still teaching. I had a long summer vacation from university which started long before the schools broke up. I'd rented a room near her new school and watched out for her, hanging around outside the school, hoping the other teachers would assume I was a parent.

I had wanted to tear her life apart just as she had torn apart mine. Was she still manipulating students the way she had manipulated me? Telling them they could trust her, that they should confide in her? She'd told me that she'd protect me, that she'd look after me. But all the time she'd only been interested in my father.

'I didn't have to do much. I already knew the kind of teacher you were. The kind who often had one-on-one time with the kids, who let them skive off their lessons and sit in your classroom, the kind who listened to their problems, the kind who didn't have any boundaries. I knew if I could just get them to investigate you, then your career would fall apart.'

When I saw Beth break up a fight between two girls at the end of the school day, I saw my opportunity. I reported her for being too physical with the girls. And that opened up a whole other load of questions about Beth's competence as a teacher, just like I knew it would.

'It did,' she says sadly. 'Because of you.' I see the undisguised hate in her eyes. And for a second I wonder if I've miscalculated, if she might get violent, if this whole evening might not go to plan after all.

'And then you went mad. You thought you were being followed, but then you convinced yourself it was all in your head, that there was no one there. Except there was.'

'It was you following me?'

'Yeah,' I say proudly. 'I enjoyed it. Making you feel afraid. Making you feel small. Alone. You left me completely on my own. My father dead. My mother in prison. Me shunted round emergency foster carers like an object. All because of you. All your promises turned to dust. You said you'd take me in if I ever needed a break from my arguments with my mother. But when I needed you the most, you abandoned me. Because it was never me you wanted. It was my father.'

CHAPTER 61

BETH

'That's not true,' I say, my face flushing. But it is, partly. I'd imagined the three of us together, a happy family. I'd got on with Sophie so well. And Nick and I were head over heels in love. I'd imagined days out together, laughter. The family I never had. But it wasn't to be. Because of her mother. And she deserved to go to jail for it. She deserved everything she got. She's out of prison now, free to do as she pleases. But Nick had a death sentence.

'Why did you hate me so much? Your father loved me, you know.'

'Why did I hate you?' She looks at me, incredulous. 'Your affair killed him.'

'Your mother killed him. You know that.'

At first I'd thought the fire was an accident, that the candle had been knocked over by mistake. It was only later I learnt that Virginia had been arrested for murder. Every scrap of evidence had pointed to her.

'If you hadn't cheated with him, it would never have happened.'

'It was my fault your parents were unhappy, was it? My fault they already hated each other? You told me what you went through in that house. You told me about your mother's temper.'

'You're so judgemental. What did you know about their relationship? You should have stayed out of it. But instead you manipulated me and my father.'

'So you got your revenge by stalking me? By making me think I was going mad?'

'It was what you deserved. Imagine how my mother felt. She wasn't an angry person before his affair. My father drove her mad. You think her anger made my father have an affair, but it was the other way round. His affair caused her anger.'

I shake my head. That can't be right. 'No – she wasn't a good person. You know that.' Nick had always said that his wife was angry, difficult to live with, that their relationship hadn't been working for a long time.

'That's not true. She was only unhappy because of him. She was fine before.'

I frown as my mind floods with confusion. I always tell my clients not to see things in black and white, that relationships are nuanced. And yet I always saw my relationship with Nick as perfect, believed that we would still be together if he hadn't died.

'None of this is my fault,' I say. 'I didn't start the fire.'

'No one would have started it, if it wasn't for you. My father wouldn't be dead. My mother wouldn't have been in jail. You deserved every punishment I gave you. That psychiatric hospital was the right place for you. I thought you'd be there forever. But you got back up again. You started training to be a counsellor. How ironic that someone who destroyed so many lives thought they could help others.'

I remember when I started training, how hopeful I'd been that I could really help my clients. It had meant so much to me. 'I'd sunk so low. I knew what it felt like to think life wasn't worth living,' I say softly. 'I became a therapist so I could help people who'd felt like me.'

She laughs. 'All about you, isn't it? Never about the hurt you inflicted on other people. And then you found Richard. Had a child. You had everything. The family you'd denied me when I was growing up. And I wanted a child then myself. But I couldn't put the past to rest. Couldn't control my anger.'

'No matter what you do to me, it won't bring your father back.' She doesn't seem to have heard me.

'Marriage counselling was just a front,'' she says. 'But I did need help. I told Peter I was going to individual counselling to sort out my anger issues.' No wonder Peter hadn't turned up for the first few sessions. He was never supposed to.

'You still need help,' I say softly. If only she could see that. She's the one that needs psychiatric support, not me.

'I knew that if I hinted that Peter was abusing me, then I could suck you in. At school you told us once you'd had an abusive partner. One who used to hurt you.'

'You remembered that?'

'Of course. I idolised you when I was at school. I hung on every word you said.'

I can't believe how far she's gone to set me up. 'So all of those hints about Peter being abusive were just to get me to break a rule and come over to your house?'

Danielle nods.

'I was worried when you cancelled the sessions afterwards, though. I thought I might have taken it too far. But that turned out fine. Because you believed me when I said I never got your messages. And you were caught off guard by Peter turning up with me and the news of the baby.' She strokes her stomach, reflectively. 'Although that was a surprise to me too. A happy one, of course. But a side benefit was that it played into your fears about Richard cheating on you with me.'

'You planned everything.'

She smiles. 'Not everything. You played quite a big hand in things yourself. You stalked me. I hadn't foreseen that. That was a real bonus in my catalogue of evidence.'

'What do you want from me?' I ask, desperately.

Danielle smiles. 'Everything you love. But I'm starting with your home.'

'Why are you buying it? Do you even want to live here?'

She winds her hair around her fingers and frowns as she makes a show of looking around the room. 'Not really. It's not very nicely decorated, is it? It needs a lot of work. No, I don't think I'll bother. As soon as you've been forced to move out, I can pull out of the transaction.'

'So it's just to get me out?'

'Of course. You destroyed my whole family. Now you're losing everything too. Your home. Your job. Richard. Charlie.'

'You've taken this too far,' I say shakily. 'This isn't the real you. You were always such a nice girl. You're nothing like your mother.' I have to please her now; pretend. I have to save myself. 'You can withdraw your complaint to social services, phone them up and tell them you got it wrong. Then I won't tell anyone what you've done.'

'You think I'm not like my mother?' Danielle says, standing up from her chair and rising to her full height. 'Well, maybe I'm more like her than you think.' She leans over me and whispers. 'It wasn't her who set fire to the flat. It was me.'

CHAPTER 62

DANIELLE

My words are supposed to sound threatening, but my voice wavers, the guilt welling up inside me. I killed my father. I feel sick with shame.

'It was you?' she says. 'You started the fire? Why?' Her face reddens and she steps closer to me. I think she might hit me, but she doesn't.

I can hardly get the words out. I'm back in the corridor of the block of flats, hearing the alarms, feeling smoke in my lungs, then running, my feet pounding down the stairs and out into the fresh air. If Dad hadn't been having an affair with Beth I would never have started the fire. He'd still be alive today.

'I wanted to hurt him. I saw the evidence of your affair. He'd told me he'd renovated the flat for me, but it was all for you. I wanted to burn the place down. I didn't realise he was inside. It was all your fault.'

Beth's gone pale. 'It wasn't my fault. You started the fire, not me.'

'I didn't mean to kill him.' I shake with regret, my body caving in on itself. I slump back into the chair. 'My mother spent all those years in prison because of me. Because of you.' I wipe the tears from my face with the back of my hand as I think of Mum. I don't even know where she is. I haven't heard from her since Peter asked her to leave and she moved out.

'You were the one who started the fire. Did you lock your father inside too?'

I stare at her, eyes wide. I can hear a ticking clock, a car on the street. I can't think straight. 'No. I didn't know my father was in there.' I feel the guilt rise inside me. I remember when I got to the stairs, I thought I'd heard screams. But I'd told myself I was imagining it. The smoke alarms were so loud it was hard to distinguish other sounds. I'd dismissed it and run away. I could have saved him.

'But when you left, did you lock the door of the flat?'

'No!' I don't understand what she's getting at, why she's saying this. Why would I have locked the door? The place was on fire.

'You didn't go to the trial, did you?'

'I did. That's how I knew about you.'

'But you weren't there for all of it. You didn't hear all the evidence.' My heart pounds.

'No.' I take a shaky breath, grip the arms of the seat. After I'd seen Beth that day in court I'd never been back. I couldn't cope with my guilt anymore, couldn't watch my mother endure the endless scrutiny, all to protect me.

'That was part of the case. Someone had locked your father in the flat. That was one of the reasons the jury was convinced your mother was guilty.'

I stare at her in shock, trying to compute what she's saying, unable to find the words.

Out of nowhere, there's a crash from downstairs. I jump. It sounded like a window breaking. I hear footsteps on the stairs. I look at Beth, and she looks back at me, her eyes wide.

Then she starts to shout. 'We're in here! In here! She's locked me in.'

A second later, there's a bang on the door of the room and a voice shouts through. 'I know you're in there, Beth. And you too, Sophie. I've seen your car outside.'

I unlock the door and come face to face with my mother.

CHAPTER 63

BETH

'Well, this is very cosy,' Virginia says. 'The two of you together. Are you having one of your therapy sessions, Sophie? Damaged by your horrible childhood?' She turns to me. 'I suppose she's telling you it's all my fault.'

'We were just talking,' I say. A moment ago I thought that whoever was coming up the stairs would rescue me. But now I smell petrol, see the cigarette lighter in Virginia's hand. I freeze.

'Beth was just telling me the truth,' Danielle says, venom in her voice. She steps closer to her mother. 'She said that you locked Dad in the flat. That you let him burn alive.'

Virginia laughs. 'The fire was already burning when I got there. And there's only one person who started that. You. And what did you do? You ran away. You let him die.'

Danielle stumbles backwards as if she's been punched. She puts her hand over her stomach, her face pale. I remember the baby. The stress can't be good for it. I feel sick with worry. None of this is the baby's fault.

'I didn't mean to let him die,' Danielle whispers. 'I really didn't mean to.'

I glare at Virginia. 'It was your mother who killed him,' I say. 'Not you.'

Virginia pushes me aside and moves closer to her daughter. 'I've spent fifteen years in prison because of you. Because I loved you.

Because, as your mother, I was willing to sacrifice my freedom for you.'

Danielle finds her courage. 'But that's not true, is it? You went to the flat when it was on fire. You must have heard him screaming. And then, instead of saving him, you locked the door. You made sure he'd never get out alive.' I can see the hurt in Danielle's eyes, the sinking realisation that her mother had completely betrayed her. A tiny part of me feels sorry for her.

'I tried to save him. Which was more than you did. You ran away.'

'You didn't try to help him. You locked him in.'

'But why would I go into a burning flat, if I wasn't trying to help him?'

'You made that up, for the court case.'

'No, I didn't. I went inside the flat. I risked my own life to try and save him.'

I remember the court case. This was her defence. That she'd been trying to save him. The jury hadn't bought it, but now Danielle looks like she's unsure.

I feel anger rise inside me. This woman took Nick from me. 'She was found guilty by a jury. She killed him.'

'But why did she go inside the flat?' Danielle asks softly, her eyes darting from me to her mother.

I think back to that day. Nick was supposed to be meeting Virginia at the flat to tell her it was over for good. I was going to be there too, for moral support while he spoke to his wife. But I stayed with a friend the night before and missed my train back to London. I was only fifteen minutes late, but by the time I got there the fire brigade were already at the flat.

'It's like I said,' Virginia says quietly, fiddling with the lighter in her hand. 'I went in to save your father. I heard him screaming and my instinct was to help him. He was my husband. I loved him.' She looks angrily at me. 'Before *she* came along, our marriage was fine.

But when I got through the door and saw him…' She shudders. 'It was so hot. And he stumbled towards me, through the smoke. The smoke was so thick he was just a shadow. I reached out to him. He was stumbling around, disorientated. I stepped towards him, grabbed his arm. I needed to get him out quickly. I could already feel the smoke filling my lungs. There wasn't much time.'

I'm transfixed by Virginia's words. If I didn't know who she was, I'd be sure she was telling the truth. She's so convincing.

'You didn't get him out,' Danielle says.

'When I grabbed his arm and started to pull him towards the door, he seemed confused. He said your name.' She looks at me with pure hatred and I shrink under her gaze. 'He called out for you. "Beth", he screamed. I'll always remember his words. "Beth, thank god it's you. I love you". And then I dropped his arm and left. I shut the door behind me, got out my key and locked it. In his final moments, when he knew he might die, all he could think of was you.'

I sink to the floor, crying. I imagine Nick in his last moments, reaching for me. And then Virginia slamming the door, locking him in.

'Nick,' I whisper. I wish I'd been there. I wish I could have rescued him. My train made me far too late. But in his final breaths, my name was the one on his lips. He truly loved me.

The guilt sweeps through me once more. If he hadn't loved me, if he hadn't said my name instead of hers, then he'd still be alive.

'You let me take the blame.' Danielle is screaming at her mother now. 'You let me believe for all those years that it was me who killed him. That you'd gone to prison for me.'

'You started the fire, Danielle. You have to accept some responsibility.'

'How could you, Mum? How could you let me live with that guilt? I was still a child.'

Danielle scratches at her arm and I see a nasty new burn and a criss-cross of scars on her wrist. She was punishing herself. I see that now. She was so filled with self-loathing. She'd always blamed herself. But really she'd wanted someone else to blame. Me. Once again I can't help feeling sorry for her. But then I think of all the things she's done to hurt me.

'I couldn't tell you I'd killed your father, could I? You'd never have forgiven me. Better for you to think I was going down instead of you. What was the use of you thinking badly of me?'

Virginia flicks the lighter and I shiver as I watch the tiny flame appear. The acrid smell of petrol fills my nostrils and I look behind her into the hallway and see a dark petrol slick running down the cream carpet towards the staircase.

'Why are you in my house?' I whisper. But I know the answer. She wants to burn it down, with me inside. She burnt her husband to death and now she wants me to go the same way.

'Why do you think? After fifteen years in prison, serving time because you slept with my husband, I come out to find out you've befriended my daughter. The daughter I've been thinking of every day for fifteen years, the daughter I couldn't wait to be a mother to again. It was all too late. She was already under your spell.'

'You were never going to be my mother again,' Danielle says. 'Not after what you did to my father.'

'You'd never have found out if you hadn't met her.' She jabs her finger towards me.

Danielle looks at the lighter and then the petrol. 'I'm not friends with Beth, Mum,' Danielle says urgently. 'I never was.'

'You won't be for much longer,' she says. 'She's ruined my relationship with you. You were all I had left. If I can't have you, then she certainly can't. Do you know what I spent my years fantasising about when I was in prison? Not that Nick hadn't died. No. That she'd died with him. She's cost me my freedom.'

'Mum—' Danielle glances from her mother to me and then back again. 'Don't do anything stupid. You're out of jail now. You don't want to end up back there.' I feel a flicker of hope. Danielle doesn't want me to die, even if her mother does.

'Don't I? What is there for me here? I thought I was coming out to see you, to be a part of your life again, but you've forced me out of your home. What's left for me? At least I had a roof over my head in prison. At least I had friends. People I could trust. Not like my own daughter, who doesn't even want me living with her.'

'Mum, it's not like that. You know that. I have to think of the baby now.'

Virginia smiles, a glint in her eye. 'You do need to think of the baby, and get out of here right now before I set fire to the place.'

I watch Danielle's hand go to her stomach protectively. I start to stand. I need to get past Virginia. I need to get out. I know she's going to kill me. She's got nothing to lose.

Danielle starts to move away towards the stairs, and I follow behind. I need to make a run for it, as soon as there's an opportunity. As soon as Virginia's distracted.

Virginia turns to me and holds a hand out to stop me passing. 'Not you.' I push past her hand and start to run, adrenaline pumping through me. But as my foot hits the ground it sticks to the petrol and then slides out from underneath me. I land with a thud. Virginia is smiling above me. She picks up a petrol can from the floor and tips the remainder over me. It sticks to my hair, my shirt, my jeans. She holds the cigarette lighter up, showing me the flame.

'Stay where you are.'

'Mum—' Danielle pleads.

Virginia lowers the lighter towards the floor. 'Get out, Danielle, while you can. I'm losing patience.'

Danielle hurries down the stairs and I hear the front door swinging shut as she leaves the house. Her mother stays behind, watching me, the cigarette lighter in her hand.

I start to stand, lifting my hands from the sticky floor, my knee throbbing.

'Don't move. I'll set light to your clothes,' she says. 'You won't stand a chance.'

She's not bluffing. I can see she'd do it in an instant.

I sink back to the ground, staying where I am, as she backs away from me slowly, watching me the whole time.

'If I see you move, I'll start the fire. The flames will speed towards you. I'll enjoy watching you burn.'

I'm frozen to the spot. I know that as soon as she gets to the bottom of the stairs, she'll set light to the petrol. She's going to kill me anyway. I won't be able to get past her before she starts the fire. My only chance is to go back into my therapy room. There's no petrol in there. I can shut the door, hope that holds the fire off for long enough for me to escape out of the window.

Virginia is near the bottom of the stairs now. I have to move. As I start to crawl away, I see her lighting a piece of paper with the cigarette lighter and throwing it onto the oil-soaked carpet. Flames lick up the steps and I run back into the therapy room and shut the door behind me.

My heart thuds in my chest, my vision blurs. I try to focus on my breathing, to stay calm. But as I breathe in, all I can taste is petrol. When I put my hand on the doorknob, I can already feel the heat of the fire. I can hear the roar of the flames. I can't escape. I'm trapped. Just like Nick was.

CHAPTER 64

DANIELLE

I stumble outside, my mother behind me.

She turns to me and smiles. 'Beth's finally getting what she deserves.'

I shake my head. As much as I wanted to hurt Beth, I never wanted this.

I look up at the house. There's no sign of the fire from the outside yet. Maybe it will be OK. Maybe Beth will get out.

I need to call the fire brigade. But I don't have my phone. It's in my handbag in the house.

'Give me your mobile,' I shout at my mother.

She shakes her head. 'I have to go now. Before they come for me.'

'Give me your mobile,' I shout.

But instead she opens her arms and wraps me in a quick hug. 'I love you, Sophie,' she whispers in my ear.

I hold her for a moment longer than she wants, digging in her pockets to try and get to her phone. She squirms in my arms.

She doesn't have her phone on her. Of course she doesn't. She's planned this. She doesn't want to be tracked down by her phone's GPS signal. She'll run away now, disappear. I never want to see her again.

Behind me, there's the sound of shattering glass, as the fire rips through the house and blows out one of the downstairs windows. I let go of my mother and turn back towards the house.

I need to do something, to get Beth out of there. But there's no time. I start to panic, my breath coming in gulps, as I gasp for air. I sink down onto the concrete path and throw up bile. I think of the baby growing inside me, the stress it must be under.

I look around for my mother, but she's already gone.

But now I can hear Beth screaming. I remember Dad's screams, how they echoed round my head for years afterwards. Sometimes I wake up in the middle of the night and still think I can hear them.

Beth's shouting now, banging against the window upstairs.

The street is empty; the fire isn't visible from outside the house and it hasn't attracted attention. I look from the house to the street and back again. I can see Beth struggling with the window catch, trying to get it open. But it's jammed shut. She's trapped. There's no time.

I can't do what I did last time. I can't run away. I have to save her.

But I can't go back in the house. It's too dangerous. I can't put my baby at risk.

Beth is still banging against the window frantically. The flames haven't reached the room yet, but they soon will. She's pushing her body into the window, trying to force it open.

I'm moving before I'm even thinking straight. I see an empty terracotta flowerpot beside the bins. And then I'm climbing unsteadily up a tree next to the house, flowerpot in my hand. I pray I don't fall. I'm not close to the window, but I'm close enough. I pull my arm back and lob the flowerpot at the window.

The glass smashes and Beth recoils, falling to the ground. For a moment I think that I've hit her, that I might have knocked her out. If I have, then she'll die in there. And this time it will be my fault.

I watch the window, desperately hoping she'll reappear.

I just wish someone would walk by. Anybody. Then they could help.

But then I see a face at the window. Relief floods me as she pulls herself to her feet. She climbs through the broken glass onto the window ledge, shards piercing her white T-shirt and bloodstains spreading through the material. In the distance I hear sirens. Beth sits unsteadily on the ledge for a second and then the fire bursts into the room behind her and she pushes herself off, landing in a tangled heap in the garden below.

EPILOGUE: 6 MONTHS LATER

DANIELLE

I stare down at my father's grave. It's become more weathered over the years and now it looks permanent, like it belongs here. Not like when it was sparkling new and stood out against the grassy landscape. Everything has moved on, but he still lies there, under the earth. More time has passed with him buried in the ground than the time he spent with me.

The tree a few metres away has grown, its roots forcing up the sides of the crumbling graves next to it, making the stones uneven in the earth. I go to sit under its shade, feeling my bump, my baby wriggling inside me. The baby my father will never meet. I feel the fresh air on my skin, breathe in the peace and quiet.

Today's the kind of sunny day you should share with other people. Peter had offered to come here with me, but I wanted to be on my own. I need to be by myself, before I move on, try my best to start my own happy family, to give my baby all the love in the world. My mother won't be involved. She'll be in prison for a long time. I don't intend to visit.

There are no flowers already on the grave today. Not like previous years, when there had always been fresh ones. I used to wonder who brought them. I thought perhaps it was his sister. But whoever it was, they must have given up.

Undoing the string on my flowers, I stand and pour water into the vase embedded in the grave and space the stems out neatly.

A car pulls into the graveyard and I glance up. A figure gets out. Brown curly hair. It's her. Beth.

BETH

She's already here. Just like I hoped she would be. For years, I've tried to avoid her. I'd always bring my flowers to the grave the day before the anniversary so that I didn't bump into her. But it doesn't matter anymore. She knows who I am now.

Since the fire at my house she's withdrawn her complaint about my counselling and her complaint to social services. She's even spoken to Richard to explain. He wanted to report her to the police for her behaviour, but I persuaded him to let it go. She has just as much dirt on me as I have on her. I behaved unprofessionally towards her and I followed her. Unofficially, we've reached a truce.

I get out of the car and walk to the passenger side to get my stick and the bunch of flowers. Since my fall from the window during the fire, I haven't walked so well, but I'm hoping the stick is just temporary and I'll eventually be able to walk without a limp.

I make my way across the grass to the grave. It's a sunny day, and I feel the warmth of the rays on my face. I imagine Nick beside me for a second, but then I push the thought away. I can't go on like this, thinking about him all the time. I need to live my own life.

I hobble up to her. 'Hi, Danielle.'

'Hi.' She looks at me as if she expects me to say something else. We haven't spoken since the fire. Instead I walk to the head of the grave, put down my stick and then lay down my flowers in front of hers. I lean down and kiss the cold stone.

'I'm sorry,' Danielle whispers. 'For everything.'

I nod. 'Do you want to be left alone?'

'It's OK. Was it you who always left flowers just before the anniversary every year?'

'Yes,' I say quietly.

'You loved him, didn't you?'

I nod. There's no doubt I loved him. But for the last six months, my memories of our relationship have been plaguing me. I no longer see them through rose-tinted glasses. I've started to question them, to wonder if everything was as perfect as I remembered.

Nick had told me so many things, had made me feel so special. But I had been young back then, just out of teacher training college. And the things he'd said; that his wife was controlling, that she didn't sleep with him, that she had a problem with anger… well, they're things I've heard over and over again when I've been giving relationship counselling. Things men say to their mistresses so often it's almost like a script. What if none of it was true? What if Nick and I were just another affair that was destined to end?

'Have you seen your mother?' I ask Danielle.

She shakes her head. 'I never want to see her again. She killed him. Deliberately. I don't know how she could do that. And I don't know how she could let me think I'd done it.'

'I was thinking about visiting her,' I say.

'Oh,' she says, looking at me curiously. 'Why?'

'I don't know. I suppose I just want closure.' But that's not true. What I really want is answers about her relationship with Nick. I want to know if she really was awful or if he had made her that way; if their relationship was so terrible that it was inevitable they'd split up. I want to hear that he loved me and not her.

She looks at me. 'I don't think you'll get what you're looking for.'

'I just need to know he loved me.'

'He called your name out when he was dying.'

I nod. That seems like such a big thing. I just need to hold onto that. 'Do you think he really wanted to be with me?'

Danielle frowns. 'Is it that important to you?'

'I loved him. I still love him, I think.'

'But you'll never know how he really felt, will you? None of us will know. He's not here to ask.'

'Oh,' I say. She's right, of course. I'll never get the answers I want, never know what would have happened between Nick and I. That possible future died with Nick. And I can't spend my life living in the past. He is gone and I am living. I have a son and I can make a happy life for myself. My happiness never should have been dependent on Nick's love.

I turn to Danielle. Her bump's really grown. The baby will be here soon. Her chance for a fresh start.

I wonder if she needs to hear the kind of reassurance I need myself. I can see in her eyes that she is not quite recovered, that a part of her will always blame herself for her father's death.

'Nick always used to talk about you. He loved you so much. He'll be watching over your baby.'

A tear rolls down her cheek. I hold out my arms and we embrace. We remain like that for a minute before we pull apart.

'We have our lives to live now,' I say. 'We have to move on.' And for the first time, I feel ready to do that.

A LETTER FROM RUTH

Thank you for choosing to read *I Know Your Secret*. If you enjoyed it, I'd be very grateful if you would write a review. I'd love to hear what you think, and it makes a huge difference in helping new readers discover one of my books for the first time.

If you want to keep up to date with all my latest releases, just sign up at the following link. Your email address will never be shared and you can unsubscribe at any time.

www.bookouture.com/ruth-heald

All of my psychological thrillers to date have explored power imbalances and vulnerability, particularly in relationships between women. In my first two psychological thrillers, *The Mother's Mistake* and *The Woman Upstairs*, I explored the vulnerability of new mothers, and how difficult it can be looking after newborns when you have no one you can trust.

As my own children exited the baby years, I wanted to use my fiction to look at other ways people can be vulnerable. There are many relationships with implicit power imbalances, and I believe one of the most interesting is the relationship between a counsellor and a client. One person is revealing their innermost thoughts to a stranger, someone they know nothing about, and who seems to have all the power. But the counsellor can be vulnerable too. The work can be very lonely, seeing client after client without the camaraderie of work colleagues. In the UK many people practise counselling in their own homes, and so the counsellor has the additional risk of letting a stranger into their home. The dynamic between a counsellor and client provides rich pickings for a dysfunctional relationship, where each party can easily manipulate the other. That formed the seed of the idea for this story.

I have really enjoyed writing *I Know Your Secret*. Beth and Danielle both got under my skin when I was writing, and I wanted things to work out for both of them in the end. They did, but not without a few difficult moments along the way. I was glad that Beth kept Charlie and that Danielle got another chance, starting her own family.

I'm always happy to hear from my readers – you can get in touch on my Facebook page, through Twitter, Goodreads or my website.

Best wishes,
Ruth

 RJHealdAuthor

@RJ_Heald

 www.rjheald.com

ACKNOWLEDGEMENTS

As ever, my thanks first have to go to my husband and children, who've put up with me through the highs and lows of writing this book. They have been there through it all. I'd also like to thank the rest of my family for their ongoing support and encouragement.

This book would not be what it is today without my wonderful editor, Christina Demosthenous, who is endlessly insightful, enthusiastic and diplomatic. Beta readers have played a huge role in shaping this book, and I'd like to thank Ruth Jones, Charity Davies and Vikki McLean, who provided such useful feedback. Many others have helped me with insight into teaching, law, psychiatry and the prison system, and I'm grateful to each and every one of you for your patience with my 'quick questions'. Special thanks to Noelle Holten, who not only works tirelessly as a Publicity Manager at Bookouture, but who also took the time to answer my questions on probation, which saved me hours of research.

Writing can be a lonely pursuit and I don't know where I'd be without the support of other authors who are on the same journey. Thanks to Lesley Sanderson, Rona Halsall and Vikki Patis in particular for acting as friendly sounding boards during the ups and downs of publishing. And thanks to the authors in the Savvy Writers' Snug for keeping me sane and being so generous with their time when I have queries. And of course the wonderful Bookouture Authors' Lounge, run by the amazing Kim Nash, who keeps everyone on the straight and narrow.

It has been a real pleasure to work with the team at Bookouture again. So much work goes on behind the scenes, and I'd like to thank everyone who's been involved, including my publicity manager Sarah Hardy, copyeditor Laura Gerrard and proofreader Jenny Page, as well as the data, marketing and foreign rights teams. Thanks to Lauren Finger and Alex Holmes for managing the production process for the book and the audiobook, and to Tamsin Kennard for narrating the audiobook.

And finally, I'd like to thank my readers. It's so wonderful to know my book is out there in the world being read and enjoyed.